HOLLOWPOINT

HOLLOWPOINT

A Novel

ROB REULAND

RANDOM HOUSE
NEW YORK

Copyright © 2001 by Robert Reuland

All rights reserved under International and Pan-American Copyright Conventions. Published in the United States by Random House, Inc., New York, and simultaneously in Canada by Random House of Canada Limited, Toronto.

RANDOM HOUSE and colophon are registered trademarks of Random House, Inc.

Library of Congress Cataloging-in-Publication Data
Reuland, Rob.
Hollowpoint : a novel / Rob Reuland.
p.   cm.
ISBN 0-375-50501-6 (alk. paper)
1. Brooklyn (New York, N.Y.)—Fiction.   2. Public prosecutors—Fiction.
3. Children—Death—Fiction.   I. Title.
PS3568.E778 H6 2001
813'.6—dc21   00-059103

Random House website address: www.atrandom.com
Printed in the United States of America on acid-free paper
98765432
First Edition
Book design by Mercedes Everett

This book is for my wife, Christine

What divides us from the universe
Of blood and seed, conceives the soul in us,
Brings us to God, but guilt?

—Archibald MacLeish, *J.B.*

HOLLOWPOINT

CHAPTER

1

Another dead body in East New York, and nobody could give a shit. Not even her family, if you can call it a family—a single half sister with a different last name and a stringy, sloe-eyed, coke-worn woman of thirty-eight but looking sixty, the selfsame crackhead mother who lay spent on the couch in the sultry midnight of her roach-spotted living room, who lay in a chemical miasma while Lamar Lamb killed the girl in her own bedroom, hardly bigger than the stained mattress on which she died.

Another dead little girl, if you can call her a little girl—with a little girl of her own.

The mother and the sister are sitting in this place, doing nothing except that. Neither seems to care about this dead girl who was not even close to the fifteenth birthday she will never see, and the funeral is no big deal for anyone at all except for me in the back, looking at them.

But in truth even I am not thinking about that girl in the box but my own dead girl and the green Oldsmobile on an ordinary Thursday afternoon, on an ordinary street one year ago.

Mine is the only white face in here—I am the only white man in these several blocks of east Brooklyn except for the detective who brought me here. He is not wearing sunglasses, but he has the look of a man who is. No one else is here.

The mother and the sister sit in the middle of the room, not too near the box with the dead girl, and the dead girl's little girl (about three months old) is crying unobtrusively. Someone's prettied her up. Her ears are pierced.

The mother now looks me over with hostility, a glint in her rheumy eyes. I walk over and seat myself in the row of folding chairs behind her, but she has already turned away and is hefting the baby around to quiet her. She tells the baby to shut up and clicks the twiggy yellow fingers of her free hand at the sister to fetch a bottle or something from a tired diaper bag on the floor. I lean over to get her attention. She tosses the baby around in her sinewy arms. I wait, looking at the back of her head, sparse hair with individual curls like a patch of dying garden. There is the smell of her and the smell of the baby.

When I say the mother's name, she swivels suddenly, swinging the baby around with her. The baby looks at me, too, with a damp, open mouth.

I tell her my name and give her the usual about being sorry and doing everything we can—a tired, threadbare line of horseshit under the circumstances but all I have. Sometimes it makes a difference. Not now. There is something drab and perfunctory about this whole sorry scene. Even the picture of the dead girl is nothing more than a photocopy from her yearbook, enlarged. I have seen this same face in Polaroids of her lying wide-eyed in death. The dead girl, unlike her child, is dark. In the photocopy, her features are obliterated by her blackness.

The mother tells me it was LL who did Kayla and everyone

knows it was LL. "Miss Iris saw him runnin outa my house," she says. "You talk to Miss Iris, Mr. D.A.?"

I tell her I haven't spoken to Miss Iris, but at this moment Lamar Lamb is in a holding cell on the second-floor squad room of the Seven-Five Precinct station house and has been there since last night, when they brought him in.

"Where you find him at?" she asks, turning back to me and genuinely surprised.

"At home," I say in a hush.

"LL ain't got no home." She tells me about LL in her full-throated scratch. "He ain't got no home no more. Last I hear, he be livin on the street. And before that he was in jail." With her free hand she fans herself with a pamphlet. The air is stifling here and moist. There is no air-conditioning. The front door is propped open, but no relief blows in with the street sounds. Atop a pole in the corner, a single fan spins without effect over the dead girl, its head hanging mournfully limp—an overtall sunflower.

"At his grandmother's," I tell her. "At Cypress Hills."

Her face takes on the hostile glint again. "I know where his grandmother live at. She don' want him there no more. She told me she had an order. From the judge. She show me the paper. He can't go there no more."

"From what I hear, it wasn't her idea."

"What you mean?"

"He just came back," I say. "His grandmother didn't have any say."

"So why you here? If you arrest him already?"

"I wanted to show our—" I start again with the horseshit but then don't bother. "I have to present the case to the grand jury. To indict him for the murder."

"So?"

"I need to speak with you about that night. I don't mean now. Not today. But I'd like you to come down for the grand jury. And your other daughter." I look at the sister, whose green gaze now focuses intently upon me. "You were there?" I ask her.

"Oh, sweet Jesus," the mother interrupts. "I already told the cops what I saw—which was nothin. And she din't see nothin. We was both sleepin."

The baby begins to act up, squirming in the dead girl's mother's arms, and she waves me away. I have no choice. I walk to the back, and the detective gives me a nod. He's right. Let's blow. But there is someone now in my way—a man with a shaved head like an obsidian bulb. He stands close to me. He stands too close to me. He stinks like liquor and there is a carnival atmosphere about him. Who he is I have no idea, but he wants to know what the D.A.'s office is gonna do about it. He, too, knows it was Lamar Lamb who did the girl. He tells me Lamar should die.

"Let me ax you," he says to me. "This nigger should'n get the death penalty for what he done?"

"That's not what I'm—"

"Let me tell you about that young lady, because you did't know her. She was a fine young lady. She was"—he says, then stops short, thinking—"in school. Beautiful girl. Never bothered no one. And the D.A. is gon—what? Gon give that nigger some kinda, some kinda plea bargain and shit? Let him out—in five years or some shit? That ain't right."

"No one said—"

He gets even closer to me, if that is possible. His right index finger is pointed at my sternum like a gun. "Don' you, don' you think they should give him the death penalty for what he done to Kayla?"

"Absolutely," I say for no other reason than to shut him up. I'm tired. I'm tired of the dead. I'm tired of the living. I'm tired of this mean-looking motherfucker with the finger like a gun. I'm tired of the dead girl's mother, who won't talk to me about the man who killed her daughter. I'm tired of the sun and the heat and these streets. But mostly I'm tired of Lamar Lamb. I was tired of Lamar Lamb before I heard his name. He's just the latest horror, and even the newspapers wouldn't have touched him except the girl was fourteen and naked and killed in her bed.

ARREST IN TEEN SEX SLAY, read today's *Post* headline over a few lines of copy on page seventeen—beneath a leggy nude virtually guaranteeing safe and effective cellulite removal.

> Brooklyn detectives last night announced the arrest of Lamar Lamb, 19, of East New York after a two-week manhunt following the August 4 murder of Kayla Harris. Fourteen-year-old Harris's disrobed body was found in the bedroom of her home in the Cypress Hills public housing project. Harris, an honor student at Franklin K. Lane High School, was remembered by classmate Lashanta Wayne as a "quiet and friendly girl" who liked English and math. Harris was killed by a single bullet to the chest. Captain Art Tobin of the 75th Precinct in East New York stated that the "possibility of a sexual motive for the attack cannot be ruled out at this time." Assistant District Attorney Andrew Giobberti, who in May prosecuted subway stalker Larry "Spiderman" Bartlett, refused comment.

I move to the door with the detective in tow, stopping short to sign the guest book in my moronic handwriting below four or five other names. Then I leave.

I walk from the funeral home, and it is very bright outside after that somber, ill-lit place. I reach for my knockoff Ray-Ban aviators.

The gray Chevy Caprice is parked on Linden Boulevard, on the sidewalk. No one pays it any mind. In this neighborhood, Chevy Caprices (gray or black or dark blue, beat to hell and missing hub-caps, laminated police placards tucked under their windshields) park routinely on the sidewalks. The detective is inside the Caprice now, pushing at the passenger door. Stuck. The handle doesn't work from the outside, so there is nothing I can do except stand here squinting and sweating in the afternoon sun, which did not abate while we were inside.

All the little businesses here on Linden are overhung with col-ored awnings, which line the sides of the street in a cheerfully optimistic progression of yellow, blue, aquamarine, and red. The sidewalks crowd together fire hydrants, fruit stands, stunted little saplings, bus shelters, subway entrances, parking signs. Dumpsters and lampposts are alive with papers that dangle and blow in a breeze sour with the city heat. Good citizens come and go—old women in print dresses and white socks and sneakers, men and boys in immaculate Timberlands and Air Jordans, Koreans in white aprons, girls in sandals with black soles three inches thick. The pace on the street is slow here, slower than the city, for instance, where people walk intently, offensively. Brooklyn walks—if we walk at all, instead of driving or just idling under awnings or on stoops, or playing dominoes before storefronts, or bullshitting on the street corner, arms on hips—as though we're going no place in no hurry. Manhattan walks behind us and wants to kick us in the ass.

But this is not my Brooklyn. These are not my streets. These places—before this job, they were places I did not go, places I did not know. Nor did their people know my places or go there. No one ever pointed out the line on a map, but we all knew where it was and we all stayed where we were. We only saw one another on the train.

The detective is cussing now at the door, and the sister appears as if from nowhere.

She is a willowy sixteen-year-old in project gold, and tall—so tall she can look me in the eye, which she tries to do. Only her eyes suggest kinship with the mother, although this one's (a violent, chlorophyll green) are merely drawn into subtle almonds without giving her the sinister look of her gargoyle mother. She tries to look at me, but I am standing with the sun at my back. I feel it through the threadbare wool of my jacket. Her gossamer dress is cut low and high, and the blue-black of her skin is stark against the white of it.

"Mister," she says. "Anthony said you got LL in jail or whatever?"

"I'm sorry about your sister—it's Utopia, isn't it?"

"Yes. What gon happen to him now?" she asks.

"Lamb? I'm gonna try him," I tell her. "For the murder."

"All right," she says. "He's in jail?"

"Yes."

"What gon happen now?" she repeats. "To LL?"

"First I have to indict him in the grand jury," I say. "And then in about a year, we'll have a trial. Unless he pleads guilty."

"All right. He'll, um, be like in jail the whole time?"

"You don't need to worry about him anymore," I say. "If that's what you're thinking."

"Yes," she answers.

"You don't need to worry about him, Utopia."

"All right."

"He's taken care of," I say, but I am thinking, *Nothing scary is going to get you, Opal. Go to sleep.*

"Mister," she says. "Can I like call you on the telephone—if I have a question to ax you or whatever?"

I give her a business card; Utopia is not looking at me but past me down Linden, toward the sun. She squints at it, and then at her mother, who stands now in the funeral doorway, watching us, with the baby. For a moment, Utopia looks back to me with her eyes bright behind the green contacts. She walks away with her spectral, long-limbed walk.

The detective starts in—an unrelenting stream of gloomy banter that doesn't let up until we are back at Joralemon Street. He is unloading what he silently ate back there. He has an Irish tan and about twenty years on the job. He drives the Caprice in the south Brooklyn style. One arm drapes limply over the wheel, steering more with wrist than hand.

"Look at this fuckin shit hole," he says. "Summertime. When it's the worst. People get all jacked up when it's warm." As he speaks, his small gray eyes dart like fish. "You'd think they'd, you know, take it easy there. Relax. Have a lemonade or some shit. Cool off. Instead, it's the opposite. Vicy versy. They get all jacked up and the guy there will, you know, say something to the other guy, and then the other guy there will be like, *Yeah, what'd you say, ass wipe?* or whatever and that's how it starts. They pop each other for that."

I nod my head.

"Not for nothin," he says, "but I ever tell youse my fuckin plan?"

"No," I say. "What fucking plan's that, Detective?"

"All right. Now hear me out. I tell youse how to cut the numbers in the Seven-Five there by, say, *half*. Ready for this, counselor? What you do is you buy every one of them sorry fucks there an air conditioner. Best fuckin dime the city ever spent. I'm telling youse. Simple as that. Get one of them fuckin air conditioners in every fuckin house there. That's why they got so much killin there. Because none of them there's got air conditioners—"

As I stare through the windshield, he is in my periphery, moving his free arm for emphasis. I hear enough of what he says to acknowledge it when I need to. I am sitting in the passenger seat, looking for green station wagons and wondering what it is the sister wants to tell me, but mostly I am still thinking about Opal. I am trying to recall her five-year-old face. I cannot.

The Municipal Building (full of right angles and columns and entirely dark with soot, smoke, stains, streaks, grime, gum, bus exhaust, bird shit, dog shit, acid rain, and other evidence of the human horde that daily flows in and out and around its incongruously bright copper doors) rises at 210 Joralemon Street in downtown Brooklyn—a gray thumb smudge on the powdery August sky.

The office of the Brooklyn District Attorney—where I do the work of the People of the State of New York.

Inside: a rabbit warren of convoluted passageways and beige walls of thin metal and frosted glass cast up in haphazard directions—a dingy den with Pepsi machines glowing and humming in the middle of hallways—file cabinets with doors ajar, inaccessible behind peeling Formica-topped tables—gurgling water coolers—artificial wood shelving—papers and notices posted here and there, left hanging long after they serve any purpose—pretzel crumbs on the floor next to pea-green metal desks and unemptied wastebaskets stuck in corners and ignored—a gritty bureau—a cockroach fantasia—with too-bright fluorescent tubes overhanging all of it.

The detective pulls the Caprice in behind another like it and

another and another parked on Joralemon Street at the foot of 210.
Here, in the gray shadow of this gray building, a caravansary of
Chevy Caprices in all their colors.

I enter through a door marked GOVERNMENT EMPLOYEES into
a resonant foyer three stories high, without daylight and dark except for a Good Humor dispenser throwing a halfhearted light into
a corner, where it is swallowed up by the overwhelming gloom.
There is no sound apart from the low, mechanical thrum of a floor
polisher pushed by a man. I don't know his name. He lifts a hand
to wave without losing the rhythm of his machine. In graceful arcs
he pulls it, a laconic pendulum turned on its side.

"Dude," someone calls out to me. "Gio. Where the fuck have
you been?"

"Homicide funeral."

"Oh. Phil, he has been searching," he says in his heavy way of
speaking this language, still new to him. His voice is like brown
leather.

"That right?" I say abstractedly, still walking.

"You did not sign yourself out on the motherfucking board," he
says. His open face says, *You didn't sign yourself out? So fucking
what!*

"That right?" I say again, aware that the great beams of camaraderie he is throwing out are missing me completely.

"There were two detectives here. There is some problem," he
says, frowning. "With your case. With the girl."

"What problem?" I say, not stopping.

"We looked for you here and there," he says.

"What problem with my case?"

"Even across the street," he adds in a conspiratorial parenthe-
sis. (He thinks I went across to Batson's.)

"That right?"

"Yes." He nods. "It was no problem, bro!"

"Thanks," I say. "Thanks, Orlando."

"Not me!" He cracks up, thinking of himself at Batson's, at any bar. Laughing some more, he bends his long body low enough that I can read his yarmulke, where the word METS is embroidered. "Phil went over. When we could not find you."

"All right, Orlando."

We walk to the elevator bank, and Orlando adds, his words drifting up to the vault above, "But of course you were not there!"

Orlando doesn't believe me. That doesn't matter.

And if Phil Bloch thinks I got myself a drink in the late afternoon? That doesn't matter either.

Coming out of the elevator onto the third floor, I walk past the detective assigned to watch the desk. He is doing the crossword, waiting for his tour to end. He looks at me with no expression. I give him a hello, which goes unanswered as far as I can tell. He does nothing to acknowledge me except let me by. I walk around him, skirting the metal detector. The hallway smells like a toilet has flooded again.

Inside, somewhere within the Habitrail of cubicles that comprise the Homicide Bureau, I hear Bloch. While the fluorescent lights still burn hothouse bright, no one else can be heard or seen. I enter my own cubicle and drop into my chair. I would close the door if I had one.

Here is Lamar Lamb's file—a heavy accordion file, color-coded pigeon-blood red (like good rubies) because it is a murder. I look at it without opening it.

I pick up the telephone—there was someone I wanted to call, a message. I've forgotten the message, and now I'm sitting here holding the telephone in midair, my index finger poised. (Nothing happens.) I am staring at Lamb's file like a good drunk. I am thinking about nothing. My only thought is that I am thinking about nothing.

The Lamar Lamb file sits untouched in the remotest corner of my desk. I'd like nothing more than to drop it in the Gowanus Canal and never see it again. I'd like nothing more than never to have heard of Lamar Lamb and the dead girl. Another dead girl.

I work on something else for an hour, avoiding home.

Now the sound of Italian opera drifts my way from Bloch's office. Several minutes later, Bloch himself appears in my doorway—a doorway with no door.

Bloch is darkly handsome, but his athlete's body is now flaccid and wide. When he was promoted to chief of the Homicide Bureau, one year ago, he moved to Jersey with his wife, a pretty nurse who loves him. His breath smells like coffee, and he's interested in stereo equipment. His office has a door.

"Where was you at, son?" he asks, using ghetto English to palliate his direct, almost accusatory, question—but also to mock himself, the Bloch he imagines for himself.

"Homicide funeral."

"Homicide funeral," he repeats.

"The dead girl," I say.

"The dead girl."

"That's right," I tell him. "You don't remember, Phil?"

"I remember," he says. (The bastard doesn't even remember.)

"I'm surprised you don't remember this case. You gave it to me last week. You told me it was a *good one.*"

"Right—with the girl." He remembers now but still thinks I

was across the street. "And the funeral was today? Wasn't she killed, what? Two weeks ago?"

"It was today."

In the neighborhood where she died, no one would take the girl's body without the cash up front, and two weeks passed before the mother hooked it up. Even then she didn't have enough for anything more than a plain box and a few hours on a Monday afternoon. For two weeks after the autopsy, the dead girl waited in the freezer for the mother to do whatever she had to do to get the cash, and the cold closed the single hole from a single bullet between her preternaturally large breasts—making her whole again in death.

"Well, anyway," he says. "Tell me the facts again?"

"Mostly I got a neighbor. Hears a shot and sees my shooter run out."

"From?" he asks.

"The apartment," I say. "Dead girl's mother's place."

"Which is where?"

"Cypress Hills," I tell him. "Out there in the Seven-Five."

"Good place to die," he says. "How old's your victim?"

"Fourteen. Just."

"Nice," Bloch says. "What's up with your Mr. Lamb?"

"Who knows," I say.

"Talking?"

"If he is," I say, "no one's told me."

"Why's he in the apartment?"

"You asking me? I'm here with you."

"No one else home at the time?" he asks. "This was her home, no? No one else sees anything?"

"Mother's there. She doesn't have anything for us, though," I say. "There's a sixteen-year-old there—a half sister or something."

"What's she have?"

"Same deal—a doughnut. Asleep, the mother says. Hears a single shot. Wakes up and finds her little sister dead."

"Anything more for the jury?" he asks. "Or we gonna have to rely on emotional value of a dead girl to prove—"

Bloch (the fucking idiot) shuts up the instant he realizes, too late, what he is saying. He sits there with a comical expression on his fleshy face, wondering what I will do or say. I ignore it, and at least he has the sense to move on. "They snatched him up last night?" Bloch says, acting breezy now on purpose.

"Yes."

"That's right," he says, trying harder. "Ran home to his mommy, and she turned his sorry ass in. Ha, ha, ha!"

"I guess he knows his Robert Frost," I say.

He senses what I have in mind is just his kind of thing; he brightens again and gives his head a quizzical shake, meaning that he wants another clue. I say, "The one about the hired man?"

"More," he says.

"Home being somewhere where—let's see," I say, making him wait for it, "where, *when you have to go there, they have to take you in*."

His laughter comes too fast. He is too ready for it, and he laughs too much. He draws in great billows of air and barks them out again. He laughs not at the joke, which is not funny, but because he wants me to know he gets it. I join him almost out of sympathy—proofing him against feeling foolish. Suddenly we are the jolly mates he imagines us to be.

But wait! I have more. "I guess *his* home is where they have to *turn* you in."

It is too much for him. His spare tire is heaving.

"Listen," he says, turning grave. "Some detective came around earlier."

"Which?"

"Little guy. North Homicide. Had to run back out, though. We have two bodies and another likely—and it's only six-thirty! Business is good."

"Did he want me to hang out?"

"That's the impression I got, brother," Bloch says. "Solano's the name. I remember now. The little guy."

"All right."

"Listen," he says, lowering his forehead but keeping his gaze on me so the whites of his eyes show. "Come across the street when you get things squared away." Bloch is happy to let me have a drink or two. He just wants to be there.

"We'll see," I tell him.

"All right?"

"We'll see."

When Bloch is gone I am tired, tired, tired.

I stare at my desk, a gray metal affair without a drawer. The drawer fell out without warning after thirty years in public service, spilling the contents—paper clips, duck sauce, pennies, china markers, green certified-mail receipts, chewing gum, yellow sticky pads, notes from Stacey, a Legal Aid Society telephone directory—on the gray-green linoleum. When I had collected them all, my knees were gray from the floor and so were my fingers. The drawer itself is now tucked away unused between my desk and the metal wall.

Atop my desk is a miniature police car. I bought it on Court

Street. The man who sells them is there every day next to the man who sells books on such topics as Malcolm X and Egypt, who is next to the man who sells incense sticks, oil ampoules, socks—whatever you need. He has several framed portraits of Queen Nefertiti in her precarious tubular headdress, and that block of Court Street is queasy-sweet with incense that mingles with the car exhaust, subway vapor, and hamburger grease. Next to him is the man who sells Ray-Ban knockoffs for five bucks. You can't tell them from the real thing. He rolls them up in a cloth when the police walk by. I own two pair myself.

Next to him is the man who sells kids' books in plastic wrap. There was one I remember. An anthropomorphic bird tries to find a better nest for himself. Unsuccessful, he comes home and sings a song:

> *I love my house,*
> *I love my nest.*
> *In all the world,*
> *My nest is best!*

Opal would ask for that one. She would say, "Daddy, read me the one I like."

"Which one, Opal? Be specific."

"What's *pacific* mean?"

"What book do you want?"

"Um, my *favorite*."

"What's your favorite?"

"Daddy. *Nest is best!*"

I would read her that book and then kiss her small blond head and close her light; she would pretend to be scared, and I would stay with her for a while on her small bed in her small room. I'd tell her to go to sleep. I'd tell her that nothing scary was going to get her. But something did. It was nothing more than a green Oldsmobile station wagon on an ordinary Thursday afternoon, but it sucked her from my car window as my arm reached out for her and felt only the empty seat.

CHAPTER

3

I t's late.

A beige clock hangs near my beige metal cubicle on the beige wall, its power cord stapled to the wall, down the wall to the baseboard below.

Seven-twenty.

The clock is fast, but even so, it's late.

Orlando sticks his cheery puss inside my cubicle and says *"Dude"* and nothing more. He stands there nodding his beautiful head. "Time to go fucking home," he says, smiling and nodding in agreement with himself. In his Castilian tenor, his gutter mouth is almost quaint—like a cabdriver shaking a fist from his cab window, calling you a donkey or a goat should you step unthinkingly off the curb into traffic.

Orlando is concerned about me. There is a dark cloud behind his cheer. He is surprised to find me sitting alone in my cubicle, doing apparently nothing except staring at the condensation bleed from the giant air-conditioning compressors outside my window. He stands there for several seconds before he walks away. In spite of what he may think, I was doing all right by myself. I have grown used to what it's like. Only now, after Orlando put his taut, brown, optimistic face in my cubicle, do I want to go across the street. I look up at the clock again. Seven-twenty-four. I have to wait—for my detective to come—for Bloch to go home. Soon, with a pantomime of manly regret, Bloch will leave his hearty crew. Until then I will sit here and do anything else.

I open another file. I withdraw a thick sheaf of photocopied DD-5 police reports and with a Magic Marker begin redacting names, addresses, apartment numbers, telephone numbers, social security numbers, beeper numbers, NYSID numbers, and anything else that would tell someone where my witnesses can be found, threatened, or killed before they can testify. Gratifyingly mindless work, but after several minutes I begin to see double from the marker. I rub my eyes and look at the wall.

Seven-fifty-eight.

Even if Bloch has blown, there still may be people who know me there. D.A.s at play are a friendly lot. They see you sitting alone and come over and say companionable things or buy you a drink or—worst of all—suck you into their little conversational groups and force-feed you camaraderie. And before you know it, you're nodding to questions and comments you can't really hear and laughing along with all of them like a jackass.

Later come the students. They gather and make themselves at home at long wooden tables. I see them from my hidden, solitary corner: self-conscious beauties smoking cigarettes with an unpracticed air and nervously peeling labels from Amstel Light bottles and letting the bits of paper fall to the floor. I am often there in my corner with the bar cat on a nearby chair, its head working industriously in the white fluff between its hind legs, one of which shoots obscenely straight into the air. They do not notice me plotting intrigues in the corner, alone and lonely, empty with love for all of them. I sit and drink and intrigue for hours. No one bothers me.

Drinks silently appear. When the cat finishes with itself it sleeps. When I run out of money I leave.

I visit the john for something to do.

A toilet has flooded.

On the metal stall partition is an exchange of graffiti between nameless cops and nameless A.D.A.s—one against the other—slur following slur, beginning with some slight, now lost, snaking its way around the partition. An arrow from LIBERAL DA leads to TAKE A TICKET STRIKE which leads to LAWYER IS ALL FAGGITS which leads to NICE SENTENCE PLUNGER FUCKER and so on. Someone has scratched at *plunger*, leaving *fucker* behind, deeming it a fair shot. They are all fair shots, I suppose. Nothing as profound as hate between the us and the them of the us and them, the A.D.A.s and the true blue of the city PD. We don't hate each other, not really. We just get sick of seeing each other—like the weariness of protracted matrimony (which I'll never know)—a familiarity that blossoms into weariness that blossoms into disdain. We are all what's made into the salami, the stuff no one wants to see—not even us. For my part, I don't see enough difference between us to choose sides and instead (with my Magic Marker) make a comma between *sentence* and what's left of *plunger*. That's better.

A fragment of a conversation in the hallway outside—somebody shot last night—no collar—no suspects. The voices and footfalls trail off to nothing, and it is quiet again.

I maneuver my foot around the upraised, enameled toilet seat, which falls forward with a sharp pistol shot. I flick my toe in the direction of the flusher handle, but there is no flusher handle. Nor in the other two stalls. In one, unflushed toilet paper floats amid a chewing-gum wrapper and a spent cigarette that trails nicotine.

In my cubicle, I lift the telephone and put it to my ear. The stuttering dial tone indicates a message. The message is from Steven Solano, the Brooklyn North Homicide detective assigned to the Lamb caper. I hang up the telephone and dial the number he left, which connects me to a machine. *Your call is very important to us; please hold and we'll be with you just as soon as we can.* And then there is Vivaldi.

Fuck you. I hit the receiver and dial again.

Nearby, an unseen woman walks briskly past on tennis shoes. The idea of her stirs me up. With the telephone receiver hooked between my shoulder and ear, I begin sorting things noisily in my cubicle, announcing my presence to her. In the process I notice for the first time an envelope lying to the side of my desk—sealed, yellow, oversize, addressed to me, and bearing a familiar seal and a case number that I recognize at once as Lamb's. A forensics lab report? I hadn't noticed it before. I have already received the medical examiner's autopsy report. I read it a week ago. No surprises. The cause of her death is "gunshot wound to the chest with perforations of the ventricle and left lung." They pronounced her at twelve-forty-five in the morning, August 4. She went D.O.A. at Kings County Hospital, which treats many gunshot wounds. Army surgeons practice there for war.

"North Homicide," says a voice in my ear.

"Solano working?" I ask.

"Who's this talking?"

"Giobberti. D.A.'s office."

"Yeah, uh, hang on," he says, then ineffectively covers the mouthpiece; through his hand I hear him say, "Hector. Hector! Stevie back there? The D.A.'s office— I don't know what the fuck— Awright."

Then to me, "Yeah, sit tight a minute there, counselor. He's in the back. Let me try to send you back there. Hang on—" and the line goes dead.

"Holy Mother," I say. I redial.

Your call is very—

Fuck you, Four Seasons.

In the yellow envelope I find a supplemental analysis report from the M.E. Here is something interesting. Inside the girl's dead body: living sperm. Now curious despite myself, I reach for Lamb's file and open it, slipping off the elastic band. I withdraw the legal-size folder marked "Police Reports," assembled neatly by Nina and left alone by me.

I've opened this file only once, when Bloch dropped it onto my desk with little fanfare but a serious, significant look. Handwritten in capital letters on the Homicide Bureau Investigation Report (enough to know this one wouldn't be any good)—AT T/P/O UNAPP. PERP DID SHOOT C/W (14 Y.O. F/B) ONCE IN CHEST KILLING HER. (*Fourteen-year-old female black.*) She was a parenthetical, an incidental detail, but that was not why I skidded the file to the farthest corner of my desk.

Fuck Bloch. Wasn't there a hard cast to his face when he said, "I have a new one for you, Gio—a good one"? This is his fat-handed way to resurrect me from the land of the lost.

Fuck him.

Fuck him and his psychotherapy. Fuck his uncluttered Cranford, New Jersey, life with his pretty nurse and his Sunday-morning garage sales. Fuck him in his fly-streamered, air-conditioned office. Fuck his door.

The telephone rings, and it is Solano. "Can't get down to you tonight, counselor" is what he says.

"You got it bad out there?"

"We had a multiple," he says, weary already. "Another guy just went D.O.A. I'm gonna be tied up for a good five, six hours."

"Give me the short and sweet, then," I tell him, but there is no answer. He is talking to someone else.

Then he says, "Here it is. On that one from last night? That collar from out there in Cypress? Lamb?"

"Right."

"The guy's talking. When we brung him in, he opened up a little."

"That right?" I ask him.

"He's got a version of events for you. I'm thinking you might wanna have a look at someone else on that one."

"Yeah, go ahead," I say. "Someone like who, Steve?"

"Listen. I gotta square some things away here. Let me come down there in the morning."

"All right," I say. "Like who you thinking about?"

He is talking to someone else again, then— "Look. The whole thing's looking like it may be an accidental discharge. I don't know. An argument and the gun goes off. I don't know. I'll stop down in the morning."

He hangs up, and the copy machine shatters the following quiet.

I push Lamb's file to its remote corner. I will give it all to Stacey in the morning. I will give her this case. Not because she wants to second-seat me, not because she thinks she's ready. And certainly not because we sleep together in plain view of everyone in the office except the oblivious Bloch, who quaintly thinks that despite my occasional predations upon local milkmaids and college students I would never, ever fuck anyone whose career I could advance—and certainly not a junior prosecutor separated from law school by a sliver of months, not years.

If he knew? (He might actually tattle, the fucker.)

The oblivious Bloch—the thought of him sitting alone and un-aware in his office on his Naugahyde couch. He has no idea that his fucking Naugahyde couch is just that, and Stacey and I fall upon it from time to time and then onto his itchy red carpeting, rubbing her pretty ass raw and my knees pink or the other way around if she wants that. He has no idea, nor does he know I still have a key to his door—my old door, my very own key, and we use it when her Midwood bedroom is too, too far away.

But it's not like that for Stacey. She doesn't fuck me for any other reason than she wants to. She does because she can.

So I will not give Stacey this case for barter, and that is not why she wants it. She thinks in her pointed zeal that she is ready for a homicide and would deserve it even if I weren't her daddy. I will give her the file because I can barely look at it.

The copy machine spills noise and white light again.

I feel myself rise. On tiptoe, I peer over a maze of glass and beige metal partitions. I see a blond head and nothing more.

I stand and walk to the end of the hallway, holding in my hand the M.E.'s autopsy report—a fig leaf. For all she will suspect, I will have come to make a copy! Perhaps she will let me cut in. "Oh," I'll say, "thank you," and then, bewildered by technology, I'll fumble with the machine, and she will say, "I think you need to push this button here" and lean over and push it for me, coming close.

(All this I think as I walk twenty feet.)

Standing by the copy machine, there is the girl, quite tall, in a boy-size T-shirt. FORDHAM LAW. Her yellow hair is held up in a careless knot by a single Dixon Ticonderoga pencil. She is standing motionless, poised. I am an intrusion. She starts slightly when I fall into her periphery. "Oh," she says, turning to face me. "I was going to do a cartwheel."

"Go ahead," I say.

"Okay," she says, and she does, hand over hand, gravity tugging FORDHAM LAW earthward at the apex. She rounds it off and lands lightly on her white Keds.

"Ta-da" is all she says.

She walks by me to the machine and lifts her papers from the sorter. As she passes, I smell soap. Walking away, papers in hand, she looks quickly back over her shoulder with a wry smile.

After that, there is nothing left to do but leave.

CHAPTER

4

Standing on the sidewalk outside 210 where the subway entrance falls into the ground, I am rooting fruitlessly through my pockets.

Almost nine now, and all has settled into a seemly silence. No one is around except the familiar man sleeping under the portico, tucked into the angle of the building and the pavement. His arms and legs splay at weird angles as though he's been dropped from a passing airplane. A rumble below sends a draft through the metal grating, humid with the mechanical smell of the train, vibrating—atop the grating—the man's assortment of found objects (dog-eared *National Geographic*s, a gooseneck lamp, a football helmet mask, flusher handles, expended toner cartridges), all spread out on cardboard.

I have no money for the train.

I walk off in the direction of home.

I turn off Joralemon onto Court Street, heading south. No people here, no yellow cabs, no cars at all except for the livery cabs—American four-door sedans painted black with whip antennas eight feet tall, barreling flat-out down the empty stretch of Court. A traffic light at Court and Joralemon blinks yellow, casting a regular pall.

The faint, cloying smell of incense drifts from the gutter, where a remnant smolders.

Walking past Batson's now, a lonely pocket of light and noise, I hear my name. Phil Bloch is at the pay phone on the darkening street corner. He hangs up and strides over quickly, first dipping a finger into the coin return. (No luck.) He is smiling and shaking his big head in mock disbelief, hitching up his trousers a notch, first one side, then the other.

"Guess who I was calling?" he asks.

I shrug, hands in my pockets.

"You!" he says. "How about that? I call you and there you are. Like fucking magic. You owe me a quarter!" he jokes, but he means it.

Bloch thinks I have come for a drink. Without another word, he ushers me inside, his broad palm pressing into the flat of my back. He parks me on a bar stool amid his crew. They sit aloof from the rest, closest to the air-conditioning. They are semi-important and self-important persons who come here to relax in the dark anonymity. Crowding here nightly, they sit and stand toasting one another and spilling drinks on one another's feet. They are, like me, career prosecutors unfit for any other kind of work, but they are also judges, defense attorneys, police detectives, local political hacks—Brooklyn boys all, but some in cowboy boots.

Inside, it is cool and dark—beer runs from spigots—people pack loud and close—girls sit on tall bar stools and bare their legs—men fall upon them with their teeth showing, for Batson's is a launchpad to many a sodden fornication, a Cape Canaveral of carnal veniality.

The place is a severe rectangle, an elongated boxcar, altogether featureless on the outside but for a plain metal door set between a pair of rounded windows allowing no light even at midday. On the door, dented at foot level, are the words BATSON BAR handwritten in black marker. The letters jostle one another where the author realized—too late—that he would come up short of space.

Bloch's crew seems glad to see me, and in no time I am nodding to questions and comments I can't really hear and laughing along with them like a jackass. I know them all, of course, and they know me. Bloch inherited them from me along with my office. He makes a joke of that. He plays that he's just squatting in my office and someday I'll come around and kick him out. "Uh-oh. Look out," he'll say when I open his door. "Here he comes. Here's Giobberti. Probably wants his office back! Gon kick my ass outa here!"

"That's right, Phil." I'll play along. "Beat it." Truth is, I don't give a shit. (I miss the door—that's all.) Bloch makes a joke because he does. He enjoys his office. He enjoys being a big fish in our little, bloody pond. He makes a joke because he thinks it *is* my office and someday I *am* going to come around and kick his ass out of it.

I'd been gone—*what was it? two months? three?*—when the boss put him in my spot. The D.A. made him chief of Homicide, without a word to me. One year ago I came back. Four months had passed. I walked into my office, and there was Bloch. There was his new desk and his new red carpet. There was the art-museum poster and the leatherette armchair. I stood in the doorway, still holding the doorknob, blinking, wondering if I'd gotten off on the wrong floor. But, no—there were the same fly streamers, dotted with the same fly bodies. There was the Naugahyde couch the color of dog shit. Bloch looked up from behind the desk as I pushed open the door.

"Gio" was what he said, dropping his *Stereo Review* to the floor. As I stood there, uncertain where I stood, the color of the Naugahyde and the sheen of the fluorescent tubes on it dialed up an inconsequential memory—a memory that was, for a change, not sickening to recall.

"The funny thing about that couch is that it reminds me of Mr. Kurtz."

"Who's Mr. Kurtz?" Bloch asked.

"He was my shop teacher. In seventh grade."

"Why Mr. Kurtz, Gio?" he asked, and the uncomfortable, self-aware look on his face dropped away, replaced by a softer one. (He no longer was thinking about his office; rather, if I'd come back too soon.)

I dropped into a chair. "Forget about it," I said—and, after a pause—"I'm out then?"

"Yes."

"When?"

"Week ago. I mean, I was running things as it was, Gio," he told me. "You know—since you left. Since—June, I mean. The boss made it official last week."

There was another pause. Bloch put his feet on his desk, and then took them back down. I suppose he didn't want to look too comfortable, but I didn't mind. The desk wasn't mine anyway—not city property—he'd bought it himself, along with the carpet, the museum poster, the bookshelf, the armchair, the American flag on a pole behind his desk. It didn't work, whatever he was shooting for; 210 sucked it all into its grungy orbit. Still, I said, "You got things squared away pretty nice in here."

"It's all Sandy. She's got a great eye, you know? Like I could pull this off myself! What do I know from decorating? You know what she does? She goes out to these garage sales, they call them. Every Sunday. I watch the kids, she goes to these garage sales out in Cranford there."

"To what?" I asked him.

"Garage sales?"

"That's funny."

"What's funny?" he asked.

"No. Nothing," I said. "It's just when Amanda came here, to New York, I mean, she wanted to know if there were any garage sales, and I had no idea what she was talking about. We don't have garage sales, I told her. We don't have garages. We have stoops. We have stoop sales in Brooklyn. She started going to stoop sales."

"Sandy's got a great eye for—you know. That sort of thing." He was talking for the sake of talking. "For what goes with what. Like I know anything about it."

"Well," I said, "it looks great, Phil."

Bloch looked around appreciatively and then, after a while, said, "No one knew when you were coming back. That's all."

"No," I said. "I suppose not."

After another while, he said, "I'm sorry, brother. I mean—all of it."

Bloch sits facing me now on a bar stool, one thick thigh angled toward his crew, the other bent protectively into my flank. He leans right in and asks what I'll take. His demeanor is moist and paternal. He is worried about me, worried that things may turn bad and embarrass him.

"She's the last of the chain-smoking judges," says someone to my right. There are three or four conversations going on now, and they come at me at once. *She smokes Chesterfields—And so he turns to me and says, "Mr. Dunbar, just what is your trial strategy?"—That's right! Right down to a nub and lights up the next one with it—And so you know what I said?—The Bar*

Committee will never—No, I want to correct myself—So I said to the judge, "Judge, I don't have no trial strategy; my trial strategy is keeping my client from testifying and then begging for mercy!"—Her fingers are all, you know, like yellow—Will never—There I go again—My trial strategy is making sure my fucking witnesses show up!

Male laughter all around.

This sort of thing continues, and then a glass appears in front of me. Just the clean, clear smell of it makes me feel better already. I take a drink and feel it sanitizing my corrupt insides. I finish off another and decide to stick around without even having to make the decision.

The usual thing. Another drink and I am tossing rude wit into the conversation. *These guys aren't so bad,* I begin to think. We are all laughing like jackasses. Bloch relaxes and gives me an affectionate sigh, no longer worried I may slip into a sullen funk and spoil his fun. He spins his tree-stump thigh around on his stool and away from me. He is letting me fly solo, pushing me from the nest of his crotch. I say something—something about someone having a face like Cruella de Vil—and we all erupt, but the reference brings the sudden hollowness that I must fill with more drinks.

Bloch beams at me, though. Another drink. Another. They come so easily. Bloch thinks I am all right. He is a good man. They are all good men. I look at each of their faces. Good men, but not much to look at: puffy, flaccid, florid, stubbly, drawn—lawyer pallor. Here is one, his longish hair swept back in a stiffly sprayed mane set off in tinted streaks. (This time I think of Simba. The Lion King.)

Recollections of Opal strike me like that, at the oddest moments—unfairly—when I am the least prepared for them. I am laughing along with this sorry crew, casting out hopeful glances for

college girls, and doing pretty well when the image of Opal's ratty
Simba forms and I can only stare ahead of me, suddenly anes-
thetized. I see Simba crammed into her little bag. She has gotten a
Barbie sticker from somewhere and stuck it on Simba's forehead—
it is matted into the yellow fur—she is walking around the small
kitchen in Windsor Terrace, swinging the bag from side to side—
she is singing something—*I'm a little aphid, watch me eat, tender
flowers are my treat* . . .

Later they arrive. Their high, effervescent voices shift the demeanor of this place, blowing away the sour cobwebs. Book bags
are dropped. Amstel Light labels are peeled. Cigarettes are lit.
They mill skittishly in their soprano girl-groups, full of hope and
dread, casting their quick, expectant glances about while they hold
on to one another for dear life. They are beautiful and horrible as
they hurl their narrow bodies tentatively into the wide world. They
are tourists here, really. They still thrill at the novelty of it all. They
plot and anticipate, and their plotting and anticipation mean as
much to them as anything more that may drop into their laps. At
twenty-one they already know what to do and what to say when it
happens, and they act like it's no big deal, but when it's over they
still think to themselves, *So that's what it is?* and they think it's real.

Bloch follows my gaze. A scornful frown shapes. He dis-
approves. He is no longer worried that I may slip into a funk; he is
thinking he cast me from the nest too early. (Here comes the thigh
again.) *Come back to us, Giobberti!*

Here is one now, a fair milkmaid. She approaches the bar,
where she looks with some dissatisfaction at her face in the mirror
while resting one foot upon its black-booted point. Pushing free of
the sourpussed Bloch, I stand. She is now two feet away, not look-

ing at me. At the end of the stretch of bar, the bartender shoots something into a glass. The girl looks straight ahead. A five-dollar bill in her hand is folded lengthwise like a stripper's tip. I look down the bar—the same bored, hopeful look I cast into tunnels for subway headlights.

Now is the time. I start to say something to the girl, something that I have said before. I open my mouth, but—

I feel the bar rise up before the words come out. The bar rises higher and higher, a glossy walnut wall. The girl has risen too. She has floated heavenward. From her perch, she finally looks at me. Her boot is right here. I could lick it. *How did she—?* From my perspective, she is swaying like Stevie Wonder—and so is the world above. Only I am held by gravity. All else has risen on some potent, giddy helium.

"Gio—what the fuck," Bloch is saying. (I don't see him, but he is up there too.) His voice is pitched as high as a girl's. I now feel his fingers like knockwurst in my armpits. I feel them draw me into the air above. I rise lightly, and at the apex my feet settle again upon their worn soles. And I stop, waiting for the return fall to earth. But gravity is my friend again. I have fallen up and landed on my feet! The floor is solid beneath me.

Bloch fills my vision. I am so close to him I can discern an ingrown hair on his neck—a rosy island on a white sea. His trim goatee moves with speech, saying nothing.

Behind him, the blank faces of his crew.

To my left, no girl.

"Mr. Kurtz," I say to Bloch.

"Jesus, Gio—" he says, walking me.

"Mr. Kurtz was a shop teacher, Phil." He is walking me somewhere. Out, maybe. But I want to tell him something. "At Xaverian. Great big guy—bigger'n you—big, big, big guy. 'Kay?"

"Yeah, all right," he says, ungently steering me.

"And—I remember this—one of the projects was an ordervound."

"A what?" he asks, not really curious.

"An *Or—Derv—Ound,*" I enunciate.

"An hors d'oeuvres—*hound*?"

"Very stupid—had a piece a wood shape like a—*hot dog*—an we had a put a head on it and ears and legs on it," I say, spitting for emphasis, "an holes on it—lil holes on its back—guess what the holes for?"

"I've no idea," he says primly.

"For the toothpicks!" I tell him. "Guess what toothpicks for?"

"Here we go," he says, opening the metal door with one arm and holding me upright with the other.

"Toothpicks for the—*oh shit! careful!*—toothpicks for ordervs!"

"All right. Here you are," he says, pushing me through the metal door onto Court Street once again.

"Fuckin thing—had a put ears on it."

"All right. You can get a car here," Bloch is saying. "Go home, Gio. Go home and dry the fuck out."

"Phil!"

"What," he says.

"I'm tryin to tell you somethin," I tell him on the quiet sidewalk. "But you're not listenin, Phil—somethin very important."

"Okay," he says patiently. *He really is not so bad.* "Tell me, Gio."

"The ears, Phil—were made a Naugahyde. Brown Nauga—fuckin—hyde! *Exact same color as your couch.*"

CHAPTER

5

I feel much better now, thank you very much. I could touch my finger to my nose, first right, then the left. I could have an entire conversation with you, and you would never suspect a thing. I walk along a line in the pavement to prove it to no one in particular. "Time to go fucking home!" (I say it like Orlando.) "Fucking. Fucking. Dude."

Who paid for my drinks? Bloch? He'll add it to the quarter I owe him.

I am walking home, angling through empty streets without giving it much thought. *What happened with Bloch's cab?*

I walk purposefully and straight.

I spit.

It lands on me.

I walk until I stop walking in front of her school.

I have stopped walking and am standing at the limestone stoop where I left Opal on two hundred kindergarten mornings—where I left her on that Thursday morning—where I saw her again in the afternoon.

Of the thousand possible paths between downtown Brooklyn and my home in Windsor Terrace, my walking feet have led me here. I have not been here for a year. I have not been here since she died—since that last afternoon when she climbed into my car. On this very spot, she climbed inside the car with the air-conditioning broken and the windows down, and as I drove off she told me something. *You're supposed to*— was what she said. *We're almost home,* I told her then, but home was farther than that, and for her it was the vanishing point on the parallax sidewalks along Prospect Park West, pushing farther away the faster I drove. She would never see it again, nor would I see it with her on my back as I ran the two flights to the apartment I can now neither afford nor leave.

The way she worked at the seat belt—her little hands struggling with the metal buckle—

I remember every detail of that afternoon. Everything is clear in my mind, except the end, except for her—she is just a cipher on the blacktop, a girl curled for sleep.

In front of her school now, I prepare myself for great emotion at this landmark of her short life. I wait for the accusatory finger to gather from the tree branches, from the limestone façade, from the dust on the windowpanes—to gather up and point at me for what I did to my own child.

I feel nothing, but it is nothing like forgiveness; it is just that I can swallow no more—I am a surfeit of blame.

I wait to see her face. I want to see her face, but I cannot picture her anymore.

There was a time afterwards when the memory of her and the sound of her and the feel of her was on my clothes and in the air, and it was so real I expected her to skip from around the refrigerator at any time, as if it were all a game, and say, "Here I am!"

I wait in front of the limestone stoop, waiting for something. But, like the premonition of an idea that evaporates with concentration, I feel nothing.

Without another glance at this sterile shrine, I move on. The alcohol has spent itself, and I am just tired. I have to pee.

Ahead a woman struggles to prop her Harley on a kickstand. Her back is to me as I walk slowly up. I see the narrow sinew flex along the dorsal side of her arms, which protrude from her sleeveless T-shirt as she strains against the handlebars of the machine—a tangle of chrome that must weigh as much as a veal calf. She turns at my approach, embarrassed now, seeing me see her. Her hair is short, there are tattoos, and she wears a nose ring, too. But despite her work to harden herself, there is a light sweetness in her eyes, and her hips are soft and maternal. She is far from home, but not that far.

I am in Park Slope, not far from home myself.

A sibling of Windsor Terrace, Park Slope is nevertheless the favored child. The streets here angle gently off Prospect Park and have names. The houses are laid down in leafy-fronted rows. They are broader here and taller, and their insides glow dully with mahogany and cherry. In this neighborhood, yellow Labradors in red bandannas run without leashes. Here, children named Jake and Jonquil call friends' mommies by their given names. Here, crew-cut women in sleeveless T-shirts blow down broad avenues at three in the morning, and softish men with longish hair can be seen carrying babies in papooses and cats in perforated boxes.

The good people here leave books free for the taking in neat piles on their stoops. They save glass bottles for homeless men to exchange for money to exchange for tiny Ziploc bags of crack cocaine. They leave bottles hanging in plastic grocery bags from delicate finials on wrought-iron fences, where Mexican men working for a dollar an hour tuck takeout menus in the metal scrollwork. An emptied grocery bag may then drift up into a tree and remain there as a fixture year in and out. Or it may loft up higher still and out of Brooklyn altogether, reposing in an elm in Queens or along the sky-line of the city that fills the western horizon like teeth.

I walk on, and Park Slope diminishes behind me to the north as I close in on my home. The brownstones grow more plain, more narrow, more squat—they lose a story or two as I walk south, as if in the shadow of Park Slope my neighborhood has stunted. The leafy canopies recede until there are no trees except the odd, stran-gulated sapling ringed with desiccated dog shit. The starless sky opens up, and under it appears a check-cashing place, a doughnut shop, an all-night laundromat.

An inviting bush presents itself, and I unzip my fly. Meanwhile, a marked patrol car rolls up. I give it a wave out of habit. It fixes me in its searchlight, and I blink and look for the command designa-tion on the rear bumper. 78 PCT. *Who do I know in the Seven-Eight?*

Soon I am in the backseat, wide and vinyl like a cab's. I turn my head from the window, open to the sobering breeze, and see the driver looking at me in the rearview mirror. His partner drapes a big arm over the seat and, turning his head, looks quickly at me through the wire cage. Neither says anything. They are both think-ing, *Lawyer is all faggits,* leaving me alone with a single thought of my own.

Thanks for the ride, plunger fuckers.

A few moments after that, I am home.

An hour after that, I am still awake.

I am drinking water and eating macaroni in my bare kitchen. There is music playing. I have the CD jewel box on the kitchen table, and I am looking at someone I don't know. (I am unhip: a civil servant in boxer shorts.) This one I didn't buy—Amanda's, left in the wake of her retreat from me like one of Napoleon's caissons in the Moscow snow. Her name is Fiona Apple, and she is an exotic piece of fruit, rare and round and sweet. I want to take a bite of her. But she is feeling sad (sullen)—something about the boyfriend.

What a fucking joke.

The telephone rings and I let it. Stacey, I know. *Who else calls me at three in the morning? Who else calls me at all, for that matter?* When the machine picks up I hear my own voice, over Fiona's, say, *"You have reached the number you dialed—"*

A beep, and I wait. *Do I need an answering machine?*

Mrs. Kretschmer now raps on the steam riser in her apartment below. I spin the volume to nothing. Fiona continues in silence. Her photograph is eight inches from me. She is beautiful beautiful beautiful.

There must be some way to meet her.

I am sitting in my kitchen with a narrow south window opening on to the backyard and the dark sky beyond. My place is more than I can afford by myself. Without Amanda's money, I can't afford it— or razor blades, or new shoes. Every two weeks, the People of the State of New York hand me a $1,374.18 check for services rendered; on the first of every month, I hand Mrs. Kretschmer $1,650.00 for these two bedrooms (one unused), this living room, and this kitchen. *But where would I go?* How would I ever pack Opal's little dresses and books and the rest?

Stacey is on the line, but she is saying nothing. In the background I hear a radio playing.

This place, this room, hasn't changed much. If Amanda were to *just drop by* (as I used to imagine she would, arriving in the same black livery cab she left in, looking a little bedraggled, like a cat that's made its way home after a rainstorm), she would find little has changed in a year, except that it is even more quiet now, quieter if possible than it was after Opal died.

We lived here together for ten years and with Opal for almost six. Windsor Terrace, where I was brought up but not born, for there are no hospitals in this neighborhood. There is not much of anything at all in Windsor Terrace except all that is familiar to me: the line of stores on Prospect Park West, the bars, the churches, the sidewalks, and the blacktop. Five square blocks of trim limestone town houses that are mostly detached and sober-colored. It is a detached, sober place. You can find parking here, but I no longer drive.

Amanda could move right back in, and it would not be any different for her. She would see right away that I have kept everything. She would say I'm sentimental, but I never threw out anything I connect with her, which consists mostly of Fiona and the little bribes from pharmaceutical companies—pens, flashlights, pads of yellow stickies, all of them featuring unpronounceable drug names and obscure, hopeful slogans. (TERAFLOXACIN MAKES CHG A THING OF THE PAST!)

If Amanda were to just drop by, she would see that I have not left her behind me.

If she were to call, she could leave a message on the machine. Maybe tell me where she is now?

I think if I were to pick up the telephone at this point, it would put Stacey in a spot; also, it would oblige me to talk to her, which would take time, and ESPN2 is broadcasting highlights from the Scottish Open in ten minutes. Nick Faldo is hosting. I am already in my boxer shorts, ready for Nick and those highland fairways beneath a gray, interesting sky.

Thank God for cable TV.

I keep eating. The long walk cleared my head. I am myself again, no longer falling down like a fucking freshman, and I am hungry. I am eating macaroni I bought from the corner bodega. The Dominican kid at the register thinks I am crazy or dangerous. He sees me come into his store and he reaches under the counter. While I shop, he stops watching Spanish TV and watches me instead.

I have to remember to pay the cable bill.

I won't remember, and they will turn it off again.

I stand and walk over to the window. Here comes a jet, headed for La Guardia. I see the landing lights of another behind it, and another behind that. They line up politely to get into New York. They turn somewhere over Staten Island and come up Eighth Avenue two thousand feet above the geometric anarchy of Brooklyn's streets. To their left, if they look, Manhattan is laid out beneath them like a cemetery in a train window, all lit up with an infinity of headstones.

Why is she still on the line? Hang up, for Christ's sake.

Stacey has not been the same lately. She is not reluctant to call me anymore. She calls me all the time. She calls me at night. She wants to come over, and she wants to know why she can't. She calls me at work and wants to talk. She sends me oddly affectionate notes that I read, somewhat embarrassed, then fold and put in my desk drawer; she sent so many that the drawer dropped onto the floor. Yesterday she called to say that she saw me reading a book in the open plaza near Borough Hall—if I had time to read a book, I should have time to have lunch with her, et cetera.

It was better with her before it was free. I don't know. If it's free, I don't want it.

Who said that?

It was Milton Echeverria—when I asked him why a good-looking guy like him had to pay for it. I was trying to needle him, fuck with his mind a little, but it didn't work. He just said that if it was free, he didn't want it. Then he smiled at me, as he smiled when I fucked up his murder case and gave him a walk.

Stacey is quiet, but I still hear the radio—the radio on the desk in her room in the apartment building in Midwood where I have been countless times, frequently drunk and always late at night, walking on tiptoe to avoid the mother sleeping in the front room with the white-noise machine on. But last night with her, it was the routine. All was familiar, yet oddly disconcerting—like stepping onto a stuck escalator. The delicious danger of the mother at the end of the hall, the girl things on the dresser, the CDs on the desk, the looming piles of *Glamours* and *Elles* and *Cosmopolitans*. Everything once imbued with the sheer pagan fun of fucking her— gone. I said I loved her, but it was just the frozen hand clawing from the ice for the tree branch that isn't there. She is nearly gone, like everyone else.

And yet for a moment I picture her reflected in a mirror. She is putting her shirt back on, and in the reflection she seems to me al-most perfect. I move to face her, but she has already turned away— unexpectedly, disarmingly, endearingly modest, face-to-face in the light.

"Stace?" I pick up the telephone after all. "Stace?" I repeat, but it is too late, and I can't hear the radio anymore.

Turn up the volume on Fiona, and Mrs. Kretschmer begins again with the steam riser.

CHAPTER

6

On the subway platform awaiting a workday-morning F train, and the platform is oddly empty. No one else is here at all except an old man in a limp windbreaker, and a mother and her child. The mother stands ten steps away from me, and the child—who is no more than five years old—circles her in ever widening orbits; the mother lets him and stands without any expression except weariness. She looks at the subway wall opposite, at the far wall above the third rail where a taped-up flyer warns DANGER POISON, evidently the same thing in Spanish, with a chiaroscuro rat crossed out to signify death. The mother stares blindly at the wall as her child swings out wider in a perilous apogee, and the blank look on her face makes me look from him to her to him. She stares at the rat-poison flyer and not (like me and the old man in the windbreaker) at the child or the single headlight now just visible in the tunnel. The approaching train pushes the underground air ahead of it like a syringe, and I feel it on my face. The old man's hair—which is thin and covers his visible scalp like a film—stirs in the onrushing air, and when the child finally, inevitably, silently succumbs to the trench grave of the open track, the old man does not move at all but seems only to say *"Oh,"* although the word is swallowed in the tear of iron against iron, and the mother still says nothing at all. Now the train is at the mouth of the station. I see the conductor in his window. When I jump, he is so close that I can see the shape of his hat, and the banshee wail of the train's brakes resonates cruelly as from the trench with the boy I climb.

(It is the sort of lurid fantasy that I have.)

On the morning F train, with the press of bodies and the heat ripening my well-earned hangover, I see Heather somebody—a Windsor Terrace girl, Opal's baby-sitter. Like a shot soldier, I feel nothing but surprise. I know I will feel more soon enough.

"Mr. Giobberti?" She is smiling anxiously—looking to me, to her friend with her, and back again to me—unable to think of what to say. She was at the funeral, crying piteously. I haven't seen her since that June day last year. Like everyone, she blames me for Opal.

"Heather. My God." I fold my newspaper under my arm and push through the peopled car. I see we both wish she hadn't said anything.

"Um, and this is Karen," she says for something to say.

"Hello, Karen," I say in reply. Karen smiles, a modern girl—pretty—only lightly pierced. "Well, well," I am saying. "Well, well."

"How *are* you?" Heather asks finally, reaching for my arm.

"Fine, good. You? What are you doing these days?"

"School. I, um—Karen and me are at FIT? Like summer school or whatever?"

"MIT?" I ask, not hearing her.

"No," Heather and Karen laugh. They are laughing at me. "It's, um, the Fashion Institute of Technology?" A lilt at the end of her sentence turns it into a question.

"Sure. You graduated high school already?"

"Yeah," she says. "In May?"

"No kidding? Well, well."

"Oh! I was like so ready to graduate."

"Tell me about it," Karen says laconically.

Heather talks to me, speaking very fast. I bend closer to her mouth and feel her warm words in my ear; I can barely hear her for the noise of her breath, the syncopated rattle of the train, and the useless blowing of the air conditioners overhead.

The F train now breaches from the earth and fills with unrelenting yellow light. Behind us, Fourth Avenue appears, and we rise higher and higher over Third Avenue at Sixteenth Street, climbing still. We all squint and blink like freed hostages. This neighborhood is an ugly stretch and uglier still from this viewpoint, from which the eye takes in not a solitary block but acre upon acre of gloom—not a slum, but low-rent and beaten down. A neighborhood in slow decline for a hundred years. Gray laundry hangs from windows. Here on asphalted rooftops are teetering brick chimneys. TV antennas—spindly anachronisms—speed past and are gone. Barely visible, the Statue of Liberty rises unspectacularly, a sordid old thing among sordid old things.

Heather goes on and on, using her hands for emphasis. Her breath smells like Cheerios and milk. I nod attentively. She is filling the air with words to avoid having to say anything. Karen is silent and dark, and she looks out the window, oblivious to this. There is a thin paperback in her hand. Camus's *The Stranger.*

Behind them both, a cemetery heaves into view: a broad spread of death nestled among the living. The dead are packed close. From the train window, their headstones make a skyscrapered city.

Here now is Karen—

She does not look at me at all. She is in a sleeveless number too small even for her slim body; it is not worn but superimposed upon her otherwise unimmured breasts, and climbs slightly at her waist to reveal white skin. There, a solitary ring is fixed, and beneath that is an indiscernible blue tattoo. Her hair—black, black like a Labrador's—is still wet from the shower. A blue vein like a wishbone is at her translucent temple. Karen must feel my frankly indiscreet examination of her, since she becomes suddenly self-conscious.

At Smith and Third Street, the F train submerges, descending into a tunnel cheerfully decorated with graffiti, visible until the dark again overcomes us.

Downtown Brooklyn, my stop, and the doors slide open. Fixed to jump onto the gum-speckled cement, I cannot move. I cannot leave them, nor can I bear to look at them for more than a moment. Instead, I am letting the doors close in front of me. I ride the train into the city.

When they step off at Twenty-third with relief and quick, embarrassed waves, I cross the platform for a downtown train and—freed now from the distraction of Karen—wait in the daze of a hangover and the sudden, staggering shock of seeing Heather so conspicuously alive.

CHAPTER

7

Back on Joralemon Street I come aboveground yawning an un-
covered yawn. Everything is addled in the hot light; nothing is
where it should be. I make my turn from the subway stairs and
nearly walk broadside into a newspaper kiosk. I look stupidly
around me, trying to make some sense of it. Everything here seems
familiar yet spun sideways and moved about. The downtown train,
I realize with relief and shame, has left me opposite my usual stair-
case.

I pass the man who lives behind a soiled column, nestled happily in the bosom of Brooklyn law enforcement. He sits on the
siamese fire-hose coupling on the wall, singing and shaking the
dimes and quarters in his waxy paper Pepsi cup.

Waiting for the elevator, which as usual is taking for-fucking-
ever, I lean against the wall. This is no good. The people and their
voices and their smells close in sickeningly. I cannot even bear to
look at them, but I hear their hellos and their morning talk of idle
friendship and hate them with the hatred of the sick for the healthy.

*If I can get moving again I'll feel all right; if I can sit down I'll
feel all right; if I can find a can of Pepsi I'll feel all right.*

Behind the reception desk on the third-floor entrance to the

Homicide Bureau sits Penny. Penny, like her desk, is forty years old
and huge. Examples of card-shop sweetness hang behind her: in-
spirational posters featuring small mammals overwritten with pastel italicized epigrams. Behind her as well, taped to the wall in a
place of special prominence, is a legal-size princess, drawn by Opal
with a light blue highlighter. Penny hates me.

"Are you in?" she asks, bringing me up short before the in-out
board. I cannot be bothered with her today, I am so hangdog. I sign
my name and turn to her, but she has already sunk her head into
her chest as she picks at a fingernail; her neck frames her face, a
beard of fat.

Waiting for me are two police detectives. One now peers over
the beige metal partition separating my cubicle from Nina's, his
arms resting effortlessly atop the frosted glass. The second cop is
seated inside, reading the *Post*. As I enter, he stands, transitioning
himself easily as small men do from one position to another. He
folds his newspaper and slaps it down atop my desk. I know him
and have known him for eight years, but that couldn't mean less to
him. He is Steven Solano. The other, I haven't had the pleasure.

"Here long?" I ask Solano. He sits again, crossing his thin legs
knee over knee like a woman. He's been up all night, but he's doing
better than I am. A .38 sticks casually from his waistband. The worn
wooden grip juts like a comma. He looks and smells like a smoker.

"It's ten-thirty."

"I take that as a yes," I say. "Who's your partner?"

"That's Carson," he says, jerking his small, shining head scorn-
fully. "The one with his dick in his hand," he adds loudly for Nina's
sake. "All right already. Sit the fuck down," he says to Carson with
effect.

Carson still hasn't closed the deal, so he pulls away with great
reluctance. He promises to catch up with Nina later, to which she

replies with a withering indifference that she punctuates with a stapler whack. Good for her. Probably looked up twice during Carson's play and not at all to say goodbye. Carson, however, seems the type that would miss the significance of that.

"Johnny Carson," he says, taking my hand. I say nothing about the name. He seems disappointed.

"Sit down," Solano says to his partner. "Let's go."

"What's your hurry, Steve?" I say. "Relax. Like Carson here."

Solano replies with a wave of his hand. Carson looks at both of us, his benign, bemused expression unchanged.

"You got anything for me?" I ask Solano.

"Like what do you have in mind?"

"On the phone last night, you said you talked to this guy Lamb. You write it up? You bring your file?"

"I got the file right here." He raps it with the side of his thumb, almost daring me to take it—*Ya wanna piece of this file?* It lies flat and neat on his knee. That's Solano—flat and neat.

"Can I see it?" I ask.

"What do you need?"

"I need your file," I say. "I need the five from the interview."

"I brought you a copy," he says, handing me the typed DD-5.

"Thanks," I say, taking the report without looking at it. "What's he saying?"

"It's all there," he says.

"Why don't you tell me?"

"It's all there, counselor."

I try to read the five. I am sweating. Above my cubicle, an underhung piece of ductwork is silent. A thread of dust trailing from a circular vent does not stir. And yet, twenty feet away, outside my window, the condensers hum and drip.

Carson is fanning himself with a narrow spiral notebook, looking for girls to walk by. I smell his Polo. His chest is very broad and entirely visible under his short-sleeve shirt. His nipples stare like headlights. His tie is draped, detective-style, over his neck and crossed at the sternum with the ends tucked into his waistband. Beads of sweat the size of ladybugs collect all over him. He even sweats big, I think.

People pass my cubicle, yet here I am trying to move as little as possible. Small beads of sweat form at my hairline. Aphids of sweat. *I'm a little aphid, watch me eat.* I hear Howard Stern on Nina's radio. (Pedestrian in the West Forties killed by a bicycle delivery-man on the sidewalk.)

Nina appears. "Sorry," she says, and I look at her, slightly embarrassed, and she smiles sadly back. She says quietly, "Gio, you know Omar Jones is on today in Part Nineteen. Mitchell wants the file over there right away."

"All right," I say absently. *"Jones?"*

"Yes."

I know Nina listens to people talk about me and about Opal and what happened. The office version is probably close enough to the truth to allow her to look at me differently if she wants to, or even to hate me. Opal spent hours at Nina's desk after school and on Saturday afternoons, fascinated by Nina's unrestrained tangle of hair, her lipsticked lips, her single-girl features so different from Opal's mother's and so like a five-year-old's Barbie notion of female beauty.

Opal had many friends here. She spent much time here with me. Amanda, in her residency, had little time for us. She was at her hospital, or if she was home, she was asleep after three days awake, learning how to take care of strangers. Opal at five and I lived almost alone. We were orphaned and widowed together. At night I put her to bed. In the morning, Opal knew not to wake her mother, and together we tiptoed around our breakfast, and I tried not to make her lunch.

"Opal, why don't you eat in the cafeteria today? Come on."

"I ate in the cafeteria yesterday. Because you forgot."

"I didn't forget, Opal. I was— How was it yesterday? What'd they have? Was it nice?"

"*Well,* they said it was pizza."

"Pizza's good, right?"

"*Well,* Daddy. Everybody and the teacher said it was pizza, but to me it looked like fish."

After school there was Heather; and if not Heather there was me. And if it was me, Opal came here. I have an image of Opal careening from cubicle to cubicle over the gray-green linoleum, bestowing her drawings as presents upon any and all. Some of them still hang taped to beige walls—princesses, whales, birds— rendered on legal pads in ballpoint pen and colored with high- lighters dug from the desk in my office with a door. I know where each of them hangs, and I have to walk carefully to avoid them all. I always speed past Penny's desk, never stopping even to sign out.

Nina, however, thinks I am *nice.*

"You're so *nice,*" she said when I turned glum after a murder conviction. We were across the street, Nina and I, alone after the usual happy riot, after the usual crew toasted me and Ireland and big tits and even the sad sack sitting alone in his Rikers cell looking at twenty-five to life. After they had meandered homeward sing- ing, Nina and I sat alone in that slow-motion intimacy of an early- morning empty bar, and I wondered aloud to her whether I'd done the right thing with the case. That was before Opal died, and I was that way then.

"Oh, don't say that," she said. "Don't talk that way."

"No. I don't know. I don't know. I don't know. It might have been that other fuckhead, that fuckhead. Crisco. What's his name? I don't know."

"No."

"It might have been him," I said. "It mighta, you know. Who knows?"

"Wait," she said. "Remind me. He's the one—"

"That was running afterwards. The one the old lady in the window saw."

"Oh, I remember," she said. "You think? No."

"You just, you just never really know, you know? No one saw shit. It's all—"

"You're just too *nice*," she said. "That's your problem."

"That's my problem?"

"Gio," she said.

"Yes."

"I want to tell you something."

"Yes."

"Are you listening?" she asked.

"Yes. I'm listening."

"Are you here?"

"I'm here," I said, putting my forehead to hers.

"No," she said, pulling back a little. "Look at me. Look at me here."

"Okay."

"God," she said, smiling, embarrassed now. "I wonder if we're going to remember this tomorrow."

"I don't know. I hope so."

"You probably won't," she said.

"Why do you say that?"

"Because you're drunk."

"What did you say?" I asked.

"You're so nice."

"I'm not nice."

"Why do you say that?" she asked.

"You don't know. Why do you say that?"

"I just think you're, you know, a nice guy," she said, shy. "I can talk to you about things, and you're like normal or whatever."

"Is that what you want me to remember?"

"No," she said. "There's something else."

"Good. I really wish you hadn't said that."

"Said what?" she asked.

"That I'm nice."

"Why not? It's true."

" 'Nice' is what girls say about a guy they'd never sleep with."

But she did. In a livery cab we went to her place. Over a suspension bridge at three in the morning we went to Staten Island, where people have lawns. The seats of the cab were maroon velour and very soft. I remember that for some reason. I can't remember her neighborhood or what it looked like apart from the cement walk over grass where we walked in the early morning while her neighbors slept. I remember her working the lock. I remember her turning off the alarm. I remember her looking inside before she let me in, and I remember she left me sitting on her bed alone for a while. I remember the way she looked at me when she came in and stood before me and let the dress come from her body while I sat in front of her. And I remember fucking her, but the next day Opal died and that was the end of Nina.

CHAPTER

8

Nina walks off, high-heeled, followed closely by Johnny Carson's impotent stare.

Then there is Stacey suddenly in the doorway of my cubicle.

There she is, but she stops short before entering and eyes the three of us eyeing her and spins her lissome self gracefully away without a word at all. There is something especially purposeful about her, and I remember her telephone call.

I trace my dampening hairline with an index finger. The thin alcohol stream in my veins has begun to percolate through my skin. My stomach feels defiled, scorched raw with liquor. There is an ache in my right knee, but that could be just a consequence of age. (I am thirty-eight already.)

In my hand the pink DD-5 interview report curls itself around itself. "He pins the whole caper on the mother," Solano says, sensing a need to paraphrase, but adding pointedly, "You got it all there."

I read it.

Investigation: Homicide #69/75
Subject: Miranda Warnings read
                      to subject Lamar Lamb a/k/a
                      "LL"; Verbal Statement by Lamar

1. On 08/20 at approx 0225 hrs, the undersigned detective along with Det Carson, 75, and Det Cortes, BNH, trans-
ported Lamar Lamb to the 75. Mr. Lamb was seated in the
Sqd Interview room.

2. At approx 0225 hrs, the undersigned read Miranda
Warnings from a card, and Lamar Lamb indicated that he
understood his rights and agreed to answer questions and give
a statement regarding his involvement in the incident.

3. The undersigned asked Lamar if he knew Kayla Harris
and he replied "Yes" and that he knew she was dead. Lamar
then stated that he was paying Kayla a social visit and had a
verbal dispute with Kayla's mother, Nicole Carbon. Lamar
stated that Nicole threatened him with a gun and told him to
leave. Lamar heard Nicole yelling and then a loud "pop."
Lamar further stated that he stayed with a friend that night
and did not go to the police because he thought the police
would beat him up. When asked where was the gun Lamar
replied he did not know.

As I read, over a loudspeaker I hear Penny's voice: "A.D.A. Giobberti, visitor at the front desk."
  "Puts himself there," I say finally, setting the five down on my
desk. "That's something."

Solano shrugs, revealing nothing.

"And the rest of it?" I ask. "His story, I mean."

"Horseshit," Johnny Carson says, and Solano throws him a shut-the-fuck-up look.

"That's why you came downtown last night?" I ask. "That's why the call?"

"He's got a story," Solano says.

"And you're buying it?"

"Let me say this. The kid don't come across half bad."

"So the kid comes across all right," I say. "You got anything more than Lamb's word on it? Or is that good enough for North Homicide?"

"I'm not taking a stand on this kid one way or—"

"I'm asking you, do you have anything more than this kid's story?"

"All I'm saying is you might want to look at the mother for this," he says.

"Because Lamb shits on her?"

"Because the kid may be straight up," he says, no longer defensive.

"All right," I say. "The kid's got a story, and he tells it pretty good. So where's the gun? You tossed the place, right? And Crime Scene was there, too. Went over it pretty good, and no gun, right?"

"No gun."

"If it was there," I say, "patrol, Crime Scene—somebody would have found it." He doesn't say anything. "Look, Steve. The way I see it, if the mother does the shoot, the gun's gonna be there when you roll up."

"Unless she hid it, the mother," Carson suggests.

"No way," I say. "Crime Scene would have been all over that

shit. Someone would have found it. She woulda had—what? Four, five minutes after the neighbor calls 911? No fucking way. Your kid has the gun. He's your shooter, Steve."

"Look," Solano says finally. "All I'm saying is, there might be some, whadaya call it? Something to what this kid's saying."

"That it's an accidental discharge?"

"Maybe, yeah."

"That's the PD's position on this thing?" I ask him. "An accidental fucking discharge?"

"No," he says. "That's just me telling you."

"So what is the department's position on this homicide, then?"

"Closed out," he says. "One arrest."

"You reopening the investigation?"

"No."

"The girl's mother, Nicole what's-her-name. She a suspect on this thing?" I ask him.

"No," he says. "Not officially, no."

"So this homicide open or what?"

"I been saying it's a closed-out case, counselor—"

"Then why are we having this conversation?" I say, too loudly. Someone walking by looks in and sees me almost standing and Solano sitting with his arms crossed. "Christ. You brought me this case. I don't want this fucking case. You arrested Lamb."

"We had probable cause."

"Don't be a lawyer," I tell him.

We are staring at each other now, but he lets it go. "All I'm saying is you might wanna look at her is all."

"*I* might want to look at her?"

"Yeah. You might wanna," he says. "In case there's something to it."

"Why not the PD?"

"I think we got a jurisdictional thing, counselor. An impediment," he says, turning sheepish—he's got a bullshit excuse, and he knows I know it. "On account of there's a closed-out case. Closed out with an arrest, so it's a D.A. thing now. In the D.A.'s office."

"So that's what this is about."

He shrugs—a bureaucratic shrug, as if to say *What are you gonna do?*

"It stays with you until I get a voted indictment, Steve," I tell him. "That's the arrangement."

"Je-sus," he says, rubbing his eyes and now looking tired. "Where are we with this?"

"I'm telling you I got my perp," I say. "You want the mother for this, then get her yourself. And get me that gun. Lamb has it."

"And what's she gonna shoot her own kid for," Carson wonders out loud. We ignore him.

"Where'd he say he went that night?" I ask Solano. "A friend's? Who's this friend?"

"He don't—" Solano starts.

"You toss that apartment of his?" I ask. "His grandmother's?"

"Yeah, but he was at the Bedford Armory before he come home."

"Nothing interesting at the grandmother's?" I ask.

"Nothing useful," Solano says. "A lot of interesting."

"What?" I ask.

"Just a shit hole is all."

"You made a mess?" I ask.

"We made a different sort of mess," he says. "And Carson ain't stopped scratching himself since."

Carson looks up. "What . . . ?"

"He says you got an itch," I tell him.

"Where?" says Carson, smiling.

"Next time use rubber gloves," I say.

"Rubber gloves," he says. "That's good."

Stacey walks by again, not even looking in this time, and Johnny Carson smacks his knee. "Now I remember where I know her from. That lady D.A. who come past."

"Who?" Solano asks without interest.

"The one that just come past. Remember?" Carson says. "That's the A.D.A. I was telling you about. The one Mikey was with that night. You remember when we were with Mikey last winter, out in Bay Ridge there. You remember?"

"That place with Jimmy Calloway?" Solano asks.

"That's right." Carson is laughing.

"No wonder you didn't recognize her. Now that she's standing up on her feet."

"I tell you what," I say, cutting them off. They are both laughing. (It is unnerving to see Solano laugh.) "I tell you what."

"What," says Carson.

"Just go—get something to eat, get some sleep. I got somebody waiting on me up front. Plus that civilian is coming down this morning, the neighbor. I have to put her into the grand jury this morning. Come back after lunch."

Solano balks. "Counselor, I been up all fuckin night."

"It's all overtime, then," I tell him. "See who's looking for me up front. Send him back if he looks friendly."

CHAPTER

9

"You A.D.A.—*Gee-o-bert?*—*berty?*"

"Giobberti?" I say, looking up into an unfamiliar face peering over the top of the glass partition on my cubicle. "Who wants to know?"

"I'm looking at this notification here from Appearance Control—"

"Who are you?"

"Archer," he says.

"Yeah."

"F.A.S.," he says.

"F.A.S.?" I ask. "The fuck is that?"

"Firearms Analysis Section," he explains.

"Okay." I play along. "The fuck is that?"

"What they're calling Ballistics now," he says, seating himself. "Since they moved us out to Queens—out to the Jamaica section there."

"Archer," I say, rubbing my sore knee. "What kind of name is that for a ballistics guy?"

"What? Oh, I see."

"Why don't you tell me about what you got?"

Archer considers the question. He draws himself up in the chair. "There's really not much to say." He is a big man with a mouth shaped like a cat's, and hands that look strong enough to crush cantaloupes. Even so, his demeanor and movements are delicate and make me reflexively look for a wedding band, which he is wearing. (I feel ridiculous for looking.)

"I took a look at the shell casing," he says. "From the scene."

"Fine, Detective. Tell me all about it."

"It's a Remington twenty-five-cal shell. Clean pin mark. Good extractor mark." He thinks for a moment about it. He actually looks at the ceiling as he thinks. He looks for so long at the ceiling that I, too, look up, wondering what he sees. The silent ductwork winds among tubes of fluorescent light. Nothing seems amiss. "That's about all I can tell you," he says finally, looking at me again.

"And?"

"That's it."

"What about the bullet? The M.E. took a slug out of the girl."

He pulls back defensively. "Like I said on the phone, my job was just the shell."

"Look, Detective, can you just call someone at Ballistics—"

"F.A.S.," he corrects me.

"At F.A.S., whatever—and find out what's up with my goddamn bullet?"

"Like I said, my job was—"

I drop the telephone in front of him and walk out of my cubicle.

A piece of paper taped to the Pepsi machine reads, "This machine eats MONEY! You have been WARNED!" in a girl's loopy handwriting.

I stand for a moment at a loss, staring at the button I wanted to press.

Lately I've had trouble with this sort of thing (indecisiveness—along with drinking too much and fucking around and crossing the street and driving cars and thinking about pulling children from the paths of trains and Chinese deliverymen). *Isn't indecisiveness an element of unmanliness—a symptom of weakness—a worrisome pussiness? Is it, and the rest, a portent of worse to come, a stone fleck in the windshield radiating slowly into an ever widening spiderweb?*

Maybe Bloch is right and I am going to crack up.

After that business with Stacey—*when was it? Sunday night?*—when I told her that I loved her and didn't mean it (we both knew I didn't), I stood unmoving at three in the morning in the corner bodega before the open refrigerator case looking at a solitary carton of milk. Inside the bodega, even at that hour, it was still hot and close, and the place smelled lightly of sawdust and kitty litter. I'd just come from Stacey's. In my pocket was a sock, and while my head still spun pleasantly from the residue of drinks circulating in my blood and the scent of her still lingered on my clothes, I knew I'd made a mistake.

Fuck me, I knew I would say in the morning, and I tried not to think about it anymore. I thought about milk. There was only the single carton, lonely and sordid, reminding me of—me. Must be sold by: tomorrow. I saw it turning into rancid cheese in my otherwise empty refrigerator. *On the other hand* . . . I walked away, wizened with indecision. I walked to the bodega door, to the relief of the lone cashier, the dark Dominican kid who'd turned away from the Spanish channel to watch me stare into the refrigerator case. He was behind a counter, framed by a Plexiglas rectangle of candy bars, paper packets of aspirin, vitamins, razor blades, and condoms.

His hand was under the counter. *What did he have there?* He was ready, in case I did something stupid.

As I walked to the door, his nervous hand was still out of view, reaching for whatever he had under the counter, as if he knew the truth—that I am a killer.

I remember the mini-fridge down the hall—a metal cube covered with oxidation and radio-station stickers, the freezer shelf a boxer's eye closed with frost. The mini-fridge is overfull with brown bags and Tupperwares and Lean Cuisine lasagnas, which at noon are microwaved, giving a warm, oleaginous cafeteria smell to this corner of the third floor. There are sodas in there too. If I took one, I could buy another and slip it back before it is missed.

A good plan, but still I hesitate. The mini-fridge, I remember, is in the cubicle next to Stacey's, and she may spot me if I am not careful. There is something on her mind, and I really can't take her in this condition.

I risk it, but as it happens she is not there. I sneak somebody's Pepsi and fumble with the metal tab, which releases with a medicinal *phit.* I take a long swig and feel the acid burning away the fuggy humors in my stomach.

I turn, and there is Stacey. Despite myself, I am glad to see her. Notwithstanding everything that is wrong with her—with us together—she is—*what is she to me?*—something important.

"What the fuck happened to you?" she asks.

"What?"

"Your face." She frowns at it.

"Oh," I say, now moving my hand over my jaw. "Shaving. Is it noticeable?"

"Only when I look at you," she says. She walks over to have a closer, proprietary look at me, then takes the can into her hand, slim and brown, like the rest of her. Her brown eyes match her eyelashes and her eyebrows and her sunned skin, but not her long hair dyed auburn to break the monotony. "What'd you shave with? A badger?"

"No, no," I say. "I need some . . ."

"Razor blades?" she suggests helpfully, taking a drink.

"Right."

"Good morning," she says, smiling at last.

"Hi," I say weakly.

"So, did you get my message or what?"

"Yes," I say.

"I guess I should say messages, shouldn't I?"

"Only three."

"You probably think I'm turning into one of those girls you talk about. Always calling. Invading your *private space*, or whatever you call it." She considers the Pepsi, waiting for something from me. "Well, anyway." She shrugs and lets it drift. "Pepsi. You *must* have it bad today. That why you didn't call me back?"

"No, that's not it."

"Where'd you go?" she asks.

"A funeral is all. Or a wake, I mean. A viewing."

"You sure?"

"Yes," I say.

"You don't sound so sure."

"It's why I didn't call," I say.

"Ran pretty late for a funeral or a wake or a viewing or whatever."

"Now you sound like one of those girls," I tell her.

"It was the girl's funeral? The fourteen-year-old?"

"Yes."

"Oh," she says. "Was it really sad?"

"No. It was— There was no one there, really."

"But that's so sad!" she says, meaning it. After a pause, she says, "I wanted to talk to you, Gio. Something important."

"Is it?" *Here it comes.*

"Is it important?" she asks, as if she hadn't thought of it that way. "Well, it's important to me. Sit down."

"You pregnant or something?"

"If I am, it's not yours, cowboy. Just sit down."

"I don't want to sit down," I say.

"It's only that you're either gonna sit down or you're gonna fall down."

"Okay." I sit down.

"I'm gonna tell you something," she says in her direct way— one of the things that keep me interested in her. "I want to work this homicide with you. The girl case."

"No," I say for some reason, although I've already decided otherwise.

"Why not?"

"Why do you want it?"

She looks down quickly. "It sounds like an interesting case."

"It's not a good one," I say.

"Get the fuck out of town!" she says, looking up.

"No. It's really not."

"What are you saying?" she says. "You have the witness across the hall, you have—"

"That's not—"

"It's a great case—a lock and load, you said so yourself—"

"Is that how I talk?" I ask her. *"Lock and load?"*

"I wasn't quoting you, asshole."

"I said— I forget what I said— Look— And how do you know so much all of a sudden?"

"You told me about it last week. We talked about it. Jesus. What do you think, I'm, like, screwing you so I can sneak a look at your secret red files?"

"I didn't mean it's not a good case," I say, knowing that I sound defensive. "I meant it's not a good case for you."

"Now remain calm, Stacey," she says aloud. "What the fuck does he mean by that? There's got to be some innocent explanation, or else we're gonna have to kick his ass."

"Just a sick case is all, Stacey. Dead girl—"

"What, do you think I can't take it?" She steps back to punctuate her disbelief.

She is small. Even standing before me seated on the desk, she barely looks me in the eye. Five feet three (just) without shoes. The fourteen-year-old is bigger than Stacey. But her proportions are fine; you don't think of her as small unless something puts her into perspective.

She is wearing a little blue suit with a little blue skirt. Grown-up clothes. This is a new thing for her, this business of waking in the morning, dressing, going to work—the business of being an adult. And although she is a year into it already, there is still novelty in it for her. As I see adulthood settle onto her in the form of little suits and handbags, I find it strangely affecting, as if she were mine, as if I were watching her grow—

And yet, on her chin, an infinitesimal blemish gives away her proximity to adolescence.

"I didn't say that," I say. "It's not that."

"Then what?"

She doesn't know, and I can't tell her—we are not that way with each other.

"The bullet's a twenty-five," Archer announces cheerfully as soon as I pass through the opening of my cubicle. He says it as if he expects a pat.

"All right. What else?"

"We can't match it up with the shell, if that's what you're asking. Until we have a gun."

"The gun I'm working on. Tell me about the bullet."

He has taken notes on a coffee-stained napkin, which he reads through eyeglasses as he speaks. "Deformed fragment—looks like a five right twist—semi-jacketed—hollowpoint. That's what killed her," he says, putting his glasses down. "Goddamn hollowpoint slug. Mushroomed when it hit her. Turned into a—a propeller, like, through her body."

I think quietly for a moment. The sucrose and caffeine from the Pepsi are beginning to have their happy effect, and I am thinking again. My telephone is ringing. "Listen. What I want you to do is run the slug and the shell in the computer." Archer looks nervously at the telephone. This is interesting: *a ringing telephone must be answered!* "Can you do that for me, Detective?"

"Sure," he says distractedly. It seems he will grab it himself if I do not. "But the database only goes back a couple years."

"Let's see if the mutt used this gun before. Okay?"

"Sure," he repeats, not sure whether he should speak or let me answer my telephone. He wishes I would get the telephone.

I pick it up, and he is visibly relieved.

"And by the way, what was that fuckhead saying about me?" (Stacey, of course.)

"What fuckhead?" I ask her.

"That—sweaty fucker, who was leering at me all morning. Johnny Walker. Something stupid like that."

"Carson," I tell her.

"Christ, is that his name? *Johnny* fucking *Carson?* Is he serious with that name?"

"Why do you think he was talking about you?"

"He was, wasn't he?" she asks flatly.

"Why do you say that?"

"Just cut it out," she says.

"Why does it matter?" I ask.

"I want to know what they were saying about me," she says. "To you."

"Let me call you later," I say.

"What did he say, Gio?"

"He didn't say anything to me," I tell her truthfully.

"What did he say?" she demands.

"The usual shit."

"What did he say?" she asks, tired of asking.

"Some shit about you and someone named Mikey something or other. To tell the truth, I wasn't listening."

She hangs up the telephone and immediately calls back. In the interval, I give Archer a shrug.

"Homicide," I say.

"What else?" Stacey asks.

"That's really it. I wasn't paying attention." I put one hand over the receiver and shake Archer's hand perfunctorily with the other. He is reluctant to go. He is enjoying the show and lingers in the doorway for a moment before he leaves.

"What else?" she asks.

"Essentially that you're a copsucker," I say, using the word she hates. "That about sums up the whole thing."

The line goes dead again.

I hang up the telephone and swivel my chair around to look out the window, doing nothing more than that for several minutes.

Then, behind the air-conditioning compressors, I see Stacey, having a smoke. She is outside now with some other young A.D.A.s— all of them women—all of them smoking like Russians, throwing their cigarette butts onto the catwalks and walkways, where they blend with pigeon shit underfoot.

Stacey eyes me, then she throws me her middle finger.

Beyond my window, beyond Stacey, beyond the smokers on their perch, a solitary plastic D'Agostino's grocery bag lifts into the sky and pauses momentarily there, hanging fire on a flaw in the wind until it lifts up again—lifting higher and ever higher—passing out of sight, and is last seen drifting in the direction of the Williamsburg Bridge.

When I look again in a moment, there is another and another softly roiling out there. There are, it seems, hundreds of D'Agostino's bags and Pathmark bags and Gristede's bags and, from the city, a Fairway bag turning now on the rising air in a laconic swirl, as if in a French movie. I see a boy of ten in brown velvet knee pants come running along the wooden walkway, shouting skyward in soprano syllables, *"Maman! Regardez!"* I imagine him sliding silently on the slick shit and cigarettes, disappearing from view. I imagine myself plucking the boy to safety from his Harold Lloyd handhold on the flagpole projecting just over the roof's edge as police Caprices—blue, black, and gray—come and go three stories below—

"Homicide," I say into the intruding telephone, which startles me with its ring.

"Mr. Giobberti," says a familiar voice, mispronouncing it (on purpose), twisting sarcasm with measured contempt.

"Yes," I say to Judge Harbison.

"This is Judge Harbison."

"G'morning, Judge."

"Good morning, now where are the fucking grand jury minutes for Unique Williams?" A pause. I am looking for my case list. "They were due in court last week," he says. I am still looking.

"I'll get them to you today, Judge."

"Yes you will, Mr. Giobberti, or I'll dismiss your fucking indictment," His Honor says before abruptly hanging up the telephone.

I look back through the window, and Stacey is no longer there. I stand and walk, as I must, to her cubicle, and when I ask her to ride along on the case she still does not understand that I need her or why. She just thinks she won.

CHAPTER

10

Miss Iris sits in the witness room and, in this unfamiliar, somewhat forbidding place (with its sooty windows and stained carpets and loud voices in the hallway beyond the door that locks from the outside), holds on to her Harrods tote bag for dear life with both hands. Still, she is a woman of some bearing. She is not *Iris* to one and all, but *Miss* Iris—slum aristocracy. She looks up when I swing open the door. Despite her size (her legs are full like taut porpoises), she seems small here.

I introduce myself to her and then add, "And this is Stacey Sharp." Stacey is my Harrods bag.

There are the preliminaries, which are pleasant enough. Miss Iris relaxes herself. She soon becomes expansive and wants to talk, but I am anxious to move it along. I don't do well with this sort of person. She is all whipped sweetness—as full of cloying platitudes as the kitten posters behind Penny's desk. I prefer witnesses who would kill me as soon as look at me: with them you know where you stand.

When it is time to get down to business, Stacey runs the interview.

"What did you see, Miss Iris?" Stacey asks.

"It was that boy Lamar," she says, her Jamaican purr putting me to sleep. "He come out of the door. I was sittin right there on my davenport when I hear the gun."

"You thought it was a gun?"

"I know it was a gun, daughter," she says seriously. "Don't I hear guns every day and night? All night long they be goin off. Poom, poom, poom. Dear Lord. A bullet come in the window, right there. It shatter like that, and wasn't nobody comin to fix it for a month. I had put a grocery bag in the window, a plastic bag for a window if you can believe it, and it bein winter and all." Miss Iris shivers at the recollection. "But this night I was tellin you about, it was next door. Poom. Just like that. Poom. I hear the gun and think, That'll be some trouble now."

"What happened then?" Stacey continues.

"That's when I seen the boy, didn't I? He was comin out the door."

"Across the hall?"

"Yes."

"How did you see?" asks Stacey.

"I got up from the davenport and walked to the door. When I opened it, there was the boy Lamar—Betty's grandson."

"How long after the noise did you open the door?" Stacey asks.

"It was real quick. When I hear that noise, I thought there would be some trouble, and I got me right up."

"Did he see you?"

"I don't know," she says anxiously. "Do you suppose he might have done?"

"You knew him, though," Stacey says. "You knew his name."

"Yes."

"You've seen him around the building or what?"

"Yes," says Miss Iris. "He was always comin over. He used to live downstairs. With his grandmother."

"He doesn't live there anymore?"

"No," Miss Iris says. "Not for some time."

"When did you see him last?"

"That night. When he come out the door."

"What?" Stacey asks. "Why would he be next door? What reason did he have to be there?"

"He have a couple reasons, I think," Miss Iris says, shaking her head. "None of them very good."

"Did he know Nicole Carbon?" I ask her.

"He know her," Miss Iris says. "Plenty of men know her, if you take my meaning, Mr. Giobberti. You can look at her and see what she's into, that woman. All sorts of activities in that place. *All sorts of activities.*"

"Lamar sold to her?" Stacey asks.

"That boy's always into nothing good."

"For how long has he been coming around, if you remember?"

"Good two, maybe three months," Miss Iris says. "And before him there was others."

"What others?" Stacey asks.

"There was several."

"Do you remember any in particular?" Stacey asks her. "Anyone else you might have seen around there?"

She considers. "I recollect one that I won't soon forget. He was the crippled one."

"A cripple?" Stacey asks.

"In a wheelchair. That's something you don't see every day. But he stopped comin on account of the elevator."

"What about the elevator?" Stacey asks.

"It stop workin," Miss Iris tells Stacey.

"What was the other reason?" I ask.

"What's that you're sayin, mister?"

"You said there was another reason why Lamar came next door."

"Well, Mr. Giobberti, he was fond of the girl now, wasn't he?"

"Utopia?" I ask.

"No," Miss Iris says, smiling. "She's too grand for any boy in that vicinity. She won't have none of that lot. I'll see to that. She's my special one, you see. No, mister. It was the other one he come for. The younger of the two sisters was involved."

"How involved?"

"For love or money, but for sure they was involved with one another."

"What do you mean?" I ask.

"Don't you listen, Mr. Giobberti? You would make a Christian woman tell you things in plain English that shouldn't be said at all? The young girl—like her mother, she was a whore for money."

"All right," Stacy says to me in her cubicle. "Now tell me the rest."

We are sitting together after walking back from the courthouse: cement, slab-sided, sixties—shaped like a shoe box and inspiring no awe inside or out. There Miss Iris did her thing. Looking stiff, still holding her Harrods bag, sitting in the witness box (the only wood in the narrow beige room), she gave her four-minute version to the grand jury. I stood in the back asking her questions. Stacey sat in front watching the Q and A like a tennis match. And the grand jury listened to Miss Iris and had no idea what it all meant.

"The rest of what?" I ask Stacey, reaching for my Pepsi, now warm and flat.

"Like what else you have, besides Miss Iris?" she asks. "Even the jury was looking at you like, What the fuck is this all about?"

"She's the first witness. That's how it goes in the grand jury.

It isn't a trial. You don't always have time to get your witnesses squared away before you begin a presentation—sometimes you have to just start throwing them on the stand."

"So there are more witnesses."

"Sure," I say. "Solano's gonna testify, maybe. I got the ballistics guy tomorrow. There's—"

"No eyewitness."

"It's a circumstantial case, Stacey."

"Right now it's not even that." She frowns. "Miss Iris sees him leave. That's all."

"A minute after the shot, she sees him leave—I'll take that. What more do you want?"

"More than that," she says quickly.

"More than that you have to work for," I tell her. "Miss Iris is free."

"You got two other civilians inside?" she asks.

"The mother and the sister."

She nods. "Asleep through all this, they say?"

"Right."

"So your theory is—what, Gio?" she asks. "Help me."

"I don't have a theory, Stacey," I say. "He fucking shot the girl. That's my theory."

"And?"

"And what?" I ask.

"He shoots her, and?"

"And nothing. Does the bird," I say. "Flies the coop, you know? What do you think, he's gonna wait around?"

She is still nodding, skeptical. "Who's working this case for you? Not *Johnny Carson,* I hope."

"No," I say. "He just does what Solano tells him to do."

"What's Solano's take on it?" she asks. "He's cool with Lamb?"

"He's—you know."

"No," she says. "Tell me."

"He's—he wants to look into another angle," I say. "Or what I should say is, he wants us to cover his ass on the kid's statement."

"What statement?"

"The kid's giving up the mother for the shoot," I say. "Solano's— It's nothing. He's playing an angle for himself, is all. Typical shit. Everyone's got an angle they want to play. Solano. Lamar."

"What's he say?"

"Lamar?" I ask her. "Says he's innocent. What do you think? That he wet his pants and apologized? He said the mother capped off the girl—an accident."

"And Solano believes him?"

"Fuck I know, but he thinks it's worth a look, just not worth his time," I say. "He wants us to look into it. It's what I'm telling you."

"Why don't you?" she asks.

"Don't I what?"

"Look into it," she says. "The mother angle, I mean."

"Because I don't feel like it, for starters, plus it's bullshit, Stace. It's— You gotta understand, this is typical. This sorta shit goes down all the time. He doesn't believe the kid, Solano. Not really. He just wants the D.A. to get his back on it—you know, so he doesn't get jammed up with his lieutenant down the road."

"Listen," Stacey says. "What's it hurt to look into his story? I mean, why the hell not? You got nothing solid on Lamar, but you, like, already decided he's your shooter." She is looking at me. "I gotta tell you, Gio," she says. "You're acting kind of weird about this."

"Fuck you, weird."

"How'd you leave it with Solano?" she asks me. "He's doing follow-up with the mother, then?"

"Look, Stace, enough with the face. Forget it. Let it go, already. It's all fucking politics."

"Your head up your ass is not politics," she tells me.

Stacey is looking at me the way she does sometimes, as if she is trying to see me better, as though I'm hiding something interesting from her—the same way she looked at me when I asked her to come with me, eight months ago, with the overt overconfidence of the undeserving, with the memory of Amanda still fresh as paint. "Come on" is what I said, and I think she did for no other reason than curiosity.

I remember her, how she was, before we touched. I remember her in elevators. I remember her smoking outside with all of them, shivering through the fall and into the first winter of their professional lives. I remember her that night, standing at the bench, announcing the People's readiness for trial at night arraignments, making her halting, unpracticed arguments to set bail. When she stood on her toes to hand up papers, I saw from my waiting spot the muscles of her calves knot into fists.

She was all business then, lowering her voice an octave as she made herself heard above the din of the courtroom—a bazaar of lawyers milling, family members thronging, defendants shuttling in and out, cuffed and uncuffed. Until well after midnight (long after my defendant had been produced, arraigned, and sent back down with a forlorn wave to someone who—despite everything—evidently loved him still, enough to wait until the small hours of the morning to see him publicly, perfunctorily accused of murder), I waited for her.

I waited because there was a single moment unnoticed by all in that midnight clamor except me, when she passed the wooden balustrade separating the gallery where I sat from the well where she worked. Her skirt caught upon a splintered baluster, and she freed it with a small, charming movement: a sinuous shift and a downcast turn of her head, making a red waterfall off her shoulders, showing her freckled neck. Untouched, still perfect Stacey saw that I saw. She smiled. I waited, and when we left, we left together.

"I don't know, Gio," she says now.

"What's not to know?"

"I just—I don't know. Don't you want to, like—"

"Oh, fuck me—I forgot," I interrupt her. "We got something in from Serology. Last night. Lamar left his what's-it in the girl."

"What's-it?" she repeats, sounding annoyed.

"You know."

"No, what? His *keys*? Can't you say *semen,* Giobberti?"

"Lamar raped her, then he shot her," I say. "That's my theory. Isn't that what you wanted from me—a theory? A simple explanation why a fourteen-year-old girl is dead?"

"Giobberti."

"Teen sex slay. It's in the *Post,* Stacey. It must be true."

"Giobberti," she repeats.

"Here it is," I tell her. "Evidence. It's as simple as that."

"Look, even if they had sex—"

"Let me tell you something, Sharp," I cut her short. "Don't waste your time trying to come up with theories, trying to make sense of why she died. People just die. You don't need to know why. All you need to know is how he did it and how you can prove it."

"Even if they had sex—" she continues, unperturbed.

"They had sex," I tell her.

"Asshole, listen. Even if they had sex, why do you think it was rape?"

"Asshole. They recovered *semen* from—"

"Asshole," she says, "even if it's his, what's that prove?"

"What do you think?" I ask.

"What if that's what they do?" she asks. "People fuck, Gio. It's fun."

"She's fourteen."

"She's a mother." She laughs at me. "And make up your mind if you're cynical or just stupid."

"It's still rape," I say with half a heart.

"It's statutory rape, moron," she says, and I know she is right. "That's all that is."

"Yes," I admit. "I'm not even sure it's statutory rape, now that I think about it—Lamb's nineteen."

"Well, if it is illegal," she says, making her naughty smile, "I've got a list of names for you."

"I figured." Stacey at seventeen—cascading curls over a dissatisfied pout—is framed next to her dead father on her mother's piano. (A slutty girl—I wish I had a copy for my wallet.) "But I'd still bet none of the pimply neighbors and second cousins on your list ever came upstairs with a twenty-five-cal semi-auto. Is that fun?"

"No," she says. "A gun takes the fun out of fucking."

"Right."

"Gio," she says to me, and seeing her, I know I'm going to do exactly what she wants. "Let's just—you know. Let's just talk to her, the mother. Play it out, and see what we see. Can't we just talk to her?"

"All right, Sharp. After lunch. Just to shut you up."

"Mm—" She comes close and palms my cheek. "You're absolutely too, too good to me, darling."

CHAPTER

11

I have my new book, and I decide to eat lunch at a restaurant for a change—a Vietnamese restaurant, where I will eat alone with my book in the air-conditioning. I do not even wait for the elevator, but instead walk down the back stairway.

On Court Street now, walking.

I am following a girl and realize I am in a crowd of boys following her. I am wearing a suit in a crowd of boys following a teenage girl, looking at her ass, staring in agony at the evident outline of panties beneath pink cotton shorts. I step stupidly into the crosswalk against the light behind the girl. Cars screech and honk at me. Inside, drivers gesture obscenely. This is not the first time. (Another sign of the spidering crack in the windshield.)

Traffic stops now because of me. I look up and blink my eyes at the Arab cabdriver. He is gesturing at me, calling me a donkey, a camel. Around me, pedestrians swarm into the crosswalk—these same people who walk aimlessly down the sidewalk, thumbs in their asses—now suddenly happy to go nowhere a little faster.

These people. *Put them behind the wheel of a car—they cut you off—they dart into traffic from a side street—*

These people. The People of the State of New York.

The Arab now shrugs—at me? at the cars honking behind him?—as if to say *What am I to do, my friends? There is a donkey here in the road.*

On the sidewalk an expressionless deliveryman, hunched in white atop a darting bicycle, jingles his bell and scatters pedestrians, then pedals away, leaving a pigeon cloud like dust behind a dirt-road pickup. I think of the dead pedestrian on Stern. That is how death comes—suddenly in the commonplace, sprouting like a monster head upon the familiar, transmogrifying the everyday.

The Vietnamese restaurant is a novelty along this stretch of storefronts, a procession of HEALTH AND BEAUTY AIDS, COFFEE SHOPPE, BARNEY'S CUT-RATE, PIZZA PARLOUR. Along here, it is still 1965. Only this Vietnamese restaurant and the Starbucks give away the passage of time, reminding us that Vietnam is friendly and that coffee is unpronounceable and costs three dollars. I don't remember that war—except, of course, what the nuns told us about the Vietcong, giving me vivid nightmares. The Vietcong were the special enemies of God because they inserted chopsticks into the ears of schoolchildren.

"Who kills a child," they told us, "there is a place in the darkest hell for them."

The cool draft from the door of the Vietnamese restaurant is almost visible. This is an extravagance. I think about my shoes, fissured with wear so that I can see my socks peeking through the tops; I can feel imperfections in the sidewalk through the thinness of my soles. Only a leathery film keeps me from the cement beneath my feet. I cannot afford new shoes. I am thirty-eight years old, and I cannot afford new shoes. I cannot afford razor blades. My face is cut to hell. I live alone in three rooms of a four-room apartment that I cannot afford alone.

Another extravagance—a six-ounce tube of toothpaste flavored with fennel, twice as expensive as a tube of Crest—four subway tokens' worth of fennel toothpaste, but I do love fennel. In an aluminum tube, it even feels expensive to hold, and there is a seemingly handwritten note from the manufacturer, a company with a homely name. "We live simply," the note begins.

They shut off my cable TV.

I haven't missed much except the Scottish Open on ESPN2.

The bill sat on my kitchen table for a while. I opened it, but inside there was a colorful insert featuring a young couple enjoying themselves. Their teeth were white, and evidently the pair had good credit ratings—they were spending money together or some such happy horseshit, not living simply. The insert promised *Concierge Service* and *World-Class Amenities for Travelers*. It was depressing.

The headlady escorts me to my table—a table for four—and pulls out my chair with a gray smile and gracious flair. *Concierge service?* I open my book, *The Fundamentals of Golf.* Another extravagance—a hardcover. I bought it at Waldenbooks on Montague Street. I saw it in the window. It cost twenty dollars—a week's subway fare, two packages of razor blades, or one new shoe sole. I walked down Montague to Chase Manhattan Bank for the twenty, but that did not work out. I went to Waldenbooks the next day. In the window, next to my golf book, was a cardboard woman sitting on a stack of law books and wearing dark oval *Bringing Up Baby* eyeglasses. *Is that where Stacey got the idea?* The author's hand rested thoughtfully under her chin, but her red dress was suggestively high. *Fuck me now,* she seemed to say, *then read my new legal thriller.* Inside, I picked up a copy of her book: *Suspending Habeas Corpus.* On the front cover (in the edgy typewriter font associated with lawyers) was written HABEAS CORPUS MEANS YOU HAVE A BODY.

"You have *the* body, actually," I said aloud to nobody.

On the flap:

Chain-smoking, gutter-mouthed state prosecutor Jane Starr is back from maternity leave, so WATCH OUT *serial killers! Jane's so smart she's* SEXY! *But when an old flame comes up dead, the results can be* MURDER— LITERALLY. *Watch Jane nab the sadist who wants to* HAVE HER BODY.

When did it become *Waldenbooks*? Didn't it used to be *Walden Books*?

When did businessmen start living simply?

When did Fiona Apple become famous?

When did all books and movies become gerundive? (*Driving, Chasing, Leaving Whomever/Whatever?*) Before, there was only *Bringing Up Baby*, wasn't there?

Things seem different now. (I am getting old.)

How did I get to be thirty-eight? Recently, a grimly aging discovery: a lone bristly hair upon the event horizon of my left ear canal, discovered by accident, by myself, as I have no one to point these things out to me. *Will I become one of those men without women, one of those feral males with strange facial hair and odd clothing? Men who buckle their raincoat buckles? Will moles grow on my face? Will hair sprout unnoticed and unplucked from my nose and ears as profusely as carrot greens?*

I turn to the first chapter of my book.

The playing field in the game of golf is called the "golf course." The aim of a "round" of golf is to get your "golf ball" into the eighteen "holes" in the fewest possible "strokes" of your "golf clubs."

The headlady seats two old women at my table for four. One, in a shapeless white cotton pantsuit, sits next to me. The other is across the table. Her face is pallid skin superimposed over skull. She is the sick one. "Sliced beef with chili," she says ruefully over the menu. "I don't think I could do that."

"How about the vegetarian?" asks the other one. "What about the spring roll?"

I am learning to play golf, a mature game requiring concentration and self-control. I am immature and lack both these skills, so I think it might be good for me. Here are some pointers from somebody whose name I do not recognize. *Think about your "stroke" before you "swing,"* he advises. In the margin a cartoon golfer in plus fours scratches his head, from which question marks lightly drift.

Aim away from trouble.
Read the lay of the land.
There's no such thing as bad luck.

These all seem sensible. These are rules that apply to all of life. (I like this game of golf.)

To the waiter the sick woman says, "We're going to share everything." To her friend she says, "This is my last day on antibiotics."

"Oh. Yes?"

"I'm feeling much better. But whenever I cough, whenever I blow my nose, there are these little—I don't know what you call them—blood spots."

One of the simplest ways to learn the ancient game of
golf is to watch it on the television.

That is very true. Before the man disconnected my cable, I
would sit in my boxer shorts and watch golf. I would make macaroni and take off my pants and look for Nick Faldo on ESPN2. An
excellent way to learn how to play the ancient game of golf.

Our lunches arrive together. *Do they think we are a party of*
three? A "threesome"?

"Gracias," the sick one says.

"I didn't get a chance to use the bathroom," says the other one,
who now stands and moves carefully away, walking as if the floor is
strewn with thumbtacks.

"Excuse me," I say to the headlady as she hurries by.

"Yes?" She smiles—her teeth are gray.

"Chopsticks?" I ask, making a pinching motion with my fingers.
"Chop. Sticks?"

"Oh, we're sorry," she says, still smiling. "In Vietnam—no
chopsticks. *Use fork.*"

"No—?" But she is gone.

They don't use chopsticks in Vietnam?

What about the Vietcong and their special place in hell? Was
that all just bullshit?

I turn back to my book, which I hold with my left hand as I eat
with the other. As I read, I see—without needing to look up—that
the sick one is looking at me. She is waiting for her friend to tiptoe
back before eating. (They were supposed to share everything.) As
she waits, I see in my periphery that she is looking at me un-
abashedly. She is craning her head to look at me. She looks directly
at my face over the book. Then she looks at my book. Then she

looks back at me. After a minute of this, she reaches out for me but
does not touch me.

"*Gawlfing*," she says, nodding—her Long Island larynx stran-
gling the lonely *O*.

"Yes," I say. "*Golfing.*"

"Do you play, then?"

"No," I say. "I'm trying to learn."

"I see," she says, seeming disappointed in my answer.

"I played once," I say, and then add—for no good reason—
"With my father-in-law." *Why am I telling her this?* I am not
normally this talkative with strangers. I am not normally this talkative with people I know. "It was kind of a disaster, though. I almost
killed him with a—what's it called?"—*should I refer to the book?*—
"with one of my '*drives.*' "

"My dead husband tried to teach me," she tells me, reaching
out unsuccessfully for me yet again, as though she were slipping off
her chair. *Should I try to grab her next time?* "He's dead."

"I'm sorry to hear that," I say, now folding the book on my index
finger. "Was it a golfing accident?"

"*Cancer.*"

"Oh," I say. "I'm very sorry."

"*Colon.*" She nods. "It was for the best."

"My daughter died a year ago."

"*Oh my gawd*," she says.

"There was a green Oldsmobile—a station wagon—it pulled
out, and I—swerved."

"*Oh my gawd.*"

"I didn't fasten her seat belt."

"*Oh my gawd.*"

"She was five."

CHAPTER

12

Johnny Carson's polyestered backside is in Nina's cubicle. Her stapler is banging away.

I squeeze into my chair around Solano's unaccommodating leg and telephone the grand jury. The line rings and rings. I sit immobilized by the heavy black receiver against my ear. The grand jury receptionist—Pauline, a relative of somebody's—will answer when the mood strikes her. It hasn't. Meanwhile, Solano sits looking tired and downcast. He's had to wait for me again—after lunch I took a long walk.

Bloch appears, eating a Jersey peach his pretty nurse in Cranford packed for him this morning (along with, if I had to guess, an egg salad sandwich?), and waits for me to hang up. I shrug, hoping he might give up and go away. The peach drips on his odd tie and on the floor—thick amber on the linoleum. A fat fly circles low.

Bloch these days is mostly bored. He sits alone in his office behind his door, listening to opera and thumbing through *Stereo Review* surreptitiously, as if it were a copy of *Screw*. For variety he comes to my cozy cubicle. Now he nods a quick hello to Solano, whom he perhaps did not notice until he stepped inside, as drawn-up as Solano is, tucked between a file cabinet and a metal wall, out of view from the hallway except for his thin leg. Another drop gathers on the south pole of the peach, gathers and falls.

I bang down the phone.

"What's the good word?" Bloch says, sitting.

"Lamb's saying the mother shot up the girl," I say.

"Whose mother?" Bloch asks.

"Hers. The D.O.A.," I tell him.

"Ouch. Why?"

"He's a little sketchy there," I say, conscious of Solano in my periphery. "A little shy on the details."

"His version is, it was an accident," Solano interjects. "The gun went off by accident, he's saying."

"An *accident*?" Bloch says, looking at Solano for the first time. "I don't think you'll find that word in the Penal Code, Detective. An accident with a gun is called *manslaughter*. Or at least criminally negligent homicide."

"That's just what he's saying, is all," Solano repeats himself. "Some beef with the mother. There's a history there, with the mother out in Cypress, he says."

"God love Cypress Hills," Bloch says. "What's the count— fifteen for the year?"

"Closer to twenty now," Solano tells him. "Plus the mother mighta been cracked up at the time. That's his story, anyways."

"That right?" Bloch asks me.

"She's a fucking skel—looks like she uses," I say. "Neighbor—I put her in the jury this morning—neighbor says she tricks for crack out of the apartment there."

Solano adds, "Real nice setup, with the two kids inside. And a baby too."

"And the one's dead now." Bloch nods.

"*Appetite is a universal wolf,* Phil," I say, "*that must make a universal prey.*"

"Oh," Bloch starts.

"*And at last eat up itself.* Something like that."

"Oh," Bloch says, almost lifting from his metal seat. "Oh, I have that one. Don't say it—damn—*Blake*? That tiger one? Burning bright and all?"

I shake my head. "Shakespeare. Bloch, forsooth."

"Damn it," he says. "I knew it too, now that you say it."

Solano looks at us both in disgust. Bloch chucks his peach pit in the direction of the trash can; it falls wide by a foot and skids across the floor, leaving a trail. When he picks it up, it is covered with gray fur.

Enter Nina, pursued by Carson. (There are now five people in my cubicle the size of an elevator car.)

Nina bends over Bloch to hand me a manila envelope. When she does so, Johnny Carson inclines his head to check out her ass, nodding with appreciation and unrequited longing. Nina gives me a significant look—a cry for help, really—then wheels and leaves. Johnny Carson turns to follow, holding a folder thoughtfully over his crotch.

For Nina's sake, I quickly say, "Detective," and both Solano and Carson turn to me. Talking to Carson, I say, "Since this case is closed out, I'm sure you guys have time to run me out to Cypress Hills."

Solano makes a face, and I add, "Just me and my assistant."

Carson nods hopefully at that. "Sure."

I open the manila envelope Nina handed me and draw out a blue form and a small packet of photographic slides, bound together with a rubber band. The blue form is marked "Evidence Receipt" and bears the return address "Office of the Chief Medical Examiner, 520 First Avenue, New York." There is the handwritten name of the dead girl, and, also handwritten, "7 duplicate Kodachromes." I know what they are—more photographs of the girl, from the inside out, this time—and I don't want to look at them. I put everything back into the envelope.

"That from the case?" asks Carson.

"Yes."

"Lemme see."

I slide the envelope across the desk to Johnny Carson. He draws out the slides and holds them to the light coming from the window behind me, filthy from the air-conditioning compressors.

"Je-sus," he says, looking anyway. "Fuck is that?"

Bloch takes a look. "Rib cage, viewed from the dorsal side."

"You know, you're right!" Carson says with surprise. "Looks like somethin I ate last week with sauce on it! Ha, ha, ha! What's this one? Looks like a fuckin—I don't know—a fuckin—liver or somethin?"

"Heart," Bloch confirms.

CHAPTER

13

As I'm stepping into the car, a blue Chevy Caprice, my left foot sinks a half inch into the sun-softened blacktop.

Carson is in the driver's seat, looking in the rearview mirror, examining his teeth. We are waiting in front of 210, and Carson thinks we are waiting for Nina. He has put on sunglasses, and I can see on the lobe of his right ear a small hole where an earring (off-duty) is put. Solano is motionless, slumping his glum self into the vinyl.

The Caprice smells. Vinyl, potato chips, bodies—and the August sun, directly above now, bears down. The tepid blast from the air-conditioning barely reaches the backseat of the Caprice. The radio is tuned to a lite jazz station. Carson's pick. For the expected Nina, he makes the Caprice into his bedroom.

Stacey instead emerges from a revolving copper door.

Behind us, a marked patrol car—a blue and white Caprice—pulls to the curb. Out come a uniformed patrol cop and his partner. They simultaneously adjust their belts, from which hang Glocks, radios, spare ammo clips, summons books, pen holders, flashlights, key rings. One of them starts with Stacey. She smiles, but it's the brush-off, leaving the cop looking stupid. The man who lives in this spot, I see, is taking it all in from his seat on the siamese hydrant—

perhaps thinking, as I am, that Stacey knows every male member of the service by his given and last names.

She drops lightly into the seat and says, "All right," to no one in particular.

"You about ready back there now, counselor?" asks Solano.

"Let's go," I say, looking quickly at Carson, who in the rearview mirror is looking back at Stacey, not altogether disappointed with the substitution.

"This one wants an ass full of radiator," Solano says as a kid jaywalks in front. The Caprice flies down Court Street at the usual cop clip. Stacey busies herself, sorting out her things and not talking. Her bag is on the seat between us and a legal pad (*a legal pad!*) on her lap. Carson has the front seat of the Caprice pushed way back, forcing me to sit with my legs in a wide vee. I lace my fingers in front of me and look directly ahead. Stacey sits with her knees virginally locked and her bare, slender legs at an acute angle to her body. Her left knee is inches from my right. *Does it mean anything?* I doubt it. Stacey is unsubtle—if she were to make a gesture, she would put her head directly in my lap.

The legal pad covers more of her than her skirt—pale blue and well hiked up. I catch myself looking downward, to the skirt, to the legal pad, and then to the elongation of her nearby thigh—as shapely as the swell of a champagne bottle. Three months ago, a month even, the sight of it would have hurt.

She is distracted. Sorting, arranging, and rearranging things. She stows the legal pad beside her on the vinyl seat, raises her behind, and pulls the skirt down a notch. Stacey still finds novelty in all this. She is still tickled to be a lawyer. *Being a lawyer is great fun*—look around! Here is Ally McBeal cavorting and having a wonderful time being a lawyer. Stacey watches *Ally McBeal.* I watch, too, but mainly to watch her watch it. She watches it, and then she turns playful with me in her Midwood bedroom, glad to be thin and small-breasted. Thinking about Ally, she goes braless to the office, drawing me into alcoves and onto Naugahyde couches. Her skirts get shorter and shorter, and yet she can carry it off. She can carry it off, just as she carries off her eyeglasses—dark ovals—the sort Cary Grant wore in *Bringing Up Baby*, where he plays against type, standing on a scaffolding in a black-and-white museum, piecing together a brontosaurus. Stacey wears them because they are an obvious counterpoint. With them, she is a fantasy-gram lawyerette jumping from a cake.

When Stacey got her shield, she showed it to her friends, and they had a good laugh. I met some of them once in the city. They were mostly thin, ironic, and articulate. They scared me to death, looking at me with the dark, carnivorous eyes of the unhappily unattached. They might have torn pieces from my body with their manicured nails. Together they looked exactly alike. I could have left with any one of them and not have noticed for days.

Carson turns the Caprice onto Atlantic Avenue, and we shoot down several blocks in silence past tidy brownstones, now restaurants and storefronts, now lofts turned into antique stores. Here is the old Ex-Lax factory, full of Irish pine cabinets and Second Empire armoires. As we drive east, however, the streets grow edgier. Men walk nowhere with paper-bagged forties. Into Bedford-Stuyvesant, and the houses grow squat and multihued—white, green, light blue—and covered sporadically with aluminum siding. There are now gas stations, flat-fixes, check-cashing places, Plexiglas-window Chinese takeouts. The Long Island Rail Road rises suddenly from the ground, its intricate profusion of red-primer latticework creating a densely shadowed blot under the midday sun where the occasional burnt-out car rests in peace and a woman talking crazy knocks around with her shopping cart brimming with garbage bags of bottles and cans and blankets.

I see a station wagon turning off Atlantic just ahead, but it is not the one. Neither green nor an Oldsmobile, it is instead a paint-peeling Ford Country Squire—boxy and inorganic—overfull with expressionless, black-hatted Hasidic men, each one of them young but then again so ancient as to make the Ford seem newfangled. They are closer to home than we are in this edgy stretch; they and theirs situate themselves on Eastern Parkway, closer to the Brooklyn abyss than ordinary white folks feel comfortable.

Deeper we go into black Brooklyn, an alien country that has no counterpart across the river. There is nothing in Manhattan—not the darkest parts of Harlem, not Washington Heights—that comes close to Brownsville or East New York. Here there is no law or order, save what from the NYPD—a distant, occupying force—is with the breezes blown. There are parts of Brooklyn that are the other side of the world. Everything's up for grabs. The thing is, it's more home to me than home anymore.

"What are those places, anyway?" Stacey says, her voice close by.

"What?" I ask, following her finger.

"There," she says, "with the red sign—*checks cashed.*"

"A check-cashing place," I tell her.

"Idiot—"

"It's, you know, a check-cashing place," I say. (In small glimpses such as this, Stacey gives away that she is not as aware of the wide world as she puts out.) "A bank for people who can't go to a bank. You know."

Carson now has the radio on local hip-hop, and I hear *"and I grabbed my three-eighty cause where we stayin, niggaz look shady."* Carson listens to their music—the same music he listens to in Long Island clubs, earring in. Solano sighs audibly, a weary father.

Stacey is not herself. She is quiet. Her self-assuredness, which both draws me to her and keeps her at a carefully measured distance, has ebbed. (She is apprehensive.) She has never been to East New York. She has never been to a housing project. She has never been to a murder scene. Her glasses stay in her bag. She could not carry them off, not here, not now. She would look and feel—silly.

I touch her leg, and she looks quickly at me, quickly smiling, as if to say *It's nothing.*

We cross the hill out of Brownsville and into East New York, turning onto Pennsylvania Avenue. We roll up to Cypress Hills, and Carson pulls the Caprice up onto the sidewalk. This is a dangerous place (very few air conditioners).

Solano pulls a brick-shaped radio from somewhere and talks into it, speaking an unintelligible police lingo of numbers and code words. A woman's voice crackles in reply.

On the street, it is no hotter than in the rear of the Caprice. I flap my jacket like a bat and peel my sweat-sticky shirt from my back. Solano mops his forehead and eye sockets with a gray handkerchief he has produced from an inner pocket, where he redeposits it when he is done. He spits. He gives a pigeon near his foot a quick kick. The bird flaps impotently on its back for a moment, embarrassed to be upside down, then rights itself and syncopates hurriedly away from Solano.

A kid pedals up. He is skinny and wearing cutoff shorts and no shirt. His hair is done back in cornrows, sloppily, as if his sister did them. "You Five-O?" he asks slyly. He pedals around in a tight circle in front of me on a girl's bike with a white plastic basket on the handlebars. "You here for me?"

"I don't know," I say to the kid. "What'd you do?"

"Ah, you ain't got nothin on me," he says good-naturedly and pedals off.

Cypress Hills. A sprawl of dark, angular, redbrick buildings rising seven stories above the neighborhood of East New York surrounding it. Cypress Hills, where this year nineteen homicides have been perpetrated, each of them less imaginative than the one that preceded it—boys shot over money—boys shot over girls— over Avirex jackets, dope, a dis. Boys shot for no reason at all. Boys shot because their friend is just fucking around, doesn't know it's loaded—dropped the clip but forgot about the one in the chamber—*it's always the one in the chamber*—"Don' be pointin that at me—that shit loaded?"—"You want to find out, son?"—and that's that.

That makes eighteen boys. (And one girl.)

This is a dangerous place, but there is nothing obvious to give it away. Trees grow, lawns are mowed. Oaks and maples thirty years old flourish and grow full and leafy along footpaths of clear, unfissured cement. The footpaths shoot in all directions, a web overlaying the fresh-mown grass, connecting the buildings, the basketball court, the parking lot. The air here is still and unforbidding. All is quiet except for a distant radio, so distant that only the muffled pounding of the bass line is heard: a regular rhythmic beat felt more than heard, but when it cuts out after a while, I notice. No one is here. The footpaths are empty. The basketball court is silent.

All seems benign until you notice (on the walkway cement and mown grass and shady-leafed playground of Cypress Hills) beat crack vials and spent .380 shell casings scattered underfoot as freely as acorns.

Solano lights up a cigarette and starts to walk without a word to anyone. We follow him along a footpath and approach the nearest of the buildings. The side of it is painted brick red to a height of eight feet to cover the graffiti, although a fresh tag, like a weed, has cropped up—an odd hieroglyph. A man sleeps on a bench alongside the walk. His mouth is open; the inside is pink and ridged like a dog's. Meanwhile, a droplet of condensation detaches itself from an air conditioner, drifts earthward, and lands upon my head. (Plop.) Moisture from above—always startling and unpleasant in New York City, but then in the shadow of these buildings I am grateful it is not a grease-smeared toaster oven. I reach up and hesitantly feel, thinking pigeon.

Solano pushes open the door at 1250 Sutter Avenue, an unpainted steel door with a shattered glass window. The glass is reinforced with chicken wire but shattered nevertheless. The lock is broken, and the door swings freely when pushed. Solano holds the door, jerking his head to one side to indicate *Come in.* Inside, two men or boys slip away without a sound and are gone before my eyes can adjust to the sudden dim, leaving behind the sweet smell of a joint and no noise at all.

Straight ahead is a single elevator; its door is open and the call button glows, a conspicuous circle of light. The car is otherwise unlit, its walls festooned with tags drawn in black, red, and silver. A sign plastered in the rear states the obvious: OUT OF ORDER.

"Here we go, people. Right here," says Solano, indicating the stairway. He drops his cigarette on the floor and gives the butt a practiced twist with the ball of his foot. From the expression on his face, he could be my father, holding open the car door for us to pile out, late again for mass.

We begin our climb. Carson dawdles and lets Stacey pass before him—the better to view her from behind, I reckon. The stairway, unlike the lobby, is well lit. Bare, circular fluorescent tubes burn on beige cinder blocks at every landing, brightening the odd crack vial dotting a corner here, a busted-up TV set there. We climb seven flights—Stacey taking each step like an impala—before Solano turns onto a hallway. He walks to a door and raises his hand to knock, then faces Johnny Carson momentarily and says, his hand still poised, "This one?" Carson nods, and Solano's hand comes down—three quick, efficient hits.

I turn to face Stacey. She is standing close to me, small.

"Just one thing," I say, still breathing with an open mouth from the climb.

"What?" Now she will do anything I tell her. Here she will believe anything I say.

"Don't sit down," I say. "Even if she asks you."

She looks at me.

"Just don't."

CHAPTER

14

From behind the dead-bolted steel door comes the sound of things being moved around, footsteps, and then, after a full minute, her voice. "Who is it?"

"Police," says Johnny Carson, sounding manly.

"It's Andrew Giobberti from the D.A.'s office, Miss Harris," I add hastily, but I feel a twinge of uncertainty. *Is her name Harris, like the dead girl's?* I've forgotten.

"Who?"

"Andrew Giobberti. We spoke at the funeral. Yesterday."

More noise from behind the door. "Just let me—just hold on one more minute." Solano shrugs. We wait. The lock then unbolts, the door opens, and there is the dead girl's mother walking away from us, barefoot on the gray-green linoleum, past low piles of cardboard boxes and down the hallway inside the apartment. Carson goes in, and we all follow Carson.

We find her, Nicole whatever, seated barefoot and scowling on a couch in an uncarpeted space. The room is spare, the walls unadorned apart from an unframed Nefertiti.

"I was sleepin," she says, but not as a complaint. For the first time I view her from this angle, and I see teeth missing. She is so small, just bone and sinew. She can't weigh more than a hundred pounds. The cocaine has taken most of her.

I say, "Thank you for letting us come by."

"I don' recall I told you you could come by, Mr. D.A. You just come." She is wearing ballooning shorts, and her spindly, blotchy legs are splayed out. Her rust-colored hair is cut in a raggedy-ass fade. She is not high—just worn down. On her is the baby.

"There are just a few questions," I tell her.

She shrugs. "You wanna sit down?"

"No thanks, Miss Harris," I say.

"Carbon."

"Sorry?"

"The name is Carbon." She withdraws a cigarette from a fissure in the couch. "As in carbon copy." She says it as if she is used to saying it. *Carbon copy,* I think, remembering that she and I are the same age—the last generation to know what a carbon copy is.

"Sorry," I say. "I think you already know the detectives here. This is Stacey Sharp from my office. She's working with me on this case. On your daughter's case."

"Yeah, I know them officers."

"Counselor." Solano nods at me, then steps outside the door to smoke and wait.

"All right now," I say, casting about for a way to start. The mother draws on the cigarette. The baby is asleep. The windows are open, but there is no breeze at all inside. The filmy curtains do not stir. In the heat, odors blossom from the cracks in the linoleum and the cushions on the couch. I feel drops of sweat form on my back and slide downward, collecting at the waistband of my shorts. "All right," I repeat.

"How long have you lived here, Miss Carbon?" Stacey asks.

"Here? In this house?"

"Yes."

"We been here in this buildin about ten year," she says. "I been tryin to get a bigger place—since the baby come."

"How old's the baby?" Stacey asks her, smiling at the child, who frowns and drools in her sleep.

"Lessee," she says. "Two, three months. She small because she was born too early."

"Kayla's?" Stacey offers.

"Yes."

"What's her name?"

"Shameeka. Meeka."

"The father, is Shameeka's father around?"

"You have to ask her," says Nicole.

"Ask who?"

"Kayla," Nicole tells her, her expression blank.

"You don't—?"

"No."

Stacey looks at me, wondering if she has made a mistake. "You have, um, another daughter?" she then asks Nicole.

"Utopia?" Nicole Carbon says. "She my oldest."

"She lives here with you?"

"Just Utopia and the baby now."

"How old is Utopia?" Stacey asks.

"She the oldest. She sixteen."

"She still in school or—?"

"She in school," Nicole says. "She go to F. K. Lane."

"Sophomore? Junior?"

"I don' know what you call it. High school."

"She was home that night?" Stacey asks.

"What night?"

"August— Was it the fourth?" Stacey asks me. "The night of the incident."

"She was here, all right," Nicole answers. "We was all here. She ain't seen nothin neither. We was both sleepin."

"Where does Utopia sleep?" Stacey asks.

"Back in my bedroom. Back in there." Nicole indicates with a quick wave.

"You were all asleep when Lamar came in?"

"Like I told that officer, we was all asleep," Nicole says. "I musta been sleepin because I din't see no one come in the door, did I?"

"Do you always keep the front door locked?"

"You kiddin?"

"Where were you sleeping?" Stacey asks her.

"When I woke up, I was right here," she says. "Right on this couch here. Where I'm settin right now."

"Ma'am," Stacey says. "I want you to tell me what you remember seeing and hearing that night."

Nicole exhales loudly and gives her story as if by rote. "Like I said already, I was here on the couch. I was sleepin. I hear a noise. A gun. Real close. I woke up. But I din't get up right away because there was like clouds in my brain. I was feelin asleep even when the noise woke me up. I din't get up right away. I was just layin on the couch after I hear the noise and the next thing I hear is Utopia screamin and she come runnin out of Kayla bedroom."

"Go on," Stacey says when Nicole stops telling her story.

"And then I get up and Utopia and me had went back there, which is where Kayla sleep. She and the baby sleep in the same room. I had went back there to see about Kayla and that was when I seen her. I seen Kayla all laid out crooked on the bed, but there wasn't no blood at all as I could see at first. But then I see it. Right here. Just a dot."

"When you went back there, was anyone else there?"

"No," she says. "Only the baby was there, cryin. And Utopia be screamin and cryin too."

"You didn't see Lamar?" Stacey asks.

"No, I told you I never seen him," she says. "But Miss Iris see him. He come runnin out after he kill my girl."

"Can you show us the bedroom?" Stacey asks her.

"Show you?"

"Yes, ma'am."

"Awright, I show you," she says, hopping up with the baby. (Nicole is wiry and moves with a nine-year-old's sharp, furtive movements.) "The police officers who come already saw it and took some pictures with a camera."

She leads us around the corner past a small kitchen: a smeared rectangle with frilled plastic curtains across a narrow window looking out into an airshaft. In one corner, empty liquor bottles sit in a white plastic bucket, and there is a pizza box with a string of hardened cheese. On the counter, I see an open bottle of something. More baby paraphernalia is strewn about—brightly colored cups and plates, open cans of formula in familiar pink cylinders. Diapers ripen in the trash. Something brown has boiled over on the stove and dripped down the front. Stacey flashes me a look of utter revulsion.

"This is my room," Nicole says as we pass a room without a door.

Across the hall from Nicole Carbon's room and slightly past it is the dead girl's bedroom. The door is closed. Nicole stands by the door and does not enter. I squeeze gingerly by her in the narrow space and push the door inward. In this room, the sour, fusty, queasy flavor of the rest of the apartment gives way to baby—the smell of baby powder, baby wipes, baby pee. Wedged in the corner is a Pack N' Play—a collapsible crib—bright red, blue, and aquamarine with white mesh along the sides.

Stacey looks in tentatively.

The walls are deep blue. A single window. The bed is a mattress on the floor. This is where the girl died. None of the floor is visible for the mattress and the scattered clothes and sneakers. The mattress is stripped. There is a small stain in the center—*the dead girl's blood?*—it could be anything. There was no exit wound—the slug flattened and did not leave her body, but instead feasted on her heart, lung, and bone.

"Ma'am, is this how the room was laid out—two weeks ago?" Stacey asks Nicole.

"Yes. Except that there was a coverlet on that bed, which the police took. Am I gon get that coverlet back?"

"Where was her head?"

"At the far end." She points quickly. "Her eyes was still open."

"She was facing up?"

"How do you mean?" Nicole asks Stacey.

"Was she lying on her back when you found her?"

"Layin on her back, yes," Nicole says. "With her legs all crooked out like that."

"Did you move her when you saw her?" Stacey asks.

"No, I just— No. She was dead."

"She was dead when you saw her?"

"Yes," the dead girl's mother says.

"How do you know?" Stacey asks delicately.

"She was dead."

I pull the door shut and step back. "Okay," I say. That's enough of that. "Thank you."

We walk together back down the hallway, past the kitchen and the living room. Nicole unbolts the door and moves her hand to the doorknob, where it stays. We three are standing there.

"You know there's been an arrest?" I ask her. "I told you that, didn't I?"

"You told me. That boy from downstairs."

"So we'll call you if anything—" I start to say.

"Did he know your daughter?" Stacey interrupts.

"Did he know her?" Nicole repeats. "LL? I suppose he see her comin and goin. They be livin in the same buildin ten years."

"I'm going to give you my card," I tell her.

"Did you ever see them together?" Stacey asks. "You know, like boyfriend-girlfriend?"

Nicole laughs without humor. "I din't never see Kayla with anyone like a boyfriend. She mostly keep to herself. Like all she wanna do is stay in her room and read her books."

"But she had a child," Stacey tells her, a little too insistently. "She must have had a boyfriend."

Nicole looks at her. "I don' know what she do when I ain't here. I ain't watch her every minute. She a grown girl."

"Okay," I say, moving to the door.

"What about you?" Stacey asks.

"Me what?" replies Nicole.

"You ever have any dealings with him? With Lamar?"

"I don' deal," Nicole says defensively. "LL the dealer. You ax anyone. They tell you. I don' deal. No, I don'. Never."

"That's not what I—" Stacey starts weakly. "Did you ever see him around?"

"I hardly see him ever. To tell you the truth, I din't know he was out of prison."

"Is it possible you might have seen him that night?" asks Stacey.

"Seen him? Seen him where?"

"Inside," Stacey says. "Maybe there was an argument?"

"No, I ain't seen him. I only see him sellin drugs. He sells drugs. That's why he in jail."

"We'll let you know if—" I try to say.

"When is Utopia coming home?" Stacey asks.

"Utopia?" Nicole and I say together.

"I thought we should, you know, talk," she explains.

"She din't see nothin," Nicole says. "What is she gon tell you? Nothin. Leave that girl alone. She and Kayla was real close. Don' go upsettin that girl on me. I have enough on my mind already."

In the silence that follows, I maneuver Stacey to the door.

"Thank you for your time, Miss—Carbon," I say. "We'll be in touch."

"What's this they sent me?" Nicole says suddenly, moving quickly to a table by the door, where she finds an orange paper, already stained. She shows it to me.

"That's a subpoena," I tell her. "A subpoena for the grand jury."

"What's that?"

"You'll need to come down to testify in the grand jury. Friday morning. Is that convenient?"

"No."

"Do you know why Lamar would want to kill her?" interrupts Stacey suddenly, and it seems to catch Nicole off guard. She hesitates a moment.

"No," she says. "Ain't no reason I can think of. Ain't no reason for it. She ain't never offend nobody. She always do what I say. She was—" And at that moment—and just for the moment—the unfathomable flatness of her drops away and there is the evident pain. She is crying now, without tears, a short, wretched noise. Stacey puts her hand on Nicole Carbon's arm.

"I'm sorry, Miss Carbon," Stacey says.

"It breaks my heart," she cries. "And I ain't have no picture of her. I been lookin. There's only that one." She indicates a small snapshot atop some clutter on the table. She walks over to it and shows Stacey. (The yearbook photo I remember from yesterday.)

"Oh," says Stacey in a way I never could. "So pretty."

"You know?" the dead girl's mother says, brightening, showing Stacey the child on her hip. "This is her baby."

Stacey says, "And you have Utopia too."

"They all I got with me now. Utopia and the baby."

"Children are a blessing," I say stupidly, and both women turn to me as if they had forgotten I was there. Nicole nods. She withdraws an asthma inhaler from somewhere and uses it.

"Yes," she says when she is done. She looks quickly at me. "That the truth."

Solano and the asshole are nowhere to be seen. No one is here at all. We are alone, Stacey and I, on the seventh-floor hallway of 1250 Sutter. There are no windows here, but every five feet, circular tubes of fluorescent light glare, making skin pale and waxy. Blemishes loom. Stacey looks apprehensive and wan.

Here I am alone with pretty Stacey, alone in an East New York public housing project. Here we are at a Brooklyn crime scene—a *nice* guy alone with pretty Stacey. Stacey, who has ceased to divert me in the same perfect way she did.

A lock cylinder spins, the sound resonates off the beige cinder block of the lonely hallway—amplified, brightened, by the angry fluorescent lights. The doorway across from the dead girl's apartment opens warily a crack. "Miss Iris?" Stacey whispers to me. Instead, an old woman appears there. Her head is in the door frame.

Her dust-gray hair is dry and combed back straight and tied in a short, stiff ponytail. Her bare brown legs sprout thinly from pink slippers. The buttons on her loose, hanging frock are mated incorrectly to the buttonholes—she started buttoning one button too high, and a distended triangle of cloth covers one knee. She walks deliberately from the door frame without a look at Stacey and me.

"Come in, come in," says a familiar voice.

Miss Iris ushers Stacey and me inside her apartment. All is neatly squared away and familiar. This could be my parents' home; it could be Windsor Terrace thirty years ago, except for the portrait of a black Jesus Christ, a crown of thorns resting lightly upon his *Mod Squad* afro. Here are the same rough wool armchairs arrayed in a pair. Here is the same plastic ivy in the same baskets suspended from the ceiling in the same macramé hangers. Here are the cork coasters on the lacquered walnut coffee table with the heavy brass fittings. There in the corner is a Magnavox console record player, with beige basket-weave speakers built in. If I were to slide the top of it and peer inside, would I find my mother's vinyl records—*Camelot, Cabaret, Man of La Mancha*? If my father were to stomp in wearing his blue uniform—tie undone, gold sergeant's shield, bottle—and collapse on the scratchy, rectangular couch and drape one booted foot over the armrest, would my mother follow to slap it down?

It is cool in here—a relief after the greasy humidity of Nicole's apartment. In a window, an air conditioner blows noisily; it is old and trimmed in walnut laminate, like the slab sides of a Ford Country Squire. Solano and Carson are inside, in front of teacups, with their knees splayed and hands folded.

"That was Lamar's mother," Carson tells me.

"His grandmother," Miss Iris corrects him.

They tell me the grandmother's story.

Lamar Lamb's grandmother's apartment is two stories below. Lamar came home Sunday night, two weeks after Solano knocked on her door looking for him. Solano looked around and left his card. When Lamar came home, his grandmother took Solano's card off the refrigerator door, picked up Miss Iris's phone, and gave up her grandson. Who can say why? All that can be said is that when her time came, she gave him up. She picked up the phone as if calling the super to snake the drain. Solano found Lamar Lamb under a rat's nest of clothes in his grandmother's bedroom closet. He had made himself so small they didn't even see him at first. His grandmother had to take them back in and say, "See, there he is. There he is. I told you." In her filmy, shapeless, misbuttoned frock, she pointed out the hiding spot with a naked, varicosed leg.

I wonder, did he sleep? Did LL sleep the dreamless sleep of the guilty man who at last can relax his guard? *The guilty shall sleep,* old detectives say. The guilty sleep, and the innocent pace and stare.

"Did he sleep?" I ask Solano, now back in the Caprice.

"Who's that, counselor?"

"Your boy Lamar," I say. "Did he, you know. Go to sleep after you snatched him up?"

"Sleep?" Solano looks quickly at Carson. "You remember, Johnny?"

Carson shrugs and drives. We are all quiet for ten minutes.

"Come to think of it, no," Solano says finally—seemingly apropos of nothing—as we pull in front of 210. "Just sat there, mostly. All night. With a fuck-you face on."

CHAPTER

15

The medical examiner, waiting in my cubicle for me to return from Cypress, is a woman reading a book. About my age but perhaps younger, she wears black fingernail polish, black jeans, black T-shirt, and her hair is short, bottle-blond, and cut like pine needles. She's nervous as hell.

"I really, I mean," she says. "I really have to testify today?"

Here is a medical doctor, board certified in forensic pathology. Her business is to take apart dead bodies, to determine the causes of their death. Here she is, having cataloged all the horror that men do to men, hugging herself in my cubicle because I have told her that she must testify today before the grand jury.

"In exactly one half hour," I say, looking at my watch. "You seem kind of nervous."

"No," she says. "I'm all right. I'm a little hungry."

"Do you want a, let's see, a mint?" I am digging through the contents of my drawer, now contained in a plastic bag on the linoleum. "Duck sauce . . . ?"

"No, thank you," she says.

"Cutting back on duck sauce?"

"Had it for breakfast," she says. A perfunctory parry (still nervous).

"Look, it's not a big deal, the grand jury."

"No. I know," she says. "It's all right. I'm okay. I'm just off guard a little. I would've worn something else. I look like a—"

"No, you don't."

"I didn't finish my sentence," she says. "What do you think I was going to say I looked like?"

"I don't know. Something disparaging. I think you look—"

"These are just work clothes," she interrupts.

"I didn't finish my sentence—what did you think I was going to say?"

"Something gratuitous. I know how I look. I usually dress down when I work. Work's sort of—messy. I should have a dress, don't you think?"

"It's not necessary," I tell her.

"No?"

"No," I say. "The grand jury's sort of—messy."

"Aren't we going to court?"

"This is Brooklyn," I say. "I think you have the wrong idea about all of this. Let me tell you what it is. The grand jury is—it's not very grand. Not here, anyway. It's just twenty-three ordinary people. There's no judge."

"No judge?"

"No," I tell her. "Plus the defendant's not there, or his lawyer. So there's no cross-examination."

"Good!"

"It's just you and me. You come in, swear to tell the truth"—I hold up my hand as though I were taking an oath—"and then I ask you some questions. That's it. You'll be in there ten minutes."

"Oh." She brightens.

"You okay with that, Doctor?"

"Yes, Lawyer." She smiles, finally.

"Gio's fine."

"Then I'm Ann."

We shake on it, and she tells me (still holding my hand, almost feeling it—clinically), "You don't look like a *Joe,* though."

"It's *Gio.* It's what people call me—I don't know. My name is Giobberti."

"Okay, Joe, what do you know?"

"You all right? You still seem kind of nervous," I tell her.

"I am, I suppose," she says. "I think that's natural, though. Don't you think?"

"I guess it's only fair. If I had to come to your office and do what you do, I'd be nervous. I mean, I'd probably faint."

She laughs again, and I see she is unintentionally pretty. "It's been known to happen."

"Let me ask you something," I say. "Do you like what you do?"

"That's kind of an offensive question," she says, taking no offense.

"Not really," I say. "I didn't mean it to be."

"Well, it sort of is. It assumes that a normal person wouldn't like forensic pathology."

"Do you think a normal person would?" I ask.

"I'm just tired of answering that question."

"At cocktail parties?"

"I've stopped going," she says honestly. "It's the way people ask it. If they said, you know, Do you like what you *do*?, it would be different. But they don't. Everyone says, Do you *like* what you do? As though I pull the heads off babies for a living."

"You sort of do, though," I tell her. "Sometimes?"

"Yes," she admits. "Sometimes."

"I know what you mean. People are always very polite when I tell them I'm a homicide prosecutor. Then they sit somewhere else." We agree and are silent for a moment. "Say, listen. What's the most disgusting thing you've ever seen?"

"How old are you?" She sighs.

"Thirty-eight," I say. "Why?"

"Because my seventeen-year-old nephew asked me that same question last week."

"Now, *that's* kind of insulting, Doctor—comparing me to a seventeen-year-old."

"He wanted me to bring him a penis in formaldehyde," she says, standing. She is as long and lean as a Texas gunslinger in her tight-legged jeans. She sets her book on my desk, a copy of *Suspending Habeas Corpus*. (Hardcover.) "Where can I buy a dress?" she asks.

"There's a Macy's in Fulton Mall. First let's talk about the girl."

"Okay," she says, sitting again.

"What happened?" I ask.

"She was shot."

"And?"

"And she was shot." She shrugs. "There's no great mystery. That's why I'm not sure why I'm here."

"It's for the grand jury," I say. "Putting a case in is one part law, nine parts Hollywood."

"I'm the Hollywood part?"

"Don't underestimate yourself, Doctor," I tell her. "M.E. testimony is killer—so to speak."

"Can't you just put in the death certificate?"

"Sure," I say. "But I think it makes a better impression with a live witness. It shows that someone really died, you know?"

"The death certificate shows someone died, Joe," she tells me. "That's why it's called a death certificate."

"You just—you just never know with juries. With Brooklyn juries."

"Why do you say it like that—*Brooklyn juries?*" she asks. "Don't they always convict?"

"Grand juries don't *convict*, my good doctor. They *indict*—and in Brooklyn, sometimes they don't even do that."

"So the indictment is . . . ?"

"Just the formal charge," I tell her. "First you get indicted. Actually, first you kill someone. Then you get indicted. Then, about a year later, you go to trial."

"Then what?"

"Then you get acquitted, because—" I start, but stop myself, knowing that I sound bitter, and that is not what I want. I abruptly, despite myself, surprising myself, want to make a good impression for a change.

"Why acquit?"

How to explain Brooklyn juries? "Let me put it this way," I tell her. "It's like—you got two and a half million people here—in thirty-one flavors, like Baskin-Robbins—and they're all pissed off—pissed off because their car won't start—because they're poor—because there's a sick passenger and the subway's stopped. I don't know. Everyone's pissed off."

"Not a melting pot, then?"

"More like a pot of Cream of Wheat. With nasty lumps in it."

"Oh!" she says, grabbing at her white throat. "Oh—good metaphor."

"And the more you stir it, the worse it gets. They get pissed off, and who're they gonna blame? The system—*fuck the system,* you know what they say?"

"Do you—like this place?" she asks. "Brooklyn? It's such a— such a dirty place."

I consider. "Sure. But it's fertile dirt."

"So, Joe. What's the problem with your lumpy old *Brooklyn juries*?"

"You know," I say. "In the grand jury, it's really not such a problem. To be honest, there's only one way to really screw the pooch in the grand jury—"

"My father told me to beware of lawyers who say *To be honest.*"

"And doctors who say *This will only hurt a little.*"

"Hey!" she says. "I've never had a single complaint."

"Now, if *I'd* said that—"

"You were about to be honest," she interrupts.

"Are you paying attention?"

"Riveted," she says.

"Because I don't tell this to every witness." I smile at her.

"Why're you telling me?" She smiles back.

"I guess—because you asked me," I say truthfully. "Most of my witnesses just want to go home."

"They're pissed off too?"

"Mostly," I say. "But I can usually get them to stay until lunchtime if I promise to feed them."

"Cream of Wheat?"

"Greasy burgers or greasy Chinese," I say. "But it's better than nothing—which is what most of my witnesses have for lunch. On a good day. No. There's only one thing that can go wrong in the grand jury, and you don't need to worry about it."

"Come on. What is it?"

"It's a technical thing. A *lawyer* thing."

"No, tell me," she says. "I thought you liked that I asked questions."

"It's like this. Anyone who testifies in the grand jury gets immunity from prosecution on that case."

"That means you can't—"

"Can't prosecute them," I say. "So when a defendant testifies— or even a perpy witness that you think might have been involved— you have to be fucking certain that he waives his immunity before he takes the stand."

"Fucking certain?" she asks. "That's even more certain than certain, I suppose?"

"Sorry—I spend all my time around cops."

"You eat with that mouth, Joe?"

"Come on, prosecutors are supposed to be gutter-mouthed," I say, tapping her hardcover.

"Oh—you're so funny." She smiles, then asks, "What happens if the defendant doesn't waive his, um, whatever?"

"He goes home," I tell her.

"Gosh."

"It'll also get you fired," I say.

"I'm sure you'd never forget to do that, though—that thing you're supposed to do."

I tell her, "But I did, you know. Once."

"Oh," she says. "What happened?"

"I forgot. The defendant testified in the grand jury. I forgot to make him waive immunity, and a couple days later we had to send him on his merry way. Tra-la-fucking-la."

"I'm sorry," she says, seeming actually sorry. "You didn't get fired, though."

"No," I say. "This was last year. It was—"

"Was he, like, a *murderer*?"

"Yes," I say. "He was a drug dealer in a wheelchair who killed the people who put him there."

"In a wheelchair?" she asks. "How do you sell drugs from a wheelchair?"

"That sort of sounds like the first half of a joke, doesn't it?"

"You don't seem to think it's very funny, though," she says. "You're all serious all of a sudden. Did he kill someone when he got out or something?"

"No," I say, suddenly finding the bottom of my shoe interesting. "He didn't kill anyone—that I know of, anyway."

"But you can't blame yourself. If you make a mistake—"

"Yes you do," I tell her too loudly. "Calling it a mistake doesn't change anything."

"I'm sorry," she says quietly, eyeing me (and wondering what just happened).

"No," I tell her. I look out the window to the verdigrised cupola of Borough Hall across the street, and I am not thinking about Milton Echeverria anymore.

"All right," she says. Then, evidently wanting to snap me out of it, she says, "It's like the Hippocratic oath, I guess."

"Right. *First, do no harm.*"

"You're supposed to say that really doesn't apply to me," she says, trying a smile. "Since my patients are already dead, I mean."

"So are my victims," I say.

"There you are."

"We're a pair," I tell her, and I may be right; we're two body snatchers, making our living off the dead.

"This murder," I say suddenly.

"All right."

"There's something fucked up about it."

"How?" she asks.

"I don't have many fourteen-year-old girls shot dead in their own beds. That's kind of unusual. Even in East New York."

"Fourteen?" She pauses.

"Yes. Just."

"That's—you know, that makes sense," she says, nodding.

"You didn't know?"

"No, when she came in, I remember—they said she was eighteen or nineteen."

"Does it matter?" I ask.

"No. It's nothing," she says. "It doesn't change my conclusions. It's just something I noticed when I was inside her. She looked eighteen, but I was thinking she was like a girl inside."

"What do you mean?" I ask.

"Her bones were still cartilage," she says.

"Why?"

"Her bones were still growing," she says. "She was a girl."

"There's something else," I ask her. "Could you tell if she was sexually active?"

"She was sexually active. She had recently delivered a child. And we recovered semen from her body."

"Right," I say. "I know. What I mean is, is there any way to tell—was she, like, very sexually active, or just—moderately?"

"That's difficult to tell," she says. "There was a fair amount of dilatation, but that may be due to childbirth."

"Oh."

"What are you looking for?" she asks.

"I don't really know. Something. Anything. I'm just fishing around. Did you see any, you know, signs of violence?"

"Sure," she says archly. "There was a gunshot wound to her chest."

"Nice," I say. "I'm looking for sexual violence."

"Check out the personals in the *Voice*."

"Good one."

"Look," she says. "Just tell me what you're looking for. What's your theory? Maybe I can help."

"Was there a fight? Was this a rape?"

"I can't say whether it was consensual, but I can say it wasn't forced," she says. "There's no vaginal trauma. No tears, no abrasions, no ecchymosis—none of the usual indications."

"Let me ask you this, then," I say. "Is there any way you can determine, scientifically, how active, how sexually active she was—like, was she ever prostituted?"

"No. Not really, no. Sometimes you'll see scarring, healed tears, that sort of thing. There may be indications of a series of abortions. There are always the common sexually transmitted diseases. Hepatitis, AIDS, those sorts of things. Those would be just indications. You can't prove with medical evidence that someone was a hooker."

"Did this girl have any of those indications?"

"No," she says. "No, she didn't."

I am quiet for a moment, thinking, and then she repeats, "Just tell me what you're looking for."

"I don't know," I say. "I don't know what I'm looking for. I'm just—trying to figure this out in my head."

"All right. But call me if—you know."

"I know."

Then she says, "I suppose we have to go now—to the grand jury."

"Forget that. You just told me what I wanted to know."

CHAPTER

16

Seven at night, and I am sitting in my metal cubicle with Conrad Gufner, a cheerfully downtrodden man about seventy years old. Here he is, sitting across from me uncomfortably on a small, hard chair. In a moment he will complain about his hemorrhoids. But for now, he is chewing the fat affably, telling me a joke about a rabbi who went golfing with an "African-American." We are waiting in my cubicle because Gufner's client, Lamar Lamb, wants to talk to me.

Gufner is working me overtime. He is spinning out his rabbi story in good form. His hand reaches out occasionally for my knee, probing with his long, translucent fingers. A cool downdraft from the ductwork above my cubicle, inexplicably blowing now, descends upon Gufner and stirs a string of yellowing hair that he has combed optimistically over his shining pink head; the strand is six inches long and blows like an admiral's pennant to his starboard amidships.

The call comes from upstairs, and Gufner revisits the can. I wait for him, holding the elevator door as he old-man runs down the long hall outside the Homicide Bureau—swinging a single arm and gingerly rotating his arthritic hips. We stand awkwardly silent in the cramped elevator, the forced intimacy making Gufner's bonhomie difficult to sustain. He examines himself without emotion in the dull reflection of the elevator wall. With his smooth, poreless skin and Vaselined red lips, he could be an old woman.

"So what's on his mind?" I ask as the elevator door opens on the seventh floor.

"My guy? Says he didn't do it."

"Did he?"

"Sure. Why not? I get paid either way."

A squad of police detectives is assigned to the office. Not a bad gig—mostly going to edgy neighborhoods to serve subpoenas on reluctant witnesses. In a sunless corner of 210, the D.A. squad has done its best to emulate the squalor of a precinct station house. It is all hard-edged and vaguely threatening, a place wholly devoid of feminine influence. Wanted posters stare from the drywall alongside a thick sheaf of persons missing. A sign advises the use of bulletproof vests in summertime: BETTER HOT THAN SHOT! Men (and one or two women) sit at desks or stand in small groups. All look at us, quickly, then look away. The men are rumpled and brown with their ties undone and tucked into their waistbands. The women are short-haired and large-assed.

The sergeant at the desk gives me the nod. He picks up the telephone.

The seventh-floor interview room is a windowless box with a table and four chairs bolted to the gray-green linoleum and otherwise unremarkable except for a length of ordinary steel pipe that runs the length of the far wall at waist height. In a chair is Lamar

Lamb, his right wrist handcuffed to the pipe and dangling limply from it. He smells like jail, and the room stinks with it.

"Hello, Lamar," I say.

"Uh-huh."

"I'm Andrew Giobberti. I'm an assistant district attorney. Okay?"

"Okay." He throws up his palms casually, as if to say *You know—whatever*. His whole demeanor says *whatever*. He catches a quick look at me, but that's it from him. He is looking elsewhere: the table, the wall, the linoleum floor. He gives me his profile. I see his incongruously weak chin. I see his ear, which is honed like oiled wood and surmounted by cornrows that trace—absurdly yet menacingly—across his skull and terminate in wormlike dangles at his neck. His black not brown skin is oddly luminous in the fluorescent light.

He lets go with an audible yawn. (The bastard is bored.) He is slumped in his chair with his manacled arm extended as though over the shoulders of an invisible bitch. He is as dull and unfazed, fastened to a pen wall, facing the man prosecuting him for murder, as I might be in front of the tube watching golf. I shake my head, but I'll be nice. I'll be his friend. I'm always their best fucking friend in the world.

"Lamar," I say. "You said you wanted to talk. So we're talking. Let's get to work, okay? Your attorney here, Mr. Gufner, he showed you this form? This piece of paper right here? Let me ask you a question. Do you know what this is right here?"

"He told me, that old man over there—the lawyer. What it say, again?"

I turn to Gufner. "Conrad, maybe you—maybe you want to just tell him what he's signing here."

"Yes. Lamar." Gufner stirs. "Lamar, listen to me. Please. Again, this is the agreement between you and the prosecutor. It lets him use anything you tell him if this case goes to trial. Okay? You understand, Lamar?"

"That what it say?"

"That's what I'm telling you it says, Lamar," Gufner says.

"I have to sign it?"

"No, you don't have to sign it," Gufner tells him, rolling his eyes at me. "You can refuse to sign it, and then this nice detective right here will put you back in the bus and take you to Rikers right now. But you said you wanted to talk to the D.A. This is the D.A. If you want to talk to the D.A. and tell him what you told me, then you have to sign this agreement first, okay? That's it."

"A'ight," he says (*all right*). "Only I ain't read it."

"Can we get those off, Detective—those, uh, bracelets?" I say, indicating with my own wrists. The detective complies. Lamar Lamb signs the sheet with a deliberate scrawl, then covertly rubs his wrist under the table.

"You hungry, Lamar? You maybe want something to eat?"

"Yeah."

"All right," I say. "What can we get you?"

"I ain't never had no supper. I was on the bus."

"You want a candy bar or something, Lamar?"

"Why you always be callin me that for?" he asks suddenly.

"Calling you what?"

"That name," he says. "Ain't no one call me Lamar."

"No one?"

"Only my moms," he says, not looking at me.

"Your grandmother?"

"No, my moms is what I said."

"What do you want me to call you?" I ask.

"You call me anythin," he says. "You want to call me that? You call me that."

"You want me to call you LL?" I ask.

He looks quickly at me. "No. No offense or nothin, but that what my boys call me."

"You have a lot of friends, Lamar?" I ask him.

"I been around, you know what I'm sayin?"

"You been around, Lamar?" I ask. "Where you been?"

"I tell you," he says.

"Tell me," I say. "Let's talk."

"Places. I seen things. I been around the world and back. I been to London," he says. Then, to clarify, he adds, "England."

"I know you have," I say. "I got it here." I tap a manila file in front of me.

"What you got?"

"Your file, brother," I say. "This is all I need to know about you. Let me sign—did you sign that, Conrad? What's the date?"

"Twentieth? I lost a day," Conrad says, laughing for some reason and rubbing himself.

"It don' look that big," Lamar interrupts.

"What's that, Lamar?" I ask.

"That file," he says. "That my record?"

"Yes."

"Dang," he says. "That ain't nothin."

"Maybe you ain't been too many places after all. Maybe you should get out more often," I say. "Outa Brooklyn, maybe."

"Yeah, I like to bust outa Brooklyn. Get out of where I'm at. Maybe I move out when I get things settled with you."

"So, Lamar," I ask. "You want something to eat? Like a candy bar or something?"

"No. I like a buttered roll," he says. "And a Coke."

"A buttered roll and a Coke," I say. "Detective, you got some-body who can get my man here a roll and a Coke? Why don't we get started, okay? Now your lawyer, Mr. Gufner, he said you had something you wanted to say to me. Is that right? Something you wanted to talk to me about?"

"What he tell you?"

"Oh, fuck it. Wait a minute. Hand me that thing. No. That. Lamar, I'm gonna turn this on now. I'm gonna record what you're saying, okay?"

"A'ight."

```
BY A.D.A. GIOBBERTI:
    This is tape number H-09254. We are
present at the Kings County District
Attorney's Office, seventh-floor interview
room. Today is the twenty-first of August.
The time is now seven-forty in the p.m. Mr.
Lamb, all right. Do you swear that the
statement you are about to give will be the
whole truth and -- ah, do you promise to
tell the truth, Lamar? You have to answer
with a word, Lamar, not just nodding your
head, O.K.?

A.  Yeah.
Q.  All right. For the record, Mr. Lamb, you
    requested to speak to me?
A.  Because I'm innocent.
Q.  All right. We'll get to that. All right.
    I'm investigating an incident that
```

occurred on August fourth of this year at
1250 Sutter Avenue, apartment 7E, at
about, uh, midnight. Ah, you were -- were
you there?

A. Yes.

Q. O.K. Is that your place?

A. No.

Q. Whose place is it? Do you know?

A. My baby mother.

Q. Who's your baby mother?

A. Kayla.

Q. Kayla Harris?

A. I think -- yeah.

Q. Are you saying you have a child in common
with the girl? With Kayla Harris?

A. Uh-huh.

Q. What happened when you got there?

A. Nothing. I just come over. I was there
for like maybe almost an hour. I was just
chilling (inaudible) and my shit was
like, I was like (inaudible) that's the
only thing that keep me, you know what
I'm saying? Keep my shit right, cause I
have a kid. A baby, you know.

Q. Lamar, I just want you to speak up a bit.
O.K.?

A. So it was like nothing.

Q. What was your relationship with the girl?

A. Kayla? You know. We was like together.
That's what I'm saying. Ask anyone. They

all know we was together. Why I gonna
shoot her for? For no reason? Just like
she a dog or some shit.

Q. You tell me.

A. I ain't tell you cause I ain't shoot her.
That shit messed up. What you say. I'm
not about that. Yeah, I'm keeping it real
about me. I did my dirt, you know what
I'm saying. I did my dirt, you know. If I
did something, I admit it. You look at
that file. You have it right there. Check
it out. I plead guilty before. I do my
time if I do the crime, you know what I'm
saying? I do my time now I'm nineteen
(inaudible) than when I'm like fifty. But
this shit is messed up. Murder and shit.

Q. Yeah, I know that about you. I see. I
know you got a, what? You pleaded guilty
to selling. Twice. You did upstate time
on the second one?

A. Yeah, I do a one to three, but they bust
me out early. Work release, you know?

Q. How'd you like Coxsackie?

A. You kidding?

Q. Not like Rikers. Am I right? You don't
want to go back up?

A. Fuck that shit, you know? I stay in the
free world. I'm not a bad kid. I get a
job. I'm working at the Wendy's out on
Rockaway. Check it out. I give you the

dude's name. I'm trying to make a better
life.

Q. All right. Kayla was there. Who else?

A. Kayla's sister. Topia. She come over.
Chill. We was having us a drink. Play on
the play station I get her.

Q. How many drinks?

A. I had, um, one maybe two. Brass monkey.
Kayla have a brass monkey too. Utopia
didn't have nothing. She's a, what do you
call her, a vegetarian or some shit. She
don't drink.

Q. And where's Nicole?

A. She was around, I don't know. I don't
remember where she was at. I don't pay
her no mind. She was smacked. She's into
smoking shit. Her head ain't right no
more, like she a cluck head, you know?

Q. What do you mean?

A. She's a trick bitch. Trick her ass for
dope and shit.

Q. The reason why I'm asking you was she
there, Lamar, is because we have
witnesses telling us something different.

A. I can only say what I remember.

Q. That's all I want you to do, brother. All
right? The only thing to do is to help
yourself, because we know what happened.
Do you understand? We already know what
happened, so you're not helping us.

You're only helping yourself. I want to
tell you that. I'm telling you straight
up, if you're going to go to court with a
half-ass story that's different than what
we already know, different from what the
witnesses are telling us, it's going to
embarrass you --

A. Exactly.

Q. -- you're gonna look stupid and they're
gonna, the judge is gonna hit you up with
some heavy time. Upstate time. You
understand?

A. Fuck it (inaudible) anything on me. I
know -- why you all scare me, man
(inaudible).

Q. What's that?

A. Why is you all trying to do me like that?

Q. I'm just telling you the way it goes. No
one is saying you're a bad guy, Lamar.

A. Shit. I done my shit.

Q. No one is saying you meant to shoot her.
It might have, you know, been like an
accident or something like that and you
didn't mean --

A. I wouldn't hurt Kayla, mister.

Q. That's what I'm saying. It's possible to
kill someone and not mean it. Doesn't
mean you're a bad guy. I'm not here to
say you're a bad guy, brother. But the
way it looks, it doesn't look good for
you.

A. I don't know.

Q. What does that mean, you don't know?

A. Just, I don't know. Shit. I'm just tired.
It's the same shit, you know what I'm
saying. You ain't got nowhere to go.
Nothing to do. You go outside and all
those Brooklyn niggers do is talk shit.
And now you want me to say I done
something I ain't do. Make me go upstate
again. I'm nineteen years old and I
already been there. That's enough, you
know what I'm saying.

Q. Lamar, why don't you just tell me
what happens next? After you get
there?

A. You already made up your mind I done it.

Q. I never said that.

A. You want me to plead guilty. I ain't.
Cause I ain't done nothing. What kind of
charge am I looking at here?

Q. You know what you're looking at.

A. I can't do no jail time. I can't -- I got
it going on. Any way I get probation or
something?

Q. Look, let's just talk about what
happened, and we'll see.

A. Same old. She never respect me. She think
I'm no good. Now look.

Q. Kayla?

A. No, Nicole. Like I was saying. She come
in and is like, to me, you no good, you

get out. Saying Kayla ain't no whore.
That's when the gun go off.

Q. Your gun?

A. Nah, I wasn't dirty. I don't carry no gun
in East New York. (Inaudible) bitch gun
anyway.

Q. What do you mean?

A. Fuck (inaudible) small, you know?

Q. You know about guns?

A. You kidding? I got guns. Not now. I
growed up in Cypress Hills. You think I
ain't know about guns? Shit.

Q. What kind of gun was it? Do you remember?

A. Chrome twenty-five.

Q. She took it out?

A. She come in and like wave it around like
she gonna scare me or something. Like I
ain't never look at no gun before. Scare
me off cause she don't like me seeing
Kayla. She come in and Kayla like stark
raving naked, on the bed. That's why
Nicole just lose it.

Q. Go on.

A. And she come through the door with the
gun. Shouting. Telling me to stay away.
Kayla started to say something in between
us, and her mother be like shouting at
her too. To be quiet. And everybody
yelling, and that when there's, like,
pow, and she fall back on the bed with a
spot right here. She fall back on her

back and look up in the air like God I'm
coming.

Q. What'd you do?

A. I left.

Q. What about the gun?

A. I snatch that shit up. After it go off,
Nicole drop it. I don't want her shooting
me in the back or some wild-ass silly
shit. I tell you she was acting crazy.
She saying oh my God, look what you done,
look what you done.

Q. What'd she say?

A. She was like bugging out, I don't really
remember. But it was like oh my God, look
what you done. Which don't make no sense.
I was just like yo, you smoke her, bitch.
And I leave.

Q. Why'd you leave?

A. Why you think? No one believe me. You
don't believe I ain't done it.

Q. Where's the gun now, Lamar?

A. I give it to my boy.

Q. Who's your boy?

A. His name Dirty. We all just call him
Dirty. His name Eve or some shit.

Q. Eve?

A. Right.

Q. As in Adam and Eve?

A. Who?

Q. You know Eve? Dirty?

A. I don't know him. We chill sometimes.

```
        Smoke us some weed. We call him Dirty
        Dread because his hair be all nasty and
        shit. I see him around Amboy Street
        sometimes, by the park there. He not
        there real regular. He don't have no
        place he have to be.
    Q.  All right. That's about it.
    A.  We done?
    Q.  Yeah.
    A.  I can go?
    Q.  You can go back to Rikers.
    A.  But I told you what happen. I didn't do
        nothing. Why I can't go? Messed up.
    Q.  That concludes this interview. The time
        is now eight-oh-nine.
```

"Why I can't go?" Lamar is asking me. He turns on Gufner, who shrugs. The detective is fastening Lamar's wrists behind him and leading him from the room while Lamar is looking at Gufner and at me and asking why he can't go. After a full minute, I still hear his voice in the hall. "Messed up, man. Shit's messed *up*."

"He doesn't get it," I say to Gufner.

"No, these kids—" Gufner starts, without needing to finish the thought.

"Anyway, maybe he'll think a little harder now."

"You think our friend there thinks much about anything?" he asks me.

"He's not stupid," I say. "He figured out how he needs to play us. Play me, I mean."

"You mean about the girl being his baby's mother?" he asks.

"The word is *babymother*, Conrad," I say. *"Babymother."*

"*Babymother*," he repeats, feeling his knee. The word makes him feel old and physically ache. "I am too old for this."

"Yeah," I say. "The way I see it, he figured out he needs a reason why he was with the girl. So the dead girl becomes the dead girlfriend."

"I don't know," he says thoughtfully. "You really think the kid's full of prunes?"

"What do you think?"

"What do I think?" Gufner raps his knuckles on the peeling Formica tabletop and says, "I think it's gonna be a short trial and a long sentence."

CHAPTER

17

Wednesday morning, and light fills my empty room and eddies on the whorling dust. A Wednesday morning (the same as any other).

In this bed, this very bed where she was conceived, Opal would sit while I dressed. On mornings such as this, her mother in the city, Opal would sit watching channel 13 and arranging her collections of treasures—shells and crayons and beads and animals cut roughly from newspapers and balled into discarded boxes or makeshift handbags.

"Daddy."

"What is it, Opal?"

"Um, Daddy, is Arthur, the Arthur on TV? Is Arthur an animal?" she asks, not turning away from the television set on the bedroom dresser.

"Yeah," I say, looking. "Sure he's an animal."

"*Well*," she asks. "What *kind* of an animal is he? Lilly, um, Lilly said he was like a little small bear, but Arthur doesn't really *seem* like a bear."

I try to picture her just like that.

Outside, Mrs. Kretschmer's dachshund woofs halfheartedly in the garden at a slug or whatnot.

A car horn nearby.

Another woof like a dry cough.

A jet engine spools up to a shriller octave a thousand feet above, inhaling great gulps of spring air, compressing it into movement.

Opal disappears before she forms in my head. I lie here in this bed of ours and try to picture her, and I cannot. I have to prop myself on an elbow to see Opal on the nightstand—framed and forever five.

Something happened last week—

I was on Montague Street at the Chase Manhattan Bank. A fragment of another age, encouraging references to thrift and industry are cut into its travertine walls. I was waiting patiently in line. I needed twenty dollars. I wanted to buy a book at Walden Books. *Waldenbooks?* (I don't know what it's called anymore.) I eyed the line discreetly, hopefully, for I am ever vigilant for beauty. But there was none. We are an ugly, unkempt people in Brooklyn. We are a dark, poor, and edgy people. Our hair is matted and our clothes aren't new. We smell of cigarettes and fried food. We are short. We are fat. We need to visit the dentist. We need to sit in the sun more often.

My turn at the machine. I inserted my plastic and saw my hand there, poised, suspended over the keypad, awaiting an electrochemical stimulation that would never arrive. I saw the eye of the machine: a lens-eye staring fixedly and unblinkingly at my own.

What in hell is my number? I asked myself. *This should be easy.* Behind me, I sensed impatience. *How do they know?*

I walked away. And in a moment, there it was—(0-8-2-3)—August 23—Opal's birth date came to me the very moment I stepped from the bank into the heat radiating up from the griddle of black-top spread out on Montague Street. There were the summer street smells—bus exhaust, garbage, and dog shit—myriad molecules of bus exhaust, garbage, and dog shit agitated by the temperature and borne aloft on the humidity into our noses, into our lungs. I stood there alone with the realization she is slipping away.

August 23—her birthday, and tomorrow her unseen seventh.

I see her in the Winnie-the-Pooh frame, Opal in yellow, peer-ing over the edge of her Pack N' Play—all I have left. I shut my eyes and the image is gone. Even here in this place, on this bed where she was, in this room where she was, even here I cannot see her with my eyes closed—I cannot hear the sound of her voice anymore—I cannot recall the shape of her when I held her on my hip. She is slipping away—as if I dreamt her for five years, and awakened by a passing airplane, the dream of her scattered and dis-persed like ash upon the ocean.

I lie here alone on my lonely bed.

Think about the new girl! (The cartwheeling blonde.) Today I will find some pretense to visit her cubicle.

I need a fresh distraction to save me from this relentless suc-cession of mornings.

CHAPTER

18

From underground I pass without qualm through the revolving door of swinging tines that will backcock violently someday and send sixteen slices of me to the speckled subway cement like so much hard-boiled egg.

I am suddenly, unexpectedly, uncharacteristically optimistic. *I am thinking about the new girl,* and I come aboveground two steps at a time. After the subway, slow as stupid—after the stifle of the tunnel (with its businessmen asleep and sweaty in their seats, their heads back, their mouths agape—low-rent businessmen wearing ties without jackets), it is good to come aboveground and know she is upstairs.

On the telephone, ringing as I sit down, I recognize Utopia's voice—her whispering, willowy, somewhere-else voice. "Mr. Giobberti?"

"Yes."

"Mr. Giobberti. This is Utopia Carbon callin." In the background, a baby cries.

"Yes."

"I talked to you at the funeral or whatever."

"Yes," I say. "I remember."

"It was my sister's. Kayla, um. Kayla Harris. The girl who got shot."

"Yes," I tell her. "I remember—Utopia."

Then there is a racket in the hallway outside my cubicle.

"—and said LL—that's what we know him as—was, um, lookin at jail time?"

"That's right," I say.

"Oh."

"We're gonna give this case everything we have," I tell her.

"Mister, um."

"Utopia. Understand me," I tell her. "We have him, and we're gonna keep him. This is a good case. It has some problems, but it's a good case."

"All right."

"All right, Utopia?"

"All right," she says, then— "What problems?"

"Don't worry, Utopia. It's a good case. I've won harder cases."

"Oh."

"All right?" I ask her.

"Yes."

"I want you to call me anytime, all right?"

"All right," she says, then again— "What problems?"

"Well. We don't have an eyewitness," I say. "You and your mother were asleep when—it happened."

"Is that like a big problem or whatever?"

"No," I say. "I don't need an eyewitness. It would be better, but it's still a good case."

"If there's no eyewitnesses, don't you like have to let him out?"

"No," I say. "Who told you that?"

"No. No one. I was just thinkin about it and everythin."

"All right?" I ask.

"Yes."

"So, please call me—"

"Mr. Giobberti?" she says.

"Yes, Utopia," I say.

"If no one, um, is an eyewitness—how do you know it was LL who done it?"

"There's other evidence," I tell her.

"Oh. What evidence?"

"It's called—circumstantial evidence," I say. "There's circumstantial evidence."

"What circumstantial evidence?"

"Don't worry about Lamar anymore, Utopia."

"Mister, I think I need to like tell you somethin," she says.

"All right."

She doesn't say anything. I hear Nicole say something, sounding far away, and Utopia slips the receiver into the cradle.

Stacey in her cubicle sees me walk by her to the mini-fridge, carrying a replacement Pepsi. She is seated facing the hallway, not the wall opposite her desk. She is waiting for me—she is *lying in wait,* as prosecutors say on TV. Seeing me pass, she says my name. She is in a good mood, and it makes her prettier.

"Again the Pepsi?" she asks, and I can't answer because she tells me, with evident satisfaction, "She's holding out."

"Who?"

"Nicole."

"You think?" I ask her.

"I *know* it, Gio," she says. "She knows more than she's saying."

"No kidding." I grab at her dangling, bare ankle—which she pulls quickly, unsmilingly away. There is a thin gold chain around it that I didn't give her.

"Just listen up," she tells me.

"All right, Stace. Tell me all about it."

"Someone let him in," she tells me. "No sign of forced entry. Did you read the crime scene report?"

"No."

"Someone let him in."

"Why Nicole?" I ask.

"Nicole's got a reason," she suggests, crossing her legs under her (a neat cat). "She's an addict, and he deals cola."

"How's that get you a dead girl? He's got a better reason to see the girl," I say. "He just got out of Coxsackie."

"Miss Iris says Nicole tricks for dope—"

"She said there were *all sorts of activities* going on there," I tell Stacey. "All sorts of activities that a Christian woman can't even talk about. Say you're Lamb—who you gonna hook up with?"

"He's no prize himself," she says, looking at his mug shot.

"Doesn't have to be, Stace," I say. *"You see somebody getting pussy for crack, he's the dopeman."*

She smiles. "Where'd you hear that?"

"Old school rap," I tell her. "Soundtrack to Brooklyn homicide. Back in the day. Good old days in the early nineties—two, three bodies a day. Not like now."

"Don't get all nostalgic on me, Gio—you can't even cope with one anymore."

"What do you think Christian women can't talk about anyway?" I ask her. "Some of them talk trash even better than you, Sharp."

"I'm half Jewish. Maybe that explains it."

"Maybe. Maybe you're just not as tough as you think you are."

"You want to hear something funny," she says. "My mother thinks you're Jewish."

"I think mostly she's glad I'm not Irish. What's her deal, any-way?"

"Fucking nuts," she says. "I don't know."

"When you gonna move out?"

"You asking me to?" she says without inflection.

"Right, that's what I need. All those magazines and crap you got thrown all around your room. My place is—very orderly. I'm a fucking monk."

"I'll take your word for it," she says.

Penny is walking by heavily, circulating a memorandum. She flashes me a look of hungry hatred. Stacey, meanwhile, withdraws a cigarette from a pack and pinches it (unlit) between thumb and forefinger, like a joint.

"So you're buying Lamb's story now?" she asks. "Is that where you are today?"

"No," I tell her.

"But you think he came up for the girl?" she asks. "Like he said?"

"Sure. Why not?"

"That's what he told Solano, so that's why I'm asking," she says.

"Yeah, to play Pac-Man and have a drink or whatever," I re-mind her. "That's all he said. He never said they were together like that."

"*Pac-Man?* You're so goddamn ancient."

"I don't know what they do," I say. "You know what a carbon copy is, Sharp?"

"What?"

"He never told Solano he and the girl were together like that," I repeat. "That's new—he's looking for a lie he can live with. He's not stupid, this kid. He comes across all right."

"What do you mean?"

"I talked to him," I say. "Last night."

She waits a moment before she says, "Nice."

"And get this," I tell her. "Get what he says—what?"

"Nothing," she says, focusing on the cigarette still pinched in her fingers.

"What?" I ask her again.

"Fuck off," she says. "Just finish what you started saying. What's Lamb say?"

"You know that kid? The girl's kid, the baby?" I ask. "She's his, he's saying now, and the girl's his babymother."

"Maybe she is."

"And maybe her name is Susan B. Anthony."

"You don't know," she says. "Miss Iris said they were together, Lamar and the girl."

"They were together like Ben and Jerry," I say. "It was business, Stacey. The girl was a pross. She's a pross and her mother's a pross. They're both giving it up for dope. Just giving it up. All sorts of activities, Stacey."

"She didn't use."

"Who?" I ask.

"The girl," Stacey tells me. "You didn't read the toxicology, either? She's clean, Gio."

"So she tricks for pocket change—like a paper route," I say. "You know how much a Tommy Hil jacket is? About twenty blow jobs."

"She's holding out, Nicole," Stacey tells me again, first sighing.

"No shit, Stacey," I say. "Welcome to the world. We're never gonna get the story from her straight up. And you know what else? I don't care. I don't need to prove why Lamar capped her. I just need to prove he did."

"You don't care why," she tells me.

"To hell with why," I tell her. "I don't need to know why he killed her. I don't even need to know that he did—the jury comes back with he did it, then he did it."

She shakes her head. "You're fucked up in so many interesting ways."

"Sharp," I tell her. "He did it."

"You don't know—"

"Why else would he lie about the kid?" I ask her. "The kid gives him something he needs."

"What's he need?"

"An excuse," I say. "He knows we can put him there, so he has to have a reason. He wants to say he was up there playing daddy. You know—it's almost funny. Lamar look like father of the year to you?"

"Like you know about that."

I don't say anything. Then I say, "The kid gives him something he needs."

"What does he need?" she asks.

"The kid ties him to the dead girl," I tell her. "Now he can bawl his eyes out and say he didn't do it. Or if I prove he did it, he can say how he didn't mean it—that it was just an accident. He came close to squirting a few last night, but he decided to save it for the jury."

"He's not gonna say it was an accident."

"Fuck he's not," I say. "You watch. Soon as Gufner sits down with him for more than ten seconds, that's exactly what he's gonna say. Gufner's gonna come around looking for a manslaughter plea—

maybe crim-neg homicide, even—saying it was an accident and all. You wait."

"He's not gonna say it was an accident."

"What do you wanna bet?" I ask her.

"You don't have anything I want."

"A gentleman's bet, then," I suggest, putting out my hand.

"Don't flatter yourself."

"You wait, Stace. This shitbird's putting it together. This kind of case—no eyewitness, no clear motive? They always come around with their fucking tail between their legs saying how sorry they all are—*Oh, I didn't know it was loaded—Oh, I didn't mean to pull the trigger—Oh, I dropped it, and it exploded.*" I look out the soot-dusted window. "Fucking piss me off. Fucking accident. Always saying how sorry they are, as if that makes any difference. People do stupid shit—someone ends up dead."

"He already said he didn't do it, Gio," she says almost under her breath. "He's kind of stuck with that version, right?"

"He'll say he was scared when he told it to Solano, that he wasn't thinking right. It won't matter," I say. "Anyway, *a foolish consistency is the hobgoblin of little minds.*"

"What . . . ?"

"Ralph Waldo Emerson."

"Whatever. That's what an Ivy League education's good for—a pithy quote from a dead white male when the topic is a dead black girl. So listen, Ralph, you think he's just gonna twist back his girlfriend's cap like that? No reason? That makes sense?"

"Fuckin A right it makes sense. You know how many people are killed by strangers in Brooklyn every year? About two and a half. You get dead in this borough, the last thing you see is your boy standing over you with a smoking nine. The last thing you say is his name."

"There's just something really wrong with this picture, Gio," she says.

"What are you, like, drawing from your great fund of experience prosecuting homicides, Sharp? You think you know how to run an investigation?"

"There is no investigation, Giobberti!" she says. "That's my point. You have three people in that apartment—and the most incriminating piece of evidence you have against Lamar is that he fucks her and runs out the door. You do that to me every other night! That's evidence?"

"If your mother found you dead in the morning, yeah!"

She shrugs. "Isn't anyone working this case for you?"

"You."

"No one?" she says. "Not Solano? Not that limp-dick Carson?"

"You."

"I cannot believe you, Giobberti," she tells me. "I don't get it. I don't know if you're lazy or stupid—or what."

"You check it out then, Sharp. You come up with something more than a little tingly feeling that something's not right, then we'll do what we have to do. Right now, the evidence I got says LL's our shooter, and that's who I'm giving to the grand jury."

"All right, Giobberti," she says. "Thanks. Thanks a lot. I appreciate your letting me work this case with you. I've learned so much—mostly how to be a prick."

"Fine, but if you want to be of some use, get some blood from Lamar. Find out if that's his kid. And as long as you're so energetic, reach out to the sister. Utopia."

"Solano said she was sleeping."

"Just talk to her," I say absently, looking out the window, past Stacey. "There's something on her mind is all."

"All right, Giobberti."

"Who is that girl?" I say abruptly.

"What?"

"That girl," I say. "There."

"Where?" Stacey follows my pointing finger outside the window, beyond the dripping compressor to the wooden walkway above a fourteen-inch galvanized cooling pipe where—with a handful of other young A.D.A.s—is the new girl.

"There," I say again.

"Which?" she asks. "No. The blonde?" There is no need for her to be more specific, for there is—unsurprisingly—only one. In Brooklyn, blondes (real blondes with blond eyebrows and skin to match) are as conspicuous as dolphins among fish.

"Good guess."

"*Guess,*" she says, shaking her head. "Her name is *Holly Nilsson,* if you can actually believe it. From *Minnesota*—what, does she like remind you of your wife or something?"

"Minnesota," I say, ignoring it.

"She's in my class. We started here together last fall, you know."

"I be doggone," I say.

"What did you say?"

"Doggone," I say. "Isn't that something they say in Minnesota?"

"You're thinking of Dogpatch," she tells me.

"Holy Mother, she really is good-looking, though. Don't you think?"

"She's super nice, anyway," Stacey says, looking at Holly. "Why're you surprised she's in my class?"

"I don't know. You just seem a lot older. In a way."

"She doesn't seem your type," says Stacey with crafted nonchalance.

"I wonder what you think *is* my type," I say.

"Not me, if that's what you're fishing for."

"Don't get all excited, Sharp," I tell her. "I'm not."

"Well, if it means anything to you, and I'm sure it does," she says archly, "I know she's got a thing for you."

"What sort of a thing?" I ask, thinking, for some reason, that the new girl has a present for me.

"Just one of those little things we girls get from time to time—like food poisoning."

"Or PMS," I add.

"Right," she says. "And then it goes away."

"I be doggone." I look out at her again, straining my eyes with redoubled interest. Knowing she likes you makes her a possibility, and when she is a possibility she is twice as interesting as before—and a possibility is nearly always as interesting as an impossibility.

"Oh, don't be surprised, Giobberti. You're very popular with that crowd." She indicates the walkway. "Those white girls."

We both are looking out the window now, looking at them—they laugh in furtive movements, smile prettily, say God knows what about what and whom, and send their spent cigarettes shooting to the wooden walkway. They all do seem younger than Stacey, but then I seem younger than Stacey.

"I don't think I've ever said two words to any of them," I say.

"Who wouldn't love you? Come on, Giobberti," she says. "You're every girl's dream."

"That right?"

"Oh, sure," she says. "You're single, you're straight, and you kind of look like George Clooney on a bad day—if I squint my eyes."

"Who?"

She shifts suddenly as she sometimes does, like a squall blowing up from a dead calm. "But what you really got going for you is you know how to make a woman feel good about herself. Like she's important to you, you know? That's a rare talent."

She stops talking now and looks at me contemptuously. She smiles slightly, sarcastically, and waves me out. "I'll see you later, Ralph."

"What?" I say to her blankly hostile face.

"Whatever," she says and turns back to her desk.

"No, what?" I ask.

"What do you mean *what*? You know goddamn well what, dickhead. Now get the fuck out of my way." She rises and shoulders past me, giving me a surprisingly strong shove—she is a tight coil of fury—but then comes back. She is ten inches from my face. "And another thing," she says. "If you want me off this homicide, all you have to do is say so. Don't worry about hurting my feelings. I think I could deal with it."

"I know you could."

"All right," she says. "Anything you don't understand about that?"

"No."

"So what is it, then?" She finally lights her cigarette.

"You better take that out there." I gesture to the dripping compressors and the walkways beyond the windows.

In answer, she sends the match, still lit, flying in my direction. "Not afraid of a little fire, scarecrow?" she says when I jolt at it. She drops back into her chair, barely filling half of it. She laughs dryly at me. The spent match sends up a gray thread from the linoleum. "What is it, then? In or out?"

"Cut the drama."

"Look—"

"Keep it down," I say.

(She doesn't.) "Put yourself in my position. You come in here this morning and tell me you interrogated Lamar Lamb last night—*the fucking defendant!*—without me. What the fuck's up with that, Giobberti? What am I supposed to make of that?"

"Keep it down."

"Fuck you, Gio. You know—listen to yourself. *Put out your cigarette. Keep it down.* When'd you turn into such an old lady? That must've been someone else I screwed on the bathroom sink at—"

"What if I said I wanted you out?"

"I told you I could deal with it," she says quickly.

"I never wondered about that."

"That's the thing, isn't it?" she says after a long moment, exhaling the words through a blue-gray fog of lung smoke. "You think we're both so tough." She laughs once and exhales again for effect. "You do whatever you have to do, but let me tell you something. Are you listening? Because I'm only gonna say this once. I think you're an evil bastard, Giobberti. You're a selfish, evil bastard. Just don't even try to say anything—this isn't a conversation. You try to get over on me again and I'll fucking castrate you. And I mean it."

And I believe her.

CHAPTER

19

Dirty Dread took a collar last week, some bullshit arrest—aggressive panhandling (a misdemeanor) in a stolen wheelchair (another misdemeanor). The wheelchair was a nice touch, but probably not enough to open hearts on the east side of Brooklyn, where paraplegia ranks on the list of social ills where trodden flower beds rank on the east side of Manhattan. The arresting officer tacked on a charge of possessing stolen property because of the chair, and now Dirty's back on the street.

At least Solano now has his name—*Yves St. Ides.* I walk to the case-tracking computer and type in the name. The screen glows a malevolent green inside its sooty beige box. A plasticized keyboard cover is worn through in places, and pretzel crumbs between the keys make them stick. I type a *Y*, and it replicates itself like a chromosome across the screen. A hundred green *Y*s.

Dirty's criminal history unfolds—a new page for each stroke of the return key, a new arrest for each page. Although long, Dirty's rap is mostly nothing. Drugs, street fights, farebeats, drugs, drugs. I can flick by his short, uninteresting life as a perp with twelve hits on the return key. He's a low-level mope. A dope-smoking dope dealer living here and there, man. This week, it's the men's shelter in the Bedford Armory, a full acre of army cots and head lice where Solano is at this very moment.

For fun, I type in Nicole's name. (C-A-R-B-O-N, N-I-C-C-C-C-C-C-C-C-C-C-C-C-C-C-C-C-C) She is a whore for money. Eleven collars for loitering for prostitution, all of them within the last year. Before that, not even a farebeat.

The case-tracking computer is in an empty corner of the bureau on a metal desk next to the little room with the slop sink in it. There is a mirror in that room, which reeks of stale coffee and mop water. A steam pipe junction fills it with an oily haze. One of Penny's unwanted posters hangs limply to one side on a single thumbtack: a kitten in a teacup, yawning, its pink tongue curling like a toboggan. Pastel italicized letters read *Be Nice to Me, It's My First Life*.

Holding my breath, I wipe the mirror with a gray towel, check my teeth and hair, and quickly walk out. (Exhale.)

"Can I borrow your *Black's Law Dictionary*?" This is what I say to the new girl.

"Oh, what—?" she says, turning around in her chair and inclining her blond head to the side to see me. An amused, startled *what*. She is startled because she expected me—just not at this moment; she is amused because she knows I couldn't care less about the dictionary.

"That," I say, indicating.

"You want to borrow it?" she asks.

"Yes. Do you mind?"

"No. I mean—well, no."

I sit on her desk, distressing her—the distress they have when they are not ready for you, when they have not been near a mirror lately. She is wondering if everything is fetchingly in order. *Don't worry,* I almost tell her. *It is.*

Instead I say, "I wanted to look up something." *Where I am going with this?*

"Oh, sure. Do you, um . . . ?"

I am flipping through the heavy book now. She looks at the book and then at me and then at the book.

"This is a very useful book," I am saying, not meeting her eyes, which I nevertheless feel casting about like jailbreak searchlights.

"Yes, it is!"

"I'm kidding," I say, shutting it audibly. "I bet you haven't opened it since law school."

"Well, not much, that's for sure." *Fer sure,* she says. (A midwesterner—Amanda's mother's flat Indiana vowels are in her voice.) *Minnesota—is that near Indiana?*

"I did use it the other day, though," she says, *relaxing?*—but her ankles and knees, wrists and elbows, are still mated. She is still all parallel lines and right angles, and her broad shoulders are narrowed forward to an octave's breadth.

"Say, listen," I say. "Let me ask you something."

"All right."

She is so pretty. I drift off for a moment—

"What?" she asks, canting her head sideways—what a dog does when you bark at it.

"Oh—" I say. "Where'd you learn how to do that?"

"Do what?" she asks, leaning right in.

"You know," I say. "That routine you did the other night. That little, what do you call it? That cartwheel maneuver."

"Oh, that!"

"You nearly scared me to death, you know."

"I've been doing that forever," she says, joints now thawed, shoulders thrown back. "Since I was a kid." *Not for very long, then.*

"Isn't it kind of—I don't know—dangerous?" I ask her. "I think if I tried that, I'd probably pull something important."

"No!"

"No. I would. I'm not very athletic," I say. "I'm thinking about learning how to play golf, though."

"Oh my God! My sister? She's, like, really good. She's almost a pro or whatever."

"No kidding," I say. "She's not a lesbian, is she?"

She laughs. She doesn't know why she is laughing.

"I heard there were a lot of lesbian golfers," I say. "I don't know."

She is still laughing. (We are having the sort of conversation in which content is irrelevant.)

"So what were you looking up, anyway, the other day?" I ask her.

"Oh my God!" she says. "I don't even remember now. Something Latin."

"*In flagrante delicto*, perhaps?" I try.

"Stop it!" She reaches out for me. "I know what that means!"

"*Necessitas vincit legem?*"

"Oh, no," she says. "What's that mean?"

"You've never heard that rule?" I ask her. "That's probably the most important thing to know—as a Brooklyn prosecutor."

"Oh my God," she says again.

I am closer to her now, looking at her left ear and how she has pushed her hair over it, achieving a careless beauty. I can't look for too long at it or things like it—I might slip off her desk and not even feel myself hit the linoleum. With a tremendous inward sigh, I draw myself back to her eyes, now widening slightly with concern that *necessitas vincit legem* somehow passed her by at Fordham Law School, even with her perfect attendance record and round, legible note-taking—or so I imagine, for her desk is Scandinavian-neat, with exclamation-pointed notes to herself on pastel stickies fixed to her books and notebooks, to her gooseneck lamp, to her heavy telephone. On her desktop, on a giant August, she has names and times and things to do all spelled out.

There is also in her eye the concern that something nasty may have reposed in the vicinity of her left ear, where an involuntary hand now gingerly pats.

"It means necessity is stronger than law," I tell her.

"Oh," she says, sounding relieved or disappointed. I can't tell which.

"You could work here ten years before you figured that out," I say. "I just told you for nothing."

She takes it as a joke and relaxes, although I am not joking. She pushes the dislodged hair back upon the ridge of her ear. I notice now, with a twinge of disappointment, that her eyes are not a pure blue, but a sort of bluish green—almost a gray-green, like the linoleum. A pellucid blue eye would have rounded out the picture nicely.

"I speak French, though," she volunteers, maybe sounding defensive—I take it as a good sign.

"Vraiment?"

"Oui," she says, now embarrassed.

She tells me all about her junior year in Paris. I don't hear a word. I am only trying not to look at her ear again, or at the line of her eyebrows, or at her heaving chest, which completely fills my periphery. Nevertheless, I start to slip from her desk onto the linoleum, and a growing numbness spreads from the primitive root of my brain as though she (by the sound of her, by the soapy smell of her, by the way she displaces the air around her) has planted an acorn within me that now sends its shoots twining around my spine, making me stupid.

"I know it's like no big deal or anything," she is saying. "But I was getting homesick, I think? I missed my mom."

"Home?" I ask automatically, although I know, although it is obvious that she is from somewhere far from here.

"St. Paul," she says. "That's in Minnesota. You know, *Land of Ten Thousand Lakes* or whatever? It's one of the Twin Cities. The other is, um, Minneapolis."

"So there are two of them?" I ask, still stupid. I continue this way, hearing nothing either of us says.

"And everyone thinks it's so cold there, but you just have to wear sweaters and we have big woolly blankets at night—"

Here is what's-her-name as clean as the good earth and spread out like a fertile prairie pasture, ready to be paved over, ready for a Wal-Mart, over easy, to be settled down upon her. Here she is filling out her blouse, her skin as creamy and wholesome as farina— isn't that something they eat, or am I in Dogpatch again?

On the other hand, for all her wholesome, fulsome goodness, will she be shy? Will she simply close her eyes and think of her long-lost prairie? Will she think of Mom?

I think better of it—I will walk away from this one. I straighten, with her dictionary in my hand, enough of her to hold for now. (There is also Stacey and that evil-bastard business.) I drop the *Black's Law Dictionary* into its place.

But then she says, with an implicit wink, "Nice talking to you, Gio."

Did I tell her my name? What is her name?

At once, I decide not to walk away. I decide that what I want right now is to wool up with her on one of her blankets, to spread her over the winter wheat and pull off sweaters and blue jeans and fling it all into ten thousand lakes.

"Hey," I say to her, sitting myself down close to her on her desktop, and then, suddenly remembering her name, I say, "Hey, Holly."

"Yes!" she says in a tenor to match my own.

"Do you know what?"

"What!" she says, and I can barely hear it.

Ask me, she is saying. *Ask me and I will say yes!*

CHAPTER

20

Milton Echeverria is dead. About time, really. They tried last year, and all they did was put him in a wheelchair.

For a twenty-year-old kid with not much ambition, Milton Echeverria had a way of pissing people off. He had a nice little heroin thing going over in the vicinity of Rogers and Martense—he sold boy in a neighborhood where crack was girl. That was in the Six-Seven Precinct, out in the East Flatbush section where he did not live. East Flatbush is where Milton set up among the Jamaicans to avoid trouble back home in East New York. Milton didn't mind violence, but he didn't like trouble. What he liked more than anything else was driving nowhere in his tricked-out Mustang, blowing down New Lots Avenue at three in the morning, setting off car alarms with the sheer noise of it. Even after the Jamaicans shot him through the spine, putting him out of the heroin business altogether, that's what he'd do—sit in the front seat of the Mustang with Gerry at the wheel, just to show them all—just to say, *Yo, check it out now, motherfuckers—look who you try to kill.*

This was last year, in the spring. Detective Anthony Lubriano, Six-Seven squad, suspected Milton knew more about who shot him than he was saying—that Milton was doing the usual, holding out so he could take care of business himself. Lubriano kept an eye on Milton anyway, on the theory that bad things happen to bad people. To no one's surprise, Jamaicans started dying with monotonous violence in East Flatbush once Milton went home from Brookdale Hospital with two legs that no longer worked.

That's when I got involved. Lubriano wanted a warrant to listen to Milton's telephone. A waste of time—seventeen cassettes of Milton talking to his girlfriend. Tired of using his brains, Lubriano ended up pinching Milton's homeboy Gerry for the hell of it one Saturday morning, shaking him out of his bed on Euclid Avenue and hauling him to the squad room, where Gerry—more scared of Lubriano than he was of Milton—just gave the whole thing up. He gave up Milton as the shooter on the three Jamaicans.

Gerry had followed Milton in his downward spiral. After Milton's smack spot had fallen apart in East Flatbush, Milton went home to East New York to push crack to the hookers on Belmont Avenue and in the buildings with working elevators at Cypress Hills and the Pink House on Linden. Milton pushed girl on hookers, and Gerry pushed Milton in the wheelchair and stayed in the hall, kicking the walls while Milton got laid. Lubriano guessed that made Gerry sore. It did.

"And he always, like, Yo, Gerry, chill, and I always, like, Yeah, whatever. I chill or whatever, and the motherfucker get his punk ass hooked up. Motherfucker in a motherfuckin chair getting his nigger ass hooked up. Every day. Every day."

"So, Gerry," Lubriano said to him. "Milton still good to go with the ladies there? I mean, that leg still walk, you know what I'm sayin?"

"Yo, man, for real," Gerry said. "He can get it on. Motherfucker Pirelli. They just hook him up."

"Who?"

"All them. Only I ain't get none of that shit."

Lubriano checked Gerry into a Suffolk County hotel with stained sheets and a uniform at his door. Ten days later, Gerry was back in Brooklyn, sitting in the seventh-floor interview room at 210 while I waited for Pauline to schedule some time for Gerry to testify against Milton in the grand jury. Gerry was in a bad mood. He had developed a taste for product, and clean living didn't suit him. He wasn't in Suffolk long enough to dry out, and he sat in front of the TV in the witness room, pacing, trying to sleep, pacing some more, not sleeping. We slid him Coors Lights and NyQuil to keep his spirits up. He paced and tried to sleep and didn't sleep. We brought him a telephone so he could call his mother. He cried. He watched Judge Judy and drank NyQuil.

"Yo," he shouted from the witness room. "I hope she not my judge, you know? She like some hard-core bitch. For real."

―――――

Milton Echeverria was the first case I picked up after Amanda left, after I came back at the end of that summer and found Bloch in my office. I remember sitting with Lubriano, thinking about everything except Milton, listening to tape after tape, and finally making him rewind one of them and play it again for me. Nothing really, just Milton on the telephone with some girl.

"Oh, come on, come on, baby," I heard him say. "Why you wanna do me like that for?"

"I did'n do nothin," she said, girlish and nasal. "Who told you—"

"Oh, come on! You think I can't see nothin? I know what you doin. You doggin on me. You doggin me out, baby. Oh, baby, baby—"

"You actin stupid," she said.

"Oh," he said. "Why you frontin? You just, you just tell me. You leavin me. *You leavin me?*"

I listened to the tape as Lubriano sat in my cubicle. He sat quietly, not saying anything but nodding at some passages, drinking Pepsis. He started to fast-forward over this one, but I stopped him. I wanted to hear it. After we heard it once, we listened to it again. I thought about Amanda with her suitcase, walking to the livery cab.

Lubriano blames me for Echeverria, as he should. I fucked it all up in the grand jury, and Milton walked with full immunity from prosecution. Milton walked because I didn't say the magic words. At first he did not understand. His lawyer explained it to him, and Milton nodded. He then put his hand on the left wheel of his chair and pulled himself fully around to face the rear of the courtroom. As he spun, he looked at me, and that was when he smiled—not a gloat, just a smile. Milton wasn't going anyplace that would explain the smile. He was just going back to where he was before, which was selling trey bags of rock coke to addicts and hookers. Inside, outside—it was much the same for Milton, but Milton smiled because freedom was preferable nonetheless.

They—his customers and Gerry too—they all called him *Pirelli.*

"Pirelli—like the tire?" I asked Lubriano.

"Fuck I know. He's PR—not a greaseball like us," Lubriano told me with a spark of ethnic pride. "I mean, he's light-skinned, but he ain't no Italian."

When I told Lubriano that we had to let him go, that I'd forgotten to make Milton waive his immunity when he testified in the grand jury, all he said was "So that's that." He may have known I wasn't thinking right and why. But he didn't let on.

Bloch said more, but unlike Lubriano, Bloch was secretly delighted. His limp-dicked rant had a perfunctory quality. Something other than the novelty of raising his voice to me overjoyed him— my mistake ratified him. He was now secure in his armchair behind his door. He also decided at that moment that I had grieved enough, that four months was enough time, and that he would no longer tiptoe around the bureau—now *his* bureau—as though it were a cancer ward. And as he went on about *accepting responsibility for our mistakes*, his fingers laced piously over his gut (larger than I remembered), I swallowed a nearly overwhelming urge to thumbtack one of Penny's card-shop posters to his forehead. BE NICE TO ME, PHIL, THIS IS MY FIRST LIFE!

I let him have his moment—what did it mean to me?

CHAPTER

21

Walking to court, crossing Joralemon Street and inhaling the sweet carbon of the blacktop softening underfoot, and there she is, the new girl, at my arm and keeping up with me on her long legs, perhaps a little too close for comfort, but with an almost touching vitality. I've forgotten her name again, and how she's come to be with me is a mystery. I'd rather not see her until tonight. I'm superstitious that way, like a bride.

"Oh, it's you," I say as she comes upon me. *What is her name?* She has me off guard, and a bus is bearing down on us. The pliant blacktop threatens to suck me down down down to hell with Stacey's thanks, to my special place alongside the Vietcong.

"I'm so scared," she says in an undertone of real and affected fear, groping for my arm as if teetering on a precipice.

"Why?" I ask, willing to be her straight man.

"I have to see Judge Harbison? He's going to *kill me!*"

"Why?" I ask again, like a moron. She draws me in with her skittish proximity and the possibility of her.

"Oh. I have this case, which is like the bane of my existence. It's so stupid. It's like— Let me tell you. It's this unauthorized-use case, and William Johnson is the defendant and . . ." And off she goes.

I give every sign of attentive sympathy, but her shower of words, her grasping arm, her imperfect gray-green eyes, are putting me in a trance again. She—*what is her name?*—has the same interrogative lilt at the end of her sentences as Heather the babysitter. They are not so very far apart. Five, six years at the most. A blink of the eye, compared with the yawning chasm of years between us.

Holy Mother! (How did I come to be thirty-eight?)

I stop nodding like an idiot to examine her face for some clue.

She is, at twenty-five, wholly unmarked. She has found her mirror since we spoke. She has put on her lipstick. Her hair is back in a fat black clip. Under the ball of sun, beneath the milk of her complexion, her heart beats like a pursued doe's—on her cheekbones, an incipient blush of color. She is thinking of Judge Harbison and William Johnson and his cousin with the same name or whoever the fuck it is that she is talking and talking about! This matters to her. They are not yet microorganisms on the petri dish of this job. They matter, I realize with a swelling sadness. The lipstick and the black hair clip and the visit to the mirror were for *them*—her heart beats like a doe's for Judge Harbison, for William Johnson, for his cousin—*not for me!*

Her lilting stream flows, each word measuring the distance between us.

There was a time when I cared about this. Now, twelve years later, twelve years that went like that: like an elevator ride in a tall building—no sense of motion whatsoever until the door opens and there are airplanes at your feet, the world turned upside down. Twelve years later, and there's very little about the job I could give a fuck about. Not the judges or the lawyers or the witnesses or the People of the State of New York.

But what about the dead girl? Not even her. I stood in the back of that place with her dead body up front. I waited, wanting to get the hell out of there, hating Phil Bloch for this case—hating even the dead girl—hating her for dying—hating her mother for giving birth to her so she could die fourteen years later. I had begun to do better. I had found a way to get up in the morning.

This morning, I got out of bed for—this one here, grasping at my arm.

Walking out of the leafy shelter of the footpath, I pass with the girl (still talking) into the open concrete expanse before Borough Hall, where it smells like a swimming pool and something else. I squint in the direction of a voice calling my name and bring the flat of my hand to my eyebrow. *Where are my knockoff Ray-Bans?* There, in the shade of a shadow of a Doric capital foreshortened by the late-morning sun, is the quiescent, somewhat menacing figure of Anthony Lubriano. He catches my eye, but makes no move to come off his perch on the high marble steps under the colonnaded front of Borough Hall.

He is a righteous bastard, utterly convinced he is the wrath of God on earth. But, truth be told, to a certain extent he is. In the right place, at the right time, no one would doubt it. In an interview room at four in the morning or giving out a tune-up in the backseat of a gray Caprice, Lubriano will make you believe. Here he is sitting on the steps, his back against a column, his short legs splayed out wide. He looks down at me with his incongruously feminine eyes—long-lashed, even pretty. His revolver is in plain view, holstered over his thigh. A snub-nosed .38, it's not much of a gun; he doesn't need much.

"D.A. Giobberti," he says. "Now, there's an ugly puss I ain't seen in a while."

"Tony," I say. I double-time it up the stairs to the detective and give his hand a shake. He doesn't stir, apart from his arm. He gives me the once-over. That done, he turns his attention to Holly below, who has an anxious fingernail between her teeth.

"Just thinkin about you, Giobberti," he says. "The other day." Jutting from the corner of his mouth is a plastic something that he holds on the side of his scowl like one who does not smoke but savors the affectation of it.

"Yeah, why's that, Tony?"

"Milton Echeverria," he says, opening his palms as if it was a self-evident thing.

I give him a blank look. "What?"

"Milton?" (He does a wheelchair pantomime with his hands.)

"Yeah, I remember. What about him?"

"Milton's dead," he says. "About a week ago."

"Get out."

"I thought you woulda heard, or I woulda called youse myself."

"You looking at anyone for it?"

"You tell me, counselor," he says. "You think Milton fuckin Echeverria was on anyone's to-do list? They probably was sellin tickets to twist back this mutt's cap. I'll tell youse this, though. Whoever done it there, they took his chair too."

"Anyone, ah—anyone see anything? How'd it go down?"

"They just choked him out. Just like that. Then shot him in the head as a fuck-you. Bango." He puts a finger to his head. "After he was already gone, the M.E. says—I guess to make sure he was outa the picture."

"Holy Mother."

"Looks personal to me. You choke someone out like that, and then you pop him too—it's personal. Someone had a hard-on for this guy, that's for fuckin sure."

"Wasn't you, was it, Tony?"

"Good one," he says. "Not for nothin, but I cross that line someday? I want youse as the D.A. on that one."

"Deal," I say.

There is a pause while he gives me a very brief but significant
suggestion of a look. "I'm just sayin you'd be fair, is all I meant."

"I'm always fair," I say, eating it. "You got anything on this Milton caper?"

"We got dick," he says. "And that's all we're gonna get. A bullet
is all we got and some forensic shit, but that's all. You wanna look at
the bullet, it's at Ballistics there."

"F.A.S. I think I will."

"Don't bust your hump on it, counselor. This mutt ain't worth
it. And just between you and me and Barbie down there, I ain't
gonna do no overtime tryin to find out who did him. Cause the way
I see, Milton got his. Someone had to give Milton his."

I eat that too. Sometimes you've got to eat some shit.

"And that's that for Milton," he says, stiffly rising. "Close out another one." He has a squat little pug's body that he edges carefully
down the steps, saying, "What you workin on these days? Nothin
good?"

"Nothing good. Mostly this and that. Got that one from the
Seven-Five couple weeks ago."

"What's that one?"

"You heard about it—got some press," I tell him. "That thing
with the, ah, the girl?"

"No, no. Who caught it?"

"Solano," I say.

"Ah yeah, Stevie's collar from—where the fuck?—Cypress
Hills there?"

"That's it."

"Right right right," he says, no longer walking, swinging the small ball of his fist into his curled palm. "That's the one I heard the girl's own mother done the shoot on. That the one?"

"Not this case. We're looking at a local mutt. Name of LL. Lamar Lamb—you wouldn't know him."

"That ain't what I hear, if it's the same case. Stevie's thinkin it was the kid's own mother there that did her. Like an accident. I don't know—some silly shit like that."

"No," I say. "No."

"That ain't right, counselor?"

"Not the way I'm looking at it."

"Well, you gotta play it like you see it. The D.A.'s always right. You the ones with all them diplomas on your walls there."

"I don't have a wall."

"Ah, good one," he says, making a gun with his fingers and shooting me dead. "I guess I gotta get back in there. They brought me down for this trial they got goin on in there. They got this little asswipe there askin me questions all mornin and I'm tellin him I don't remember nothin. He looks like a kid with the tie on and the jacket and everythin. You should come on by. It would fuckin kill youse, this kid and me."

When we have shaken hands and he is already in the bright plaza, I call after him suddenly, remembering something he said.

"Tony, what's that you said about Milton's chair?"

He turns, facing me and squinting into the sun. His hand comes over his eyes. He looks oddly small and pale in the light, vulnerable and exposed on the concrete—like a pill bug under a lifted log. He's out of place in the blunt daylight. I know him from the small hours of the wilds of East Flatbush and from cramped, humid cop places like car seats and paint-thickened cinder-block rooms.

"Yeah. They choked him out and took his chair there," he says as he walks away. "You believe that?"

Yes, I do. You can't make this shit up. "Someone should write a book," I say haphazardly to no one when he is gone.

"Why don't you!" says Holly brightly.

"Don't I what?"

"Write a book!"

"Yeah, right," I say. "Plus no one would believe it anyway."

CHAPTER

22

Waiting for His Honor in His Honor's courtroom, there's not much to do. I'm here to stand up on a sentence, but looking at the long calendar, I realize I'll have a wait before they get to my guy. So I wait with Holly—what the hell.

I've run out of things to say to her sober, so I read the back of the wooden bench in front of me. We are sitting in the gallery behind the well, where there are rows of wooden benches like church. In crude capitals, scratched into the wood by perps and their perpy families and their perpy friends: LITTLE DANNY E.N.Y.—SOGGY—HOWIE—FUCK YOU—BUSHWICK '94—FUCK THIS SHIT!—EDDIE—6 DEEP—SHORTY—BO BO—CHINIA—FUCK THIS—QUEEN BITCH—MENACE 2—D SQUARE—SPARKY—DIRTY ONES—BAY PARKWAY '88—KILL 6—B.L. CREW—GANGSTA KILLA BLOODS—STERLING ST MOB—FUCK YOU JUDGE WHO IS YOU?

I smile at this last one and point it out to her.

"F— *you judge*—," she says (she can't even *say* fuck), "that's terrible. Who would write that on there? *Who is you.* It's not even good English."

"Wait a couple years," I say. "Then you'll want to have it tat-tooed on your forehead in big blue letters."

"No," she says. "They're disgusting. And they never come off."

"Sometimes they're nice."

"Oh my God!" she says, turning quickly and reaching out to me with her tentative arm. "I didn't say something really stupid, did I? You don't like have a tattoo or something, do you?"

"Oh," I say. "No, no."

"Oh my God," she says. "Sometimes I talk without thinking."

"I had a girlfriend with a tattoo," I lie, thinking about Heather's Karen and the F train. "It was right here." I point to her navel, overcoming the sudden temptation to stick in my finger and leave it there.

"Oh," she says.

"And she had a ring. Right over it."

"Oh," she says again, and her lower lip curls almost imperceptibly— despite what she knows about me, and knowing nothing at all about Karen, she is still disappointed. "I suppose it can be cool," she says, looking away. "I'm just scared of needles."

The courtroom is filling up. Court officers in white shirts sit doing nothing or stand swinging their fists into their palms. Defen-dants on bail wait in the back, bored. Soon they will start drawing tags into the wood. Lawyers and police, looking not much better than those in the back (just whiter), sit in the front. Next to us, a police officer sits in uniform with his hat on his knee. There are fu-neral cards in his hat—dead put there to keep him alive.

Here is Judge Harbison now, robed and grave over half-frames, seating himself next to a filthy flag.

"All rise," says the clerk perfunctorily, and so the afternoon ses-sion gets under way. An A.D.A. begins to run through the day's cases. "People serving and filing the supporting deposition," he says by rote, and he hands over a stapled packet. This is how a case starts, but the judge wants it to end right now.

"Is there an offer, People?" His Honor asks. "People . . . ?"

The prosecutor (new to this) is fumbling, looking for the offer on the file. In a moment, he finds what he needs. "The offer is an A.C.D. and five days community service."

And the court: "Do we have a plea?" Not to the prosecutor or the defendant but to the defendant's lawyer. There is a huddle between the defendant and his lawyer, and soon there is also a plea. His Honor says, "Five days community service, and you are to stay out of trouble for six months. Do you understand, Mr. Velazquez?"

Mr. Velazquez understands. He will pick up trash along the Interboro Parkway for five days. He will stay out of trouble for six months, or at least not get caught doing it.

And then—a boy is in his place.

And a different lawyer with the boy. Only the judge and the prosecutor are the same. The boy's lawyer is a Legal Aid Society attorney—young, wearing a short, tight black skirt that squares her ass into four corners. She's in a cheap-looking blouse, a T-shirt really. Her head is a cap of black curls, and a bandage on her knee explains the way she walks. She, too, is new at this, but when she turns to the gallery—looking for the boy's mother? (someone is waving now)—I see she is already hard. It doesn't take long.

The boy has done something to violate his probation. He was on probation, but then he did something stupid, and now he's back in court. He was unable to stay out of trouble for his six months. He got himself snatched up, and they put him on Rikers and now he is back before the judge who sentenced him. The boy does not want to go back in. He does not want to go back to Rikers, which His Honor is considering.

Here before the judge is the boy in the navy blue corduroys and white shirt with a collar that somebody, his mother maybe, brought to Rikers for him for this very appearance before this judge. He certainly was not wearing this churchgoing getup when he was arrested. This is for the judge. This is how the boy's mother wants the judge to see her son—not in the oversize, crotch-hanging baggies or the sleeveless Iceberg T-shirt he was arrested in. Here he is, not wanting to go back in, wearing his mother's outfit as if he's nine years old. His head is bowed, and behind his back his hands are coupled involuntarily in bracelets, enhancing his appearance of contrition. The chrome cuffs contrast nicely against his skin, like jewelry. He is shaking with emotion without seeming weak. His bowed head forms a perfect right angle to his body.

When the judge puts him back in, the boy's head comes up and he stops shaking so much.

I am not thinking about the boy now, but about Mr. Velazquez and the six months. When you put it that way, it seems so easy to behave. *Who can't behave for six months?* Except, evidently, this kid here with the mother now making a scene. Easy to lead a good life if you break it into manageable bits. I wonder if I might try that. I am still thinking about what Stacey said. I think I might try to be good for a while—I'll be good, *but not just yet.* Not just yet.

I sit with Holly and wait for my sentence guy.

CHAPTER

23

Back in my office, back in my cubicle, Penny has placed a telephone message slip on my desk.

Amanda called. (I haven't seen her in—a year.)

I sit down and look at the phone and think about how my wife made it ring.

On the slip, with her fat blue marker, Penny has checked off *Please call*. And while Amanda did not write these words or necessarily even say them, the precatory look of them on the paper is strangely touching. (As if she herself had said them to me.) In that instant, it seems the easiest thing in the world to talk to Amanda again, perhaps even to see her again and be with her. But as soon as the absurdity of that picture forms in my mind—a picture of Amanda and me together, without Opal—the moment collapses into emptiness, and I ball the message slip and send it arching into the corner.

The number she left is not familiar—a 212 number—Manhattan, for the love of God. *Is she living in the city now?* She could do that. She could plant herself in Manhattan and fit right in. She could leave all of Brooklyn behind, me included, and set up on the Upper West Side or somewhere and start shopping at Fairway or Zabar's

as if she'd done so all her life—as if she'd never heard of Windsor
Terrace.

Even so, Windsor Terrace was her idea. She liked the idea of
Brooklyn. I wanted out of Brooklyn, but I got only as far as Columbia. I came back to Brooklyn for her. I would have followed her
wherever she wanted—even around the block.

Brooklyn wasn't her home. Her home was a midwestern place
I visited once—a flat expanse where shopping malls and tire stores
cover the flat earth as if poured from a milk bucket—a place so far-
flung that children learn to drive at fourteen—a town with no dis-
cernible downtown where houses dot the once-farmland—cubic
yellow houses with no trees at all and minivans and pickup trucks
on the fresh blacktop driveways cut into the new-laid sod.

I never told Amanda, but I was fascinated by that place. Fascinated by its newness and its niceness and how the houses and shopping malls touched nothing else but instead sat surrounded by
orderly parking lots or plots of lawn, each a yolk in its own spreading white. Everything spread flat across the blacktopped farmland,
spreading into ever wider and flatter rectangles according to its
own entropy. All fresh and orderly. The blacktop black, and everyone white with blond hair parted in the middle. But mostly I was
fascinated by the thought of her there. I never pictured Amanda at
home there with her blond brothers. She does not even speak like
them, with their flat voices—an accent of no accent at all.

In truth, I never could picture her as a child anywhere. I can
picture her in the city; I imagine her born fully clothed at twenty-
four on the corner of Columbus and West One-fourteenth Street.
She came to Brooklyn for the novelty of it, because it was New York
and not Indiana. The dirt, and the stuck trains, and the women who
spit, and the bricks that fall from buildings upon those who live
here almost waiting for the brick to fall—that was all part of the

allure—mile markers on her headlong flight, and she savored every-thing that made me want to get away. Amanda made Brooklyn new for me; and for ourselves we made a little Indiana in Windsor Ter-race. I had a blond baby. I set an air conditioner in the window. When I came home at night, it smelled like a home. But Amanda was only a tourist here, looking at Brooklyn from the top of a double-decker bus, and when the trip ended, of course she had to leave. I had no choice except to stay.

I've seen Amanda, though, as an Indiana girl. Her mother showed me an album—neat pastel squares with white borders in a book of faux tooled leather. She sat next to me on the couch when Amanda brought me there. Her arm was sunspotted from tennis playing. She paged through the album. Under each picture, writ-ten on black construction-paper leaves with a white wax crayon in a neat, feminine hand, were dates, places, and wry comments end-ing in exclamation marks, such as *Lake Tomahawk, Summer 1971* and *"Hey, that looks good enough to eat!"* and *"Don't worry, I don't bite!"* There was Amanda's yearbook photo, too—all glossy color with straight teeth. With each page, her mother would incline her head toward me, measuring my reaction, waiting for clues.

I was a curiosity—an out-of-place thing. Perhaps even forbid-ding. She sat there, doing her best, but it wasn't working and we both knew it. I sat with her mother on her peach-colored, over-stuffed living room couch, and I felt dark in my gray corduroys and short black hair. I felt like a spot on that couch—as though some-one might have spilt me and run into the kitchen for a damp cloth. (I felt Italian.)

Amanda's mother reacted to what I do like most people do—with a genuine but carefully delimited interest, a willingness to be horrified, but only to a certain extent. I kept it well within the pa-rameters of TV's insipid reality and steroid glories. She wanted nothing of the everyday sickness. She wanted only to hear me say, "Brooklyn's pretty rough in places." She nodded with approval when I told her that, giving her at least one satisfaction in me—that I do what they do on TV.

"I'll bet," she said, giving me a significant look. "I'm sure you've seen a thing or two."

"Yes, ma'am." There was something about her, about Indiana maybe, that made me say *ma'am,* although it sat as awkwardly on my tongue as *Brooklyn* did on hers.

But she didn't want to know about what it's like. She didn't want to hear about the man who, with a half-shaft from his Subaru, beats the woman to death in front of her ten-year-old daughter, the same daughter who repeats to the 911 operator, *"He's killing her!"* over and over and over again. "Who's killing your mother?" says the operator, tired of asking. *"Daddy!"* the girl finally says before the line goes dead.

Amanda's mother wasn't looking for that, so I said again, "It's pretty rough, ma'am."

I played golf with her father. He was seventy years old and deaf as a furnace. I told him I had never played the game. "What?" he asked. "What's that?" He didn't believe me. He was the sort who could not picture a world without golf featuring prominently in it, and probably imagined fairways and greens interspersed among the skyscrapers of lower Manhattan or at least somewhere in Central Park.

On the first tee, the old man sent the ball flying. His swing seemed a little crabbed and idiosyncratic to my eye, but it worked. The ball soared and then landed to the side of the fairway. "Get up, ball" was all he said.

"Now," he said too loudly, coming over in his barrel-chested way, fixing me with his eye—Amanda's eye—"now, what you want to do on this one is not worry about smacking the hell out of it. Just concentrate on keeping this arm straight and your eye on the ball."

"All right," I said, feeling about nine years old.

"All right, then. Now, swing at it."

I swung at the ball. I caught the top, and it hit the bluegrass fairway twenty feet ahead of where I stood and hissed angrily as it bled off speed. I was happy just to have hit the goddamn thing, but all I said was "Get up, ball."

"Now, what you did there," said the old man, even before the ball had come to a full stop, "was you took your eye off the ball."

"I didn't want to lose it," I said.

"Not much danger of that," he said as he pulled the golf cart around. He did not even trust me to drive it.

The sun climbed. A blister began to fill on the pad of my thumb. Behind us, four sixteen-year-old boys encroached. They had reddish-tan limbs and blond hair parted in the middle. No matter how quickly the old man and I moved on, the foursome behind us would reach the tee at the moment I was preparing to swing. They would stand there, quietly watching me as I sent the ball into the bluegrass or—as it happened once—almost perfectly perpendicular to my aim and into a wooden bench where Amanda's old man was sitting.

"Christ Almighty," he said, the first thing he had said in about an hour—long enough to have eyeglasses made.

He let the boys play through.

The next afternoon we sat by the pool. (I didn't know how to swim, either.)

Drifting thistledown lit up like phosphor in the sun, and in the trees around us cicadas ground out their mechanical whir: a varied, unceasing backdrop that rose octave upon octave, redoubled in volume, then fell away to nothing—like a thrumming radio beat, the bass sound of bad neighborhoods.

Amanda's littlest brother was there, killing wasps with a plastic golf club. When the wasps landed on the water, he would smack down the oversize club with both hands onto the surface, sending up a shower of spray. When he tired of that, he came to me, lying on a lawn chair, already burned pink.

"You want to see something funny, Gio?"

"You bet," I said.

He pointed his finger to a corner of the lawn, where his hemorrhoidal pug, having no finger to scratch itself with, had planted its flowering pink anus on the crew-cut grass and commenced to spin in fervent ecstasy.

"Joey," said Amanda's mother, looking at the smiling dog and then at me and then back at the dog. "Don't bother, Andy."

They all watched the irresistible dog, slightly embarrassed, but I saw nothing shameful there. To a certain extent, we all do it. Despite our deficiencies, we contrive to make ourselves happy. We fail, but that's no surprise. We still look for moments of relief.

CHAPTER

24

From my unemptied trash can, next to Bloch's peach pit, I take Amanda's message slip, fold it carefully, and put it in my wallet. Then I have to go outside.

Midday, impossibly hot, and I sit on a bench in the plaza, an open scalene triangle bordered on its three sides by the Supreme Court, Borough Hall, and a line of high-rises along Court Street. I have my new book. I feel the heat of the wooden bench under me, but soon I do not notice the heat anymore or the sun.

The benches circle a fountain where, at night, people who have no bathrooms bathe and pee. They frolic and pee under the moon, under the rococo cherubs that arc heavily chlorinated water down upon them. I smell it from my bench—the eye-watering chlorine overlaying human urine. The chlorine brings to mind Amanda's father, who never swam but walked around the pool in his gray trunks, dropping chlorine cookies in the deep end, where they sank.

The fountain is the centerpiece of the plaza. Due to the chlorine or some indefinable other, the fountain has a shoddy, secondhand quality, soaked up by the entire plaza. But then all of downtown Brooklyn has a shoddy, secondhand quality. Here, the

high-rises seem cast off from across the river, as if Manhattan discarded what it didn't like and Brooklyn is where it all landed.

I open my new book. I am reading about making "chip shots"
from the "rough" when a woman approaches. She sits next to me,
although there are several open benches. She is softly talking, not
making a scene, but she is clearly nuts. She takes out a small spiral
notebook and a box of crayons and begins to draw. I see words and
numbers on the page and drawings of simple fish. She is saying:
"And North Carolina and South Carolina and North Carolina and
South Carolina—"

*Hold the "pitching wedge" like a bird; don't let it fly
away, but don't break its neck either!*

"Golf?" Stacey asks me, appearing from nowhere in her sunglasses and sitting close to me on the bench. I feel her thigh against
mine. She has already forgiven me, and we won't say anything more
about this morning. That's how it goes with us lately: we fight—it's
my fault—she lets it slide—and I try to be nice for a while.

"Who you kidding, Giobberti?" she asks me.

"I golf," I say, trying to be nice.

"And I cook," she says, sipping the straw of an iced coffee,
black. "Listen, I want to tell you something, and don't be mean."

"All right."

"You promise?" she asks.

"I promise."

"You were right about Kayla's kid," she tells me. "It's not
Lamar's."

"Go on."

"I didn't need his blood," she says. "I just realized, the baby is
what—three, four months old?"

"Looks like it."

"Lamar was upstate until May," she tells me.

"No possibility of a conjugal visit?" I ask after considering it.

"With a fourteen-year-old?"

"Right." I laugh at myself. "Okay, Stace."

A young man walks by us. He is small and looks like a young Jesus. His shirt reads JEWS FOR JESUS—the O is a Star of David. He is darkly sad-eyed, and his hair hangs long and Christlike. "Jesus is coming," he says to us.

"Jesus is here," I whisper to Stacey, and she laughs out loud—a wonderful sound.

"I was thinking about Nicole," Stacey says to me, suddenly serious. She puts a hand on my forearm momentarily. "I was thinking, you know, even if it went down like you said—I mean, even if Lamar shot Kayla, why doesn't Nicole admit he was there? Why's she say she doesn't see him?"

"Because she doesn't see him."

"That place is so small, Gio," she says. "There's no door to her room. She's gonna see him, or hear him at least."

"She's a crack addict, Stacey. A rock star," I say. "Half the time, she couldn't see her own ass with a mirror."

"Don't you think it's weird, though?"

"You're a Jewish boy," a passing woman tells young Jesus, loudly. "How can *you* be for Jesus?"

Stacey and I both turn. He is inauthentically Jewish, the woman seems to say. He is unnatural, and what is unnatural cannot be trusted. She wishes he would take off his dangling crucifix so she could deal with him as a Jew. If they were more different, they might get along better. This is Brooklyn, and we know how to digest difference, although it may go down like lumpy Cream of Wheat. It is sameness we abhor; in sameness we probe for schism.

Christians don't kill Jews here; the poor don't rob the rich. In Brooklyn, husbands kill wives with Subaru half-shafts. Bloods kill Crips.

"Your mama know you out here?" the woman asks. "And dressed like *that*—in that *shirt*?"

Meanwhile, the fish lady is saying, "—and the police told them they could beat me and beat me and they beat me because it makes them feel powerful and when they beat me up they feel powerful—"

"Why doesn't she—" Stacey starts back in.

"Brother man, 'bout a shine?" Someone new is talking now. To me. I look up into the sun rising over a cast-off high-rise, into a silhouette of lanky homelessness. He is all but featureless—all knees and elbows and hanging gray rags. "Shine 'em up," he says while I feel his smell.

"No, thank you," I say quietly, ignoring him as we do.

"I don't know, Gio," Stacey says.

"Brother man."

"No. I'm okay," I say to the man, looking involuntarily at my ruined shoe. I need more than a shine—I need a new fucking shoe. But I see that he has no polish; there is nothing in his hands. Given the chance, he would spit slobber on my shoe and wipe it off with a forearm.

"Give me some quarters. You have quarters."

Three Black Muslims glide past, distributing copies of *Muhammad Speaks*. They are clean yet frightening, like Gestapo assassins. I haven't seen them this closely before. They walk mostly among the stoplight traffic along Adams Street, walking with the men selling roses in cellophane.

"Listen, Gio," Stacey says. "I want to go back out."

"Where?"

"To Cypress."

"Brother man."

"All right," I say. "Why?"

"I'm not comfortable with this," she says.

"With what?" I ask her.

"This case," she says. "The way it's going down, I'm not comfortable with it."

"All right."

"You have quarters," the man says.

"Without you," Stacey tells me. "I want to go by myself."

The Black Muslims now approach a young woman, soft and Bensonhurst white. I wouldn't be surprised if she'd never been this close to a black man before. Her eyes cast out instinctively to me. The tribal bond. Together we are different, but juxtaposed against them we are the same. Without the other, we are the other to each other. With the Black Muslims, I am her big brother.

"All right," I tell Stacey.

"It's just she may open up to me," Stacey says. "Without you there."

"Fair enough, Sharp," I tell her.

"Okay?" she asks me, and I can't see her eyes because of the sunglasses.

"And we are born in sin—we are all guilty," young Jesus says. "We suffer because we are guilty, and we are guilty because we are born."

"Brother man!" says the silhouette. "I'm trying to survive in the world."

I give him his fucking quarter and tell him to beat it. When he turns out of the sun, I see he is the man from the portico.

"Oh, Solano called," Stacey says. "He's got Dirty down at the house."

"You gonna let me ride along on that one, at least?" I ask her, still being nice.

"Sure." She smiles at that and tells me, "I'll let you see Dirty."

"We could go to Cypress. After."

"No, Gio," she says. "I want to go alone. Let's do Dirty now, and I'll go out to Cypress tonight. Maybe Utopia will be there then."

"—and beat me in North Carolina and South Carolina and North Carolina—"

"You talk to her yet?" I ask.

"Not yet."

"But don't you see?" young Jesus is saying now. "Guilt is not a burden. Guilt is a blessing. Our guilt is what makes us human—our guilt makes us brothers."

"Gio," Stacey says. "I want to tell you something."

"What do you want to tell me?" I smile at her for some reason.

"What I said—about father of the year or whatever? That was mean, and I'm sorry."

"No, Stacey," I say. "Truth is an absolute defense to slander. Didn't you learn that at Brooklyn Law?"

"It's not true, Gio," she says. I don't say anything. "Gio."

"Yes."

"We need to talk," she tells me.

"All right."

"Not about the case, I mean. About you and me."

"Okay. Not now."

"Not now," she says, as if she agrees.

CHAPTER

25

In the swelter of the midafternoon, the blacktop and rooftops bend the air and send it higher and ever higher, pushing up incongruously clean clouds that boil and grow under the East New York sun. Stacey is at the wheel as we head to the Seven-Five house at 1000 Sutter—only a few blocks from Cypress Hills, it eats from the same plate of shit. Stacey herself is obscure behind opaque shades. At a stoplight I turn to her, but she says nothing more. She drives like a girl with a badge, flogging the Caprice until the potholes on Pennsylvania Avenue set up reverberations that linger from one to the next.

She is driving too fast—on purpose, I think, knowing what it means to me and knowing about Holly. Someone—one of the rooftop smokers, probably—told her. Fucking office. (We know too much about one another, and one another is all we talk about.) She knows about Holly, but she hasn't said anything about it.

She turns onto Sutter Avenue. The tires shriek, but she is silent.

We stop in a traffic snarl compounded by two or three livery cabdrivers jockeying for a few feet of blacktop. A horn behind—another sounding out "La cucaracha!"—a verbal exchange—hands, arms gesticulate—*Donkey!* (Wait for the guns!) Men fight and die for inches here—a Verdun.

I don't want to be here—in this car—on these streets—among these people. Across the median, traffic moves fluidly in the opposite direction. Around us, civilians mill. Boys, mostly, boys looking like men. Boys half my age already exceeding their life expectancy. Old men at eighteen for whom anger, fear, and spite is a necessary acclimatization, like Sherpas breathing thin Himalayan air. They breathe the air of their streets and harden into stringy vessels of tightly sprung hatred. They grow as long and skittish as hares, their bodies attuned to predators' footfalls. Their hearts beat faster and boil up the pressure of the blood in their veins. They develop ulcers. Their cuts do not heal. Their teeth blacken and fall out. They walk with canes, the bullets still in their bodies. On a Dumpster outside a bodega, sprayed out in a silver scrawl—FUCK THE SIS-TEM. Their lives here, in these places—Holy Mother. We could never understand it; we don't even want to know about it. With Amanda, at dinner parties in Park Slope and on the Upper West Side, among her collegial overachievers, among our classmates from Columbia, in their town houses and apartment buildings, walking on their streets and driving in their cars—the hours spent on affirmative action and the death penalty and Al Sharpton, but nothing about this. They don't want to know about it. They ask me what I think, and I change the subject.

Fuck the system. I am the system, I realize, and Stacey, and the Caprice, and these streets, and the heat, and the useless ambling on street corners, and the gunfire that erupts in the playgrounds nightly, culling them once and for all.

Here is Brooklyn in all its storied nostalgia. Our noble piers, once wombs to battleships, now house strip joints. Ebbets Field is a housing project. In Red Hook, lattes can be found amid large art. Double-decker buses bring Germans to see it all. Under the Brooklyn-Queens Expressway, a Home Depot spreads out—there, Hasidim from Borough Park and Russians from Brighton Beach rub against one another. The Hasidim are in frock coats, the Russians in Members Only jackets tight over their round bellies. They all wait patiently with orange trolleys of plywood and drywall and paint buckets, and no English is spoken at all.

There is no longer a Brooklyn of unwritten rules and corner conspiracies—there are no barbershop back rooms here anymore—there are no stickball-playing, card-tossing, take-no-guff mugs cracking wise here. Their line has moved on, to Levittown or Massapequa. Some still are seen in south Brooklyn—in Dyker Heights or Gravesend, for instance—but they are not the genuine article. They are parodies of their fathers, driving tricked-out Camaros with red horns dangling from their mirrors and NO FEAR decals plastered to the rear window. Some of them have even gone over to the other side—they say "Whasup, son?" when they see one another and drive cut Toyota Supras—they tune their radios to hip-hop stations—they wear earrings—they shave the sides of their heads and pull back what's left into trim topknots like Puerto Rican samurais—they even grow neat little pencil beards like them, and sometimes befriend them and marry their sisters. And four generations of dead grandmothers would gasp in collective dismay if they knew who now sat in their parlors and what they did in them.

Those who know old Brooklyn, like my father—who used to deal with precinct lowlifes by dropping them bodily into the Gowanus Canal—are dead.

"You really don't give one shit about me, do you?" she says finally. She looks straight ahead, and so do I. I can't say anything.

When it gets to that—when it gets down to her saying you don't give a shit about her, there's nothing you can say that she would hear. Her father, *William* (as she always says it), killed himself perfunctorily when Stacey was thirteen, and that left her with no patience for happy horseshit. He actually went to the garage and let the car run. What small imagination the poor bastard had. Poor *William.* His Mercedes ran so cleanly that even after several hours, all he had accomplished was a violent seizure. Stacey, home from school, saw him there on the garage floor, flounder-eyed, and shut the door.

I see him as the upright, gray, costive, misplaced, overtly Irish forty-year-old atop the unplayed piano (next to Stacey, slutty at seventeen) in her mother's Midwood home, a place where the scent of Lysol and accustomed despair hangs like Spanish moss amid bad art in garish greens and turquoise blossoms, in the cushiony armchairs, and on coffee tables in the form of liver-shaped swimming pools of pale veneer on tapered spindle legs.

"Have you seen your father?" her mother asked her that day.

"Daddy's sick," Stacey said, using the well-worn euphemism. And when Daddy did not appear for dinner, that was nothing new. William's unexplained absences and countless other failures as husband, father, and man were attributable to his thirst, without question, by his wife. She found him splayed on the garage floor the following morning. The Mercedes still idled quietly, efficiently. He had lingered into the night, and with a pencil had started to write something on the gray cement.

Stacey later lay down in the very spot William died. She lay down and stared up at the ceiling. In that position she contemplated life and death, good and evil, guilt and innocence. She decided that she had no responsibility for her father's death; what she had seen in those eyes was fear—not fear of death, but fear that the girl might fetch her mother. She calls him *William,* as her mother still does, but with a thinly veiled humor that implies he belongs dead. She will tell you all about William's great dining room silences, his basement bouts of inconsolable weeping, his odd and unwanted presents, his sitting on the edge of the mattress at four in the morning while she smelled his drinking and tried to play dead—as campers are told to do when confronted by a bear. So William on the cement was afraid Stacey might save his life out of spite.

Stacey would tell you this herself in a hallway or an elevator, in her matter-of-fact way. To have her tell it, she is not a recovering anything. The thing happened and then receded entirely, leaving no trace—as the roiling tide runs in then out again, a deepening in the color of the sand the only sign that it was there a moment before.

She told me about it that first night in her room. We lay there in the dark. The only light was from her alarm clock. I was waiting to leave. I thought another ten minutes would do it. I wasn't sure what to make of her. She gave it up without a fight, but it was just sex. An appeasement of biology (for me), of curiosity (for her). We went in her room, and when it was over she lay there without clothes. We stayed like that for a while, Stacey silent on her stomach and I next to her. I reached over and ran my hand along her back. I felt large and out of proportion to her. My feet hung off the edge of the bed, and when I moved, it sagged. She lay there for the longest while. Then she told me about her father. I can't remember how the topic arose.

I don't know why she chose to tell me then or what she was thinking as she lay there quietly in the dark. Certainly she knew about Opal, dead then for half a year, and Amanda gone too. Did she know she was the first woman I had touched since? I don't know what was on her mind then—perhaps it was me, but it may have been her father or what she had read on the garage floor as she had lain there when she was thirteen. *Forgive* was all he had managed, scratched out in pencil on the cement before he died.

CHAPTER

26

Stacey jams the Caprice onto the sidewalk outside the Seven-Five house and walks off without a legal pad to hide behind, leaving me pushing on the stuck passenger door. Inside, she is circling with crossed arms, and the desk sergeant waves me over to ask what her problem is. "I'm here with you," I say and shrug, and he bites his hand. Cops linger and talk nearby and a telephone falls abruptly onto the floor. Stacey jumps, and the sergeant shoots a look at me. Then some uniform comes up to Stacey, and she is too friendly with him all of a sudden. I ask the sergeant if Solano's upstairs, and instead he points me to the muster room. I tell him I'll see him around, and to Stacey I say, "This way."

Dirty Dread's stinking, ass-length, aptly named locks fall down in thick, matted coils behind him. He is standing before me, an emaciated shrimp with cheekbones gaunt from eating nothing you want to know about—a real sorry-looking motherfucker, cracking his life away.

"Yves St. Ides?" I ask him.

Dirty's mouth shapes *yes*, but no sound comes. He coughs, embarrassed, then tries again.

"How you doing today?" I ask, already knowing.

"I'm awright."

"I'm the D.A., Yves. They tell you that?"

"Yes, sir."

"This is Miss Sharp," I tell him, and he looks quickly at Stacey. I look quickly at her too, and I almost wince when I tell Dirty, "She's with me."

"Awright."

"You know why they brought you down here, Yves?" I ask.

Dirty is nervous—like a cat, he seems in a perpetual, skittish state of incipient flight.

"Sit down, Yves," I say, indicating a bench where Solano is busy with a fingernail clipper. The tables here are affixed to the blue-painted benches and feature obscene high school graffiti— enormous peckers, pendulous breasts, and the like.

"You know what this is about? Why you're here, Yves?"

Dirty shakes his head no. "No, sir," he says under his breath.

"You hang with Lamar Lamb sometimes?" I ask.

"Who?"

"Lamar Lamb," I say.

"No," he says.

"No?"

"No, sir," he says, thinking I wanted the *sir.*

"What do you mean, no?"

"I don' know no one by that name."

"Detective, you got a mug shot by you?" I ask. Solano opens the flap on the neat file beside him and deliberately withdraws a paper that he places on the table in front of Dirty.

"Him," I say. "What do you think, Yves?"

"Yeah," he says slowly. "That my boy LL. I don' call him that other name you say."

"When was the last time you saw him, saw LL?"

"I don' know for sure."

"When?" I ask.

"What's today?"

"Wednesday," I say. "August twenty-second. You gotta be somewhere?"

"No," he says. "Sir."

"So when was it?" I ask.

"Ah, maybe like, maybe a month ago."

"Maybe less?"

"Maybe," Dirty says.

"Maybe a couple weeks?"

"I dunno," he says. "Maybe. I dunno."

"Yves, listen up," I say. "Your boy popped a fourteen-year-old girl two weeks ago. He gave you the gun."

"I din't kill nobody." For some reason, he looks at Stacey.

"No one said you did," Stacey says to him.

"But you have the gun," I say.

"How you know I have the gun?" he says, turning back to me.

"LL told us," I say. "Yesterday."

And Stacey adds, "He said he gave you the gun."

"You say," Dirty says to no one.

"What?" I ask.

"You say he told you," he says, sensibly, but pissing me off anyway. "How I know?"

"What are you, smart?" I ask him.

"No."

"Who do you think told me?" I ask him. "Maybe you think you're such a player I'm gonna come see you every time someone gets it in Brooklyn?"

"No, man. I'm just sayin," he says. "Where he at now, LL?"

"Jail," Stacey says.

"Why he in jail?"

"I put him there," I say, fast.

"Why?" he asks. "He din't do her."

"Do you know anything about that?" Stacey asks almost kindly. Dirty is looking to her more and more. She is an inadvertent good cop.

"Only what he say."

"What'd he say?" Stacey asks. "How do you know he didn't shoot her?"

"Come on, why he gon snuff his girl?" he asks. "She don' offend him never. She his bottom ho."

"But he gave you the gun," Stacey tells him, and he nods. "Tell me about it."

"He just like, Yo, do me right," he says. "What I gon do? I owe him my life. I owe him my *life*."

"And you hid it," she tells him.

"Yeah. I hid it," he says. "What I gon do?"

"Where is it?" I ask him too forcefully. Stacey glances sideways at me.

"I ain't seen it for like a week or somethin," he says, shutting up again. "I think someone mighta take it."

"Why do you owe Lamar your life, Yves?" Stacey says, trying to get it back on track.

"That's somethin different, miss."

"Tell me about the gun, then," she asks. "When'd he give it to you?"

"Um. It was at this place we sometime chill at over on Pitkin."

"A house?"

"Apartment. Apartment. LL live there, but it not his. No one livin there. It don' belong to nobody. It just a room and another room attached to it. So, like, I was asleep and LL come in. He come in and is like, Yo, Dirty, wake up, wake up."

"He tell you anything about what happened?" she asks him.

"He don' say nothin, really," Dirty says. "Except what I already told you—that his girl get herself snuffed. He, like, was just like, you know."

"Where is it now, the gun?" I ask him again, and Stacey presses my foot with hers under the table. Hard.

"I dunno. I told you," he says. Then, looking at Stacey, he asks, "I in trouble?"

"Look, Yves," Stacey says. "You hid a murder weapon—that's tampering with physical evidence, hindering prosecution—felonies, you know."

"Plus you got that stolen property beef," I tell him. "For the chair."

"You A.C.D. that," he tells me, meaning the case is bullshit and we'll dismiss it when we come to our senses. "Bullshit, man. You dismiss that."

"No way, man. That shit's messed up." I frown. "You pushing your narrow ass around in a wheelchair? What's up with you? You don't got any self-respect, Yves? Steal some crippled brother's chair?"

"No, man. I just found it."

"Messed up, man." I shake my head. "I'm telling you."

"No, man, for real," he says. "Someone give it to me."

"Give it to you?" I ask.

"Straight up," he says.

"Dang, Yves. People just giving you shit all the time," I say. "Like that gun, for instance. What are you, like a fucking pawn shop?"

"No."

"Where is it?"

"Dunno."

"Where is it?" I ask. Here comes Stacey's foot.

"Dunno, man," he lies to me. "Been a while."

"You could get charged with that," I lie to him. "Accessory to murder, you know. Maybe you can look for it. With Detective Solano here."

"I dunno if I find it for you. I look for it, if you want. If I get some free time. I ain't seen it in a while, though, so I might not find it."

"You should be more careful with guns," I tell him. "Smart guy like you."

"Should'n I get a lawyer?" he asks Stacey.

"You know, maybe you should get a lawyer," I say. "You shouldn't talk to us without a lawyer, Yves. You got rights, you know. You want a lawyer?"

"I can't afford me no lawyer," he says.

"No, man, they're free," I tell him. "Worth every cent, too."

"You think I should get me a lawyer?" he asks Stacey again.

"Dirty, man, I'm telling you," I say. "You never heard of the Constitution? You got rights."

"I know I got rights," he says. "Be silent and shit."

"You gotta check it out, my man," I say. "You get yourself one of them free lawyers, and then you tell him everything you want to tell me. And in about two months your lawyer calls me on the telephone and tells me to go fuck myself. Really a great system. So what do you say?"

"I ain't tell you go fuck—"

"Of course you'll be in jail," I say. "And you'll have to wait another year for your trial. Waiting in jail, you know what I'm saying?"

"Oh, snap," he says. "For real?"

"It's your right to go to jail," I say. "Fucking Constitution, man. Don't they have the Constitution where you're from? Where the fuck you from anyway, brother? You from Indiana?"

"Port-au-Prince," he says.

"Where?"

"Port-au-Prince," he says again.

"Porta-John? That's in like Haiti or somewhere, am I right?"

"Haiti," he says. "Yeah, man."

"Haiti—forget about it," I say. "They don't have the Constitution there. All they got going is a beach. Lots of white-sand beaches. You miss Haiti, my main fucking man? You are my main man, aren't you, Dirty Porta-John? Are you my main fucking man? You miss Haiti?"

"No, man."

"No?" I ask. "You don't like beaches? You like these dirty fucking streets with shit blowing in your eyes more than beaches and sand? You like living in this stinking fucking hood where the shit's blowing in your eyes all day long?"

"They kill my father in Haiti."

"No shit."

"Yeah, man," he says. "Macoute."

"Man, that's tough," I say. "The old man dying like that? That's a tough break. How old was he?"

"Dunno. Not like old-old."

"Was he fourteen?"

"What?" he asks.

"Did I stutter? Was your old man fourteen years old?"

"No, man," he says. "What—?"

"I don't suppose he was a girl, either?"

"What?" he asks, looking to Stacey and even to Solano. "Man, I don't—"

"What's your fucking problem? Don't you understand what I'm telling you, Porta-John? You think you can play me? You think you can hold out on me?"

"No, man," he says. "I just don' understand why you ax me—"

"Gio," Stacey says, and Solano has put down his fingernail clipper.

"Understand this," I tell him, ignoring Stacey. "Unless your dead father's a fourteen-year-old girl named Kayla Harris, I don't give a shit. I don't care if Baby Doc Duvalier drove a tractor up his asshole. Do you understand me, Porta-John?"

"Gio," Stacey tells me. "Why don't—"

"You think you're gonna play me? Hold out on me? Listen to me. Fuck you. You play me, and I'll fuck you like a bitch."

He says nothing.

"Listen to me now, Yves. Help me with this, else I'm gonna come for you, I'm gonna convict you, and then I'm gonna buy you a ticket on the cheapest fucking cargo flight to Haiti. Fuck, I'm gonna squeeze your punk ass into an envelope and fucking mail you there, because that's where you're going—sure as you're sitting there stinking up this place. You ain't a citizen, Yves. I convict you, you're gone. Gone. *Au* fucking *revoir. Comprenez-vous,* dick?"

"*Oui,* man."

"You still think you're one sharp-ass motherfucker?"

"No," he says.

"Who's the sharpest motherfucker you know?"

"Dunno," he says.

"Aw, Dirty," I tell him. "You're looking at him, brother!"

"All right."

"So I'm gonna ask you again. Do you want to exercise your constitutional right to be represented by counsel pursuant to the United States Supreme Court's landmark 1963 decision in Gideon versus Wainwright? What do you say?"

"What?" he asks.

"Do you wanna lawyer up?"

"No, man. I'm workin for you."

"In that case, brother, I have just one more question for you today," I say, quiet again, and everyone is quiet and the air conditioner too. "Where's the gat?"

An hour later, with the gun—a candy-ass chrome .25—sealed in an evidence bag, Stacey, driving the blue Caprice, says, "I thought you were only a prick to me."

CHAPTER

27

Blond Holly sits next to me in a corner banquette in a dark place in the city where drinks come and go with delicious ease, and the antiseptic smell of vodka is on her breath. I am getting drunk, yet I am still in the good part—the slow, numbing stupor is far off. She is doing all right herself, but she is at that tiresome point where I am altogether too fascinating to her—where she hangs on my every word with unflinching, unquestioning enthusiasm. After she rolls her head at something unfunny, she must then refocus her gray-green eyes on me.

We cabbed after work to her building, and while I waited with the driver in front as the sun went down, she went inside, tossed off her work suit, and reappeared *just moments later*, wholly transfigured in a thin, simple dress the color of butter. She ran like a boy down the sidewalk to the cab with her wide-open exuberance—overtly, perfectly pert—her perfume freshened and her hair combed out straight. "I'm ready," she said, and with that, the night opened like a present.

She is a big girl, with swimmer's shoulders, and the cab knelt under the weight of her. She is sleeveless and bare-legged; a fine muscle swells her naked thigh, and its shape continues unobstructed under the dress that falls high on her leg. Her upper arm is firm. She could snap Stacey in two, I think, but in a fight to the finish I would bet on Stacey—if only because Stacey wouldn't fight fair.

Holly now looks optimistically at me over the cosmopolitan in her hand. The delicate stem, top-heavy, is poised in midair—her care in holding it the only sign she is feeling the effect of it. The vodka is a sheet, set shimmering by a narrow cone of white light from high above her that brightens the girl but leaves all else in darkness about her. Even me. I sit in the dark, watching her as she drinks (moving her head and not the glass), and as she does so, a fair lock falls forward and alights along her cheek. She does not draw it away but instead inclines her head at a different angle and looks from behind that veil—from there she smiles, knowing that she has me now.

The glass joins her lips, and she drinks, her lipstick doubled in the reflection. She is drunk but still pretty, and as she slumps languidly backward out of the light, I lose her momentarily until she reappears to my accustomed eye in a posture of feral submission, her neck bare to my teeth.

"*What?*" she asks me in that way that they do.

All around are couples paired, and there is music playing. Women pass with aprons wrapped like shifts, longer even than the skirts they wear. They move tentatively. They glide. One passes and stands nearby; her features dissolve as she moves from light to dark so that all that remains is a glint from her glistening shoulder.

"What?" she says again.

"Nothing," I say, but I am thinking wicked thoughts featuring her, and she knows it. We are at the beginning, when I will concede anything to her—but she, because she is young, is prodigal with her advantage. She asks for nothing. She yields to me wordlessly, knowing the drinks are a prelude and that more will follow. She seems willing to be led.

   She is too willing to be led. *When did girls start giving it up without a fight?* I feel a sudden hint of letdown. (If it's free, I don't want it.) In the morning, she will awake still convinced she has found it at long last, the real deal, only to find instead the mattress empty. If I were to explain that I had nothing against her, she would still take it to heart. Sentimentality is a woman's first weakness. The need to be loved is her second. Her third is that she will take any rejection personally.

   Amanda never looked at me like Holly—in the end, she never looked at me at all. She left me without a sentimental thought. A doctor, she amputated me like a gangrenous leg in a single, certain cut. She went to the city and left behind me and everything that was Opal's except the memory of her face.

Holly stands and tosses back what's left in her glass, attracting the attention of a man at the table opposite, and of the woman with him who follows his gaze. They are each equally fascinated with my date's wondrous, braless chest, which is covered only by the film of her dress. And it is a thing of beauty—unfashionably voluptuous.

   "Now don't leave," she says happily, too loudly.

   I watch her walk deliberately and self-consciously erect until her broad, bare back disappears around the darkened corner.

   Left behind with me on the banquette is a yellow bag containing a CD. Earlier, still sober, we walked like a couple past the record store on Broadway where Fiona is among neon. (I thought I knew her in the moment before I realized she is only famous.) I bought the CD for Holly. I open the bag now and sit alone with Fiona again, thinking of the night's inevitable outcome—how we will stumble back to her apartment, up the stairs to where the roommate waits. The dress will become a buttery pool on the floor, and the novelty of her naked will melt away with it.

Does she live alone? I imagine her with the inevitable roommate—the ironic species of fattish brunette that attaches like pilot fish to free feminine beauty. I see her in front of the TV in a T-shirt, waiting for us, waiting for me. She'll discreetly slip away, but not until she's given me the coy roommate hello and the once-over, storing up demerits like nuts for the winter, so that at the end she'll offer Holly not consolation but *"You know what? I never liked . . ."* The apartment itself is a dorm room—it will look and smell like a dorm room—it will smell like girls with their sprays and underwear drawers and synchronized menstrual cycles.

I suddenly want out. I want the carpet to roll me up and pack me off to oblivion. I want to be alone with Fiona at my kitchen table.

How quickly can they reconnect my cable?

A sentimental thought for Stacey—about what it was like before it became a routine. She was never led. She never played dead (except for William). This place was one of ours. There was a time, in the darkened corner—she was on top of the sink with her small, freckled shoulders pressed against the mirror. I wince at the abrupt recollection of opening my eyes and seeing myself atop Stacey atop the sink. (Her idea.) She had said to me, "Wait a minute—then follow me," and I did.

The man and his wife are sitting apart. His legs are crossed in front of him—a cap-toe oxford dangles laconically from his knee. He gives it a shake now and then. The shoe is handsome in the English way and polished. They are a happy couple and enjoy world-class amenities when they travel. He is eating without talking. A cuff-linked wrist pivots with a chicken wing attached. The woman's hands are folded, as if in prayer, before her pursed lips. He offers. She shakes her head no, almost imperceptibly.

The throng of humanity with its myriad relationships and needs and problems—

I see them on the street and on trains, and I cannot even imagine where they sleep, much less understand how people can be happy except in sporadic fits.

Stacey thinks I'm an evil bastard, but what the hell does she know?

I am a hemorrhoidal dog on the grass—

I wait a minute, then follow Holly around the corner.

I am in the darkened corner.

A door opens, filled with light and Holly.

We fall together back into the small room.

I fall upon her and say nothing at all.

Soon her dress is up and down. She is atop the sink. Her back is pressed against the mirror and I am angling to avoid my reflection, except there I am—over her shoulder, looking desperate, but not for this.

I look away and hold the door closed with a wrecked shoe.

She shuts up now and wants to sit closer to me. I really don't mind. I even put my arm across her and bury my nose in her thick hair that smells like shampoo. But it is an unearned intimacy that becomes wearying. My arm falls asleep, and I can't reach my drink. There it is on the table, without a ripple on its clear meniscus, as thick as mercury—there, just beyond reach, with the special attraction of the unattainable thing. No use. In the mirrored panel, her eyes are closed. (She's either passed out or thinks this is a magic moment.)

The man and his wife are unspeaking still, and she looks openly in my direction. I am staring at her now. She is staring at me. We are looking each other in the eye, and we have each somehow lost the instinctive reflex to turn away. We look at each other un-abashedly for several drawn-out seconds until she comes to her senses and turns away, turning to her husband, who abruptly puts his mouth on her neck and makes her laugh. I feel unjustifiably be-trayed by her and outright hatred for him.

In the mirror I see the girl, and I see my awkward left hand dip into my jacket for my wallet, which slips like a fish and falls from my fingers upon the tabletop, displaying the heavy gold shield in the shape of a twelve-pointed star that catches the light from above and radiates it gaudily. The wallet is empty of money, the last of it gone on Fiona. Some canceled credit cards, a yellow MetroCard, and something else—something paper and creased over. I sit for a moment until I snap out of it. (The message slip with Amanda's name.) I withdraw the paper with my free hand and unfold it with my thumb and forefinger.

Carefully—with the exaggerated, self-aware care of a drunk—I move Holly's still, solid body deeper into the corner of the banquette. Her face presses against the leather bolster and she sleeps soundly, with parted lips, on a nest of blond. I silently slide from there and out the front door.

Nearby, there must be a telephone. There must be a bank—or something?

Why did I leave?

What do I need?

I need money.

I need a telephone.

Under a streetlight, a couple walks toward me. I look at my watch for something to do. They pass, and I sheepishly catch the man's eye where a chrome stud is in an eyebrow (and another in his lip). She is a female version of him. They pass away in a cloud of arms, talk, and cigarette smoke.

I am running now, in the opposite direction. Not running, really—sort of jogging in a hampered, unathletic way. I trip and nearly fall into open sidewalk. A man in a white restaurant jacket is bringing up cabbages in a cardboard box; he stops in his tracks and looks at me. I see the box—JUBILEE CABBAGES.

I turn the corner, and I am on Broadway. Astor Place—right?

I slow to a walk and tuck my shirt back into my pants. I see my reflection as I pass the glare of the record store, burning nine colors of neon. I am hunched and haunted in the pane, framed by music I've never heard. My fly is open. No one seems to notice or care, except Fiona. We are old, sullen friends now. She sees me and says, "Holy Mother, Gio."

I want to sit down somewhere now.

I need money.

I am walking.

I am staring into the lens-eye of the cash machine.

In the corner, under the stark fluorescents, the guard is sitting. Square badge.

What is that number?

And then, my mind disgorges it all like a violent vomit—0823—the stinking daylight—the bank on Montague—August 23—Opal's birthday—the message slip—*Please call*—

The skin of my forehead touches the linoleum, and my head rests on a paper carpet of discarded receipts. The guard is over me, bent at the waist with impatient fists on hips. I can barely see his face from the glare of the fluorescent lights behind him. I hear him very clearly. I can't understand a word. The message slip is in my hand, unfolded. I try to show it to him, to help him understand. I try to explain, but I only hear myself repeating—

It's her birthday.

CHAPTER

28

Bloch wants to know about it. He is hanging expectantly around my cubicle, as subtle as a dog under the dinner table.

Where in hell does he get his information? No one in the Homicide Bureau talks to Bloch voluntarily, as far as I can tell. Not about this sort of thing, anyway. But Bloch thinks I'm his friend. He thinks we are friends because he buys me drinks, watches me fall down, picks me up, and puts me in a cab. He thinks we share something that men share, and this means I'll tell him everything he came to hear. He already knows what happened with the girl. Somehow, he knows.

No doubt everyone knows. This bizarrely incestuous place. We know each other's business. We know far too much. We know who is fucking whom. We know because we fuck each other and we talk about it. We fuck each other and we talk about it, and then we fuck police officers who listen to what perps listen to on their car radios. We fuck cops and they talk about it and call us copsuckers. We fuck defense lawyers and they talk about it. Defense lawyers fuck each other and court officers and sometimes their own clients. Defense lawyers fuck perps, too, and you better believe we all talk about that. They come into court or we see them walking on Montague Street and we say, *"Is that?"* We all fuck around and we all talk about it, and we all talk about the perps who fuck their own mothers, notwithstanding the gossamer thread that runs between the perps and their lawyers, between the cops who arrest them and the A.D.A.s who prosecute them and the mothers who gave them birth. We all fuck each other and we all talk about it in the morning. It's like high school—we even have guns.

Bloch knows about the girl. He just wants to hear it from me.

He is talking around the subject, shifting uncomfortably on the undersize chair while I make busy and respond occasionally, distractedly, through the veil of sordid recollection.

Meanwhile, someone has traced on the outside of my sooty windowpane a single word—ASSHOLE—in reverse for my benefit, in five-inch capitals. Yet whoever wrote it neglected to mirror the *L*, and with the *L* written that way it seems like a five-year-old's writing. The author is likely one of the young assistants (all women) gathered out there at this moment, smoking and looking at me. This will be the end of my interest to them, as the word now frames me like a filthy halo.

Holly is not out there; nor is Stacey, who stepped onto the elevator with me earlier and said nothing at all. I said nothing in reply. She knows too.

In a moment, Bloch gives up and changes the subject.

"What's on today?" he asks.

"Grand jury. Dead girl case."

"Oh, right, right," he says. "Dead in the bed. Who's your shooter on that one? Remind me."

"Nobody."

"Wasn't this some sort of accidental discharge case?" he asks me. "Weren't you looking at the mother on this one?"

"The mother? No," I say. "Who told you that, Phil?"

"I thought you told me— Didn't you say—something?—I can't remember." He laughs at himself, acting stupid to avoid looking stupid.

"Not the mother," I tell him. "I got her testifying. She's subpoenaed to the grand jury tomorrow."

"What's this case about again? Why's she shot?"

"Fuck I know," I say, now annoyed and wanting him gone. *What am I going to do about that damn word?* I should do something about it. "Because it was hot," I tell him. "Because she didn't have an air conditioner."

Bloch looks slyly at me. He thinks I'm leading to something. "Ah," he says.

"Ah, what?"

"Give me another clue," he says happily.

"What clue?"

"Go ahead," he says. "This is a hard one."

"What?"

"Wait—don't say anything," he tells me. "It's that book, isn't it? That one by—Sartre?—however you pronounce it."

"Phil . . . ?"

"*The Stranger,*" he says, pleased with himself, smacking himself. "That's what you were driving at, weren't you—Merlot kills the Arab—*because of the sun.*"

"Meursault," I say absently. *I need a Pepsi.* "Camus."

"Right," he says, happy anyway. "Camus."

After a time, he says, "Weren't you looking for the weapon on this case?"

"We got that," I say. "A Lorcin twenty-five—I sent it to F.A.S. yesterday."

"What the fuck's F.A.S.?"

"Ballistics, Bloch," I say. "Where you been?"

"*F.A.S.,*" he says thoughtfully. "Any history on the twenty-five? They run it through their computer yet?"

"Matter of fact," I say, handing Bloch the report, "just got this. Match on an attempt robb a couple years ago. And this—this is interesting—a strong probable on a body a week after the girl. Someone I know."

"Any connection to your shooter here?"

"On the homicide maybe," I say. "But probably nothing on the robb. Somebody Massiah something or other copped out on that already. Couple years ago."

"Massiah," he says, considering whether to do something fun with the name, but he lets it go.

"I got Sharp checking it out anyway," I tell him.

"Who?"

"Sharp." *Does he know about her too? Do I care?* "Stacey Sharp. She's riding along with me on this one."

"One of the new kids?"

"Right," I tell him. "One of the new kids."

"The red hair?"

"Yep."

And then—

—Holly suddenly fills the doorway of my cubicle. A wrathful Valkyrie, she discharges a lightning bolt at my head. I duck. So does Bloch. It misses and cracks loudly against the windowpane.

"You can keep your fucking CD—and you owe me eighty-nine dollars." She stands there while Fiona spins on the linoleum like a coin.

I open my (still empty) wallet for all to see. "Phil—?" I ask.

He rolls obediently, heavily, on the creaking chair and from his rear pocket pulls a money clip bearing a Detectives' Benevolent Association seal, from which he peels twenties, handing them to me one by one like a father. "Three, four . . ."

"More," I say, then hand five of them to the girl.

"I don't have change," she tells me, softening, breathing heavily, looking puffy.

"Forget about it."

"I owe you eleven dollars," she says, not leaving.

"Holly—" I say, standing now. "Holly," I say again, and I want to say more, but her name is all I can say.

Standing in front of me, she hesitates for still another moment— a brief moment in which she might have said something more herself, if I had said something more, but when I say nothing she spins away down the hall, her blond head bobbing over the glass partitions, all eyes upon her (the day's topic), leaving me feeling like something the color of Bloch's Naugahyde couch.

Stacey is in the entrance to my cubicle. I am alone doing nothing. I smell her perfume before I see her, and I see her in my periphery before I turn my head. She stands in the entrance. She rarely comes into my cubicle, thinking perhaps that the same crime scene tape I have strung around the whole of Windsor Terrace extends here, too, keeping her from getting too close.

"Just . . . don't," I say. I am weak, and she could overbear me easily—I am a licentious and debauched Rome bare before the Goths. But she is in no mood for that. Brown is visible at the roots of her red hair, which hangs limply. Her complexion is sallow. She's wearing too much perfume. I'm probably not much to look at, either, but we've reached that point where it doesn't matter. I see her look quickly at the word on the window, but she leaves that alone too.

"I'm not arguing with you, okay?" she says flatly. "But just answer one question for me, okay? I don't want to argue—let's just say it's part of my education or whatever."

"All right," I say. "Shoot."

"What are you doing with Lamar Lamb?"

"You know."

"Pretend I don't, then," she says.

"I'm going to indict him," I tell her.

"For murder," she says.

"For murder."

"Giobberti," she says. "You can't do that. You know you can't. You know he didn't do it. It doesn't make any sense."

"Doesn't make any sense?"

"No!"

"You think it needs to make sense?" I ask her. "What kind of people do you think these are? It never makes sense."

"That's not what I mean," she says.

"Look at this."

"What's that?" she asks.

"These are open homicides from last week," I say. "Male found in apartment, shot once in head, once in foot, removed to Brookdale, D.O.A. Female found on rooftop suffocated with bag over head, panties in mouth. Removed to Kings County Hospital, D.O.A."

"Giobberti."

"Man found handcuffed and shot once in head," I continue reading. "Dog in apartment found shot once."

After a moment she asks, "Dead?"

"What dead?"

"The dog," she says. "You didn't say whether the dog was dead."

"I don't know," I tell her. "It doesn't say."

She sighs, asking, "So what's your point, Giobberti? That horrible things happen to people in Brooklyn?"

"No, Stacey," I say. "That horrible things happen to dogs in Brooklyn."

"Don't."

"Stacey, do you really want to hear it from me—what I believe?"

"Yes."

"No, you don't," I tell her. "You'll have to learn it for yourself. You're too full of—whatever it is twenty-five-year-olds are full of."

"Not me, Giobberti."

"Even you, Stacey—but I'm gonna tell you anyway," I say. "Here it is. People die for a lot of reasons here, and most of them are really shitty reasons. You try to figure it out and you lose your mind. Stop thinking about *why* people die and spend more time on *how* they die and *when* and *where* and who the fuck did it—that's all you have to prove. That's all that matters. You're not a goddamn philosopher. You don't have to prove *why*. Why is for TV. It's for movies. It's for—Jane fucking Starr who just got back from maternity leave. Fuck *why*, Stacey. We never know why people die—they just do."

"Gio," she tells me, coming closer, touching my shoulder. "I talked to her."

"Who?"

"Utopia," she says. "She told me."

"Utopia told you what, Sharp?"

"Gio," Stacey says. "That she saw her mother shoot Kayla."

"Utopia saw her mother shoot Kayla," I repeat.

"She told me. An accident."

"She told you," I say. "When?"

"Last night. I told you I was going out." And then she asks me, "She told you, didn't she?"

After a moment, this is what I say: "I knew."

"Gio. What a goddamn mess," she says, leaning her small body on the edge of my gray metal desk. "What do you want me to do?"

"Get Utopia down."

"All right," she says.

"I want to talk to Utopia."

"And Nicole?"

"Leave her alone," I tell her. "She's coming tomorrow morning for the grand jury. Get Solano for that. I want to talk to Utopia."

"What are you gonna do?"

"I don't know."

"Are you all right?" she asks.

"I'm all right."

"I mean, you all right with this?" she asks.

"It's not like that anymore. I'm all right."

"You sure?" she asks again. "You don't look too good."

I tell her (not thinking), "I just had a bad night."

And, looking at the window and then back at me, sadly, quietly, she says, "You really are an asshole, Gio."

CHAPTER

29

Utopia Carbon looks at me with baleful, reproachful eyes as dark as shotgun bores. They are not as I remember them. They are different, and not subtly different—they are entirely different, as though another person is looking at me from her sliplike body, looking from behind her chemically flat, straightened hair.

There are girls in the world like this and entire hidden civilizations of people that live their lives in all their complexities under our very noses, unnoticed. Utopia at the reception desk, seated next to the table with the tissue box, is now in my world, an unopened bottle on my shore. I want to tell her that I know why she is here, but I do not know. I know only what she came to do. (She came to give up her mother.)

I walk and she follows. I sit her down in my cubicle on a small metal chair. She places one thin leg over the other and sits there. I sit. She does not look at me. She is examining her fingertips distractedly. A sheet of hair covers one eye. She is not wearing her alarming chlorophyll tints, I realize.

"Why?" is my first question to her. "Why'd she shoot her?"

"It was, um, stupid," she says. "It was nothin. It was somethin between them."

"Who?"

"My mother and him," she says. "Him. LL. Lamar, whatever. She din't want LL being with Kayla."

"Why?"

"You know—how mothers are," she says. "They was in the bedroom. My mother, um, be hittin on the door tellin Lamar he have to go, and Lamar just like ignore her or whatever. That's when I woke up, when I hear all the noise and everythin or whatever."

"What happened then?"

"That's when she bugged out," Utopia says. "I saw her kick on the door and go off to the kitchen."

"Why?" I ask.

"That's where she keep the gun," she says.

"What kind of gun?"

"Automatic?" she asks. "That's what you call the kind without the round thing here?"

"Right."

"All silver with brown handles," she says. "It was small. She had it there since, um, since Mass give it her. She say it's for protection and everythin and whatever. I never really look at it exactly, but I knew it was behind the refrigerator."

"Who'd she get it from?" I ask.

"From Kayla father. His name is, um, Mass."

"Oh, right," I say. "You recognize the gun if I showed you?"

"You got it here?" she asks, moving suddenly, as if I'd told her there was a copperhead coiling on the floor behind my discarded desk drawer.

"No," I say. "I have a picture, but finish what happened first. What happened after she got the gun? Where were you?"

"I was in the other room, in the back. Which is where I sleep with my mother."

"You could see all this?" I ask.

"I was right there. It's small. There's like no door on my room."

"I know," I say. "What then?"

"And she had went over to Kayla room, to the door, and is like keepin bangin on the door, tellin Lamar to come out and get dressed and go and everythin or whatever. And that's when the door opens fast and Lamar is standin there and they like yellin and—oh my God—that's when I hear the gun go like pow or whatever."

"You saw the gun go off?"

"It happen just like that," she says.

"Was your mother holding the gun when it went off?"

"Yes, she was right there," she says. "She was like wavin it. Like this." She indicates with her long arm, thin as rope. "It wasn't like she aimin it or nothin. She just— It just go right off. And after it did, um, she had went onto the floor. And LL left."

"My God."

"You know, for real, mister. I ain't—" she starts but can't finish.

I wait for her. I am looking through the photographs taken by the Crime Scene Unit, then I show one to the girl. "Is that your room?"

"Yeah." She nods, brushing at a cheek. "And my sister room is down this way."

"This one?" I show her another.

"Yes," she says. "But the door was like more open. Can I see those pictures, mister?"

"I don't think you want to."

"Why not?" she asks.

"Your sister is in them."

"I still want to see them," she says and means it.

I hand them to Utopia. She goes through them, one after another. The dead girl is sprawled naked on the bed in pictures taken from various angles and distances—all of them with a clinical detachment, as though she were a blood smear or a murder weapon or any other piece of physical evidence. She is Exhibit A. In some, her entire body can be seen. In others, her lifeless pupils stare. Apart from her eyes (and a hole the size and color of a lipstick tip on her sternum, between her fully flowered breasts), she could be asleep. She has the body of an adult, with thickset thighs and the wide, circular areolas of a new mother.

"She's so beautiful," she says after a long while. Her head is down so that I cannot see her face. "So beautiful."

"Yes," I say, looking again. Posthumously pretty.

"Her hair look so nice," Utopia says, and then she lifts her head and looks at nothing. I take the photographs from her hand.

"What's gonna happen now, mister?" she asks. "You got to arrest her, right?"

"Yes," I tell her. "You gonna be all right with that?"

"I don' hate her, if that's what you mean," she says. "You know what I mean?"

"No," I say.

"I suppose you wouldn't," she says. "I don' blame anybody. I don' blame her, I mean. It's nobody's fault. She was just acting stupid. It's not her fault, the way she is. She wasn't always like the way she is now."

"No?"

"No, mister," she says. "You din't know her before. Once she started with all that, after Mass went up—it was like, boom. Everythin changed."

"When was that?"

"Shoo. I say like a year ago. Maybe less," she says. "After Kayla father went upstate. It was in the summer, anyway."

"That was Massiah Harris?" I ask. "Her father?"

"Shoo—you know?" she says. "You know all about us. It's funny."

"You'd seen it before, you said? The gun?"

"Just like once before that night," she says. "I din't even know it was loaded. When she broke it out, I thought she was like playin. You know. Tryin to scare Lamar to leave or whatever."

"Did your mother know? That it was loaded, I mean?"

"I don' know," Utopia says. "I only seen her with it once. She told us leave it alone. Guns kill you, she say. I guess she was right."

"When did you see her with it?"

"I just saw when she tried to pawn it on this guy. I was there. I just looked at it. I din't touch it or nothin. I just looked at it, and I never seen a gun up close before so I looked at it and I was like, So that's what it's like."

"What guy? Lamar?"

"No. He just some— He nobody, really," she says. "He just came around a while ago."

"A friend?"

She laughs without meaning it. "He nobody friend. He just came around, you know? He the dopeman, you know. He the one that like push the rock on my mother or whatever, before Lamar come back around."

"Why'd she show him the gun?"

"It was like—once, she ain't got no paper. She din't have any money, I mean, to pay him with. After a while, you know, she was doin like maybe fifty a day."

"Fifty? How'd your mother cover fifty a day?"

"How do you think, mister?" she says, almost laughing at me. "You know what they do."

"In the house she did it?"

"No," she says. "Not at first. I guess she went on Belmont Avenue with the rest of them and everythin. But this guy I was tellin you about was like her regular or whatever. Sometime she brought him in, when she din't have no money to give him. They were regular for a while. Like every other night, maybe. But after a while, he was just like, Yo, forget about it."

"What do you mean?"

"He was like disgusted— That's when she was like tryin to pawn everythin on him. Some chain Mass give her. The VCR. She gave him that. She tried to give him that gun, like I told you. But he wouldn't take it, so then she get like desperate. That's when she was like, Go in there. Go to Kayla room. Go in there, but I don' want to hear nothin."

"What do you mean?"

"The way her mind worked or whatever, it was like all right so long she don' hear no noise. But it was Kayla who make all the noise. Sayin no and everythin. At first, anyway—after a while, she was quiet. Kayla always do what my mother tell her. She's like that."

I am quiet.

"I just acted like I din't know anythin or whatever," she tells me. "But I knew."

"My God. My God."

Utopia frowns at her fingertips. "Look at these fingernails!" Then she says, after a pause during which I say nothing and she is looking at nothing except her nails, "Dope do that to you, you know what I'm sayin? I know. I seen it. I had a friend too. Not just my mother. You do anythin to get it, and money, family—they ain't nothin to you."

"I'm sorry."

"Yeah," she says. "So that time I was tellin you about was the only time I seen it before, the time she try to pawn it off on Pirelli."

"Who?" I ask, feeling suddenly queer.

"The guy," she says. "He was like, Shoo, why I want some bitch gun for? Because it was too small for him. He was always like he was too cool for everybody. He always frontin like that, you know what I'm sayin? He think he like all that. He ain't about it, though. He ain't nothin but a cripple. Fuckin disgusting and shit. I hate him."

"What do you mean, *cripple*?" I ask, already knowing.

"Yeah," she says. "He think he so the man or whatever. But he ain't nothin. All he do is like roll down Sutter in his wheelchair."

"What's his name?"

"They all call him Pirelli or whatever," she says. "Because he have tires for legs."

"Puerto Rican?" I ask.

"I guess," she says. "He was pretty light, anyway. He was always frontin like he a Ñeta or somethin. But it was like a joke, because he nobody really."

"Do you know his name?" I ask. "His—actual name?"

"*He* the one, now I think about it," she says, brightening and ignoring my question. "Before—I said it was nobody's fault? Now I think about it, it was *Pirelli* fault—he who got my mother on that."

"Did you know his name?"

"Pirelli who kill my sister, you ax me," she says.

I don't need to ask his name again. I know that Pirelli is Milton Echeverria, just as I know I freed Milton, just as I know Milton addicted Nicole, just as I know Nicole is no more to blame than Milton—for if they are guilty, then so am I, who freed Milton and set in train the progression of events that led to Kayla's death. I don't want to hear Utopia tell me anything more about it. I know enough.

In the quiet, though, my question catches up with the girl, and she says, "We only know him by Pirelli. You know him?"

"No," I say. "It's probably—just a coincidence."

"Well, he got what he had comin to him, anyway."

"What do you mean?" I ask despite myself.

"What I hear from this boy I know on Dumont is they snuffed him," she says. "That was over on Euclid, like about a week ago. You seem like you know him."

"His name was Milton Echeverria," I confess. "He was—just a dealer. Like any other dealer that could've sold to your mother. He was just a nobody. It wasn't his fault."

"Now he a nobody for real," she says. "He got his."

"That's what a detective on his case said."

"What case?" she asks me.

"There was a case against him. About a year ago. Murder."

"Oh, snap," she says. "Who he kill?"

"Some—Jamaicans. Some people who tried to kill him, really."

"Shoo," she says. "Why ain't he go to jail?"

"There were problems with the case," I say. "Legal problems with the case. When did you last see him? When did he come around Cypress, I mean?"

"Shoo, I ain't seen him in a while. Not since Lamar come back. Lamar got out in like May and started comin around again. Seein Kayla. Lamar came around before—what you call Pirelli?"

"Milton?"

"Before Milton or whatever left. Lamar kicked him out, on account of he and Kayla was close."

"They were together, Lamar and Kayla?"

"It wasn't like they was married or nothin, but they like chill sometimes, you know? Lamar always being nice on her, even when they was kids. Always bring her stuff. Even when the baby come, they always go for walks almost like Meeka was his. Lamar was the only one Kayla ever like that way that I seen. She never saw no one else for real. She mostly keep quiet. You know it's funny, because I think Pirelli was the first boy she ever had like sex with and everythin or whatever."

"What happened when Lamar came back?"

"When Lamar came over—what happened?" she asks herself. "It was before the baby was born, I know that. Because Lamar was like, Shoo—he ain't say shoo, but he was like, Shoo, girl, who done that to you?"

"Who did?"

"Who you think?" She smiles. "You know all about us—you ain't never seen the baby? How light she is?"

"Milton? Pirelli?"

"Uh-huh. And when Lamar find out, he be like, I gon kick that nigger ass. But I don' know if he ever did anythin about it. Lamar mostly act big. Only I know Pirelli din't come around again. Maybe Lamar snuff him out after all."

The girl shudders with some sort of emotion.

"You all right?" I ask.

"Yeah, I'm all right," she says. "It's like it's not really happenin. I can't explain it." After a moment, she tries anyway. "Did you hear about that hospital where they gave the two babies to the wrong parents? I don' know. Maybe you heard about it?"

"No."

"Anyway, that's what happened. And then they realized they made a mistake later when they was like five and one of the babies had this, I don' know—like an illness or whatever, and it died. You sure you din't hear about the two babies? It was in the newspaper."

"No."

"I mean it's bad enough that you have a baby that dies, but now your real baby is livin with someone else. What I'm sayin is, a lot of people—they're good people, too—you know what I'm sayin? People make mistakes. We don' live in a perfect world."

"No," I say.

"That's what I'm sayin. I don'— I can't blame my mother for what happened. She just, she just make a mistake, you know? She make a mistake and she keep on makin mistakes. Look at what happen. She like feel bad or whatever because she trick Kayla on Pirelli, so when Lamar come around she try to scare him away. She think LL was doin Kayla like a ho when it wasn't like that with them. It's like a joke almost. Like she had the right idea, but it was too late—too late for Kayla."

"You don't blame her?" I ask.

"How would that help me out? She still my mother. I can't be like I don' have a mother because of what she done. Who else do I have?" She looks at her fingernails again. "Anyway, maybe she clean up now. I ain't seen her touch it since that night—Kayla clean her up, dying."

"You think you can just let it go?" I ask her. "I mean, I'm not even involved and—"

"You think you're not involved?" She smiles. "You're involved, mister. Listen to yourself—you know all about us. The way you talk about us, like you was part of the family! Shoo. You part of the family. You part of the family now."

"And Kayla?" I say.

"It's like this," she says after a while. "I went to this movie about, um, the world was explodin and everythin. It sounds pretty stupid, but it was all right. Did you see that one?"

"I don't really watch movies," I say.

"Anyway, the world was like gonna explode or whatever because there was this volcano or thing inside the earth, and like everyone in the movie is like sad and everythin and whatever because they was gonna die. But I'm like, How do you know? You don' know what it's like in death. Death could be better. It could be a better place where Kayla at."

She looks at me. "So you think I'm like stupid or crazy or whatever?"

"No," I say. "I don't think that."

"Did you ever wish you was dead?" she asks.

"No," I tell her. "No."

"The funny thing is, I don' either. But sometimes I think maybe they give me to the wrong family when I was a baby and someday maybe they come lookin for me and tell me. It's just somethin I think about. Like a daydream or whatever."

CHAPTER

30

Prospect Park gives a name to Prospect Park West, a broad avenue that in turn gives an address to several blocks of buildings and town houses that front on the park itself; Prospect Park surmounts the rise that slants away to the west, and together the park and the gently yielding topography give the neighborhood a name: Park Slope.

But the southernmost tail of Prospect Park West continues after the park ends, and what is left of that avenue shrivels to two lanes that cut through the center of Windsor Terrace with no trees whatsoever to mitigate the afternoon sunlight that beats heavily down onto the west-facing storefronts, making them naked and sullied and ordinary.

Here a couple walks, enfeebled by age and infirmity. On the corner, a man straddles a fire hydrant, shirtless and unmoving. A motherless, giddy child bursts from a door, his terrible voice rising over the monotonous throb of air conditioners making sidewalk puddles. A teenage girl follows, grasping futilely at his shirt and shouting his name. She is slatternly and strung out. He thinks it's a game.

I am in that neighborhood I never see—the neighborhood of

the weekday afternoon. A vampire haunting my home, I stay away until late at night to avoid even sunset here. Now the sun is still thrown up high and there is only the young, the old, and the unemployed. They all walk on the streets and sidewalks and have no idea where they are.

This hateful, oblivious place. How I wish it had all fallen off the map of the world when Opal was taken from it, yet on it goes, breathing its ordinary existence, and people walk upon it and circulate within its bodegas and pork stores and check-cashing places, unaware that not fifty feet from where they do what they do, my beautiful girl died. *How can they not know?* What an exotic notion—that there is a place in this world where she was and then she wasn't. That place, that merest circle of ordinary blacktop, the axis of the world; and around it, the world ceased to spin. (But only for me.)

In this place, on such a brilliant afternoon, with the summer sun just so, and the air conditioners bleeding onto the sidewalks, a girl died. She slipped away in a horror made more horrible by the insignificance of the time and place—the horror of an ordinary Thursday afternoon.

There was a green Oldsmobile.

I remember every detail. I see every ordinary, mortal aspect of that afternoon—

I am driving—I am in my car—my crappy Honda—the air conditioner is broken, and the windows are down—there is traffic on Fourth Avenue—it's hot, and I'm breathing car exhaust and thinking about Nina and her bedroom twelve hours before—I am aware of what I am now, and I am thinking about what to do about her, but I can't get around how easily that dress fell from her body, which I am also thinking about.

I don't want to be here—picking up Opal at three in the

afternoon—Heather is away—I haven't seen Amanda since Tuesday—

Opal's kindergarten teacher is waiting now on the school stoop—impatient—I am late—Opal forgot her lunch box—she starts down the stoop but then has to run back inside—I double-park and wait in the car—someone behind me keeps honking—*Go around, moron!*

Opal comes now, holding her *Little Mermaid* lunch box in the air to show me—the teacher is waving—Opal climbs into the seat beside me—she wants to know where Heather is—she wants to know where Mommy is—she wants to know why I'm mad—

She is trying to work the seat belt herself—*Daddy!*

I turn onto Prospect Park West—*I know, Opal—be quiet*—her small hands are still working—she can't get the two ends together—*Daddy!*—and a station wagon at a stop sign on a side street noses into my lane, a block away—*Daddy, you're supposed to*—the station wagon is green, an ugly Oldsmobile—the driver is impatiently edging forward—*We're almost home, Opal*—

Then it is abruptly in front of us, the station wagon—

I put the wheel hard over—a blur of motion as the Honda slides sideways, toylike, and abruptly stops, facing storefronts, and all is quiet once again under the sun.

I reach out my hand to Opal, but nothing is there—even the station wagon is nearly gone now, rattling hurriedly away down Prospect Park West and barely visible in the open window through which she went.

I pause now under the awning of the corner Korean market. I had something in mind, but I've lost the thought. I am looking, looking, standing stupidly, looking at the blacktop.

On the sidewalk a Mexican man sits on a purple milk crate with his back against a parking meter, shucking peas. He is opening pods and dropping the pale green beads into a steel water bowl on the pavement, where they bob and float. He shoots the empty pods at a cardboard box nearby. I see neither a misdirected pod nor so much as a single fallen pea. He appears neither happy nor unhappy. His cheekbones are set wide on a broad Mayan face under a shock of matted, blue-black hair covered by an incongruous baseball hat: DALLAS COWBOYS. I turn away only when he looks at me.

Wheeled out onto the sidewalk are mobile fruit stands draped in vivid Astroturf with pears and oranges and grapefruits piled into pyramids. Here, too, are buckets of flowers. I select a cellophane wrapper of carnations and pull them, pink and dripping, from a bucket. The cashier asks, "You want?" indicating the stems. I nod, and he trims them and places the carnations onto a waxy square and rolls it all into a cone.

I begin to think about Amanda and what I am going to say to her. I drop the flowers onto the vinyl seat of the livery cab and am still thinking of what it will be like when I see her, and then there she is. I recognize her before I can even see her face. She is standing by the doorway of the limestone porter's lodge near the entrance of the cemetery where she said she would be. I recognize her as the cab slows. A full minute passes while I walk to her. *Does she see me?* For a moment I believe I could leave and she would never know that I had been here. She is standing there in that familiar way—upright with her knees together, her arms folded as if it's cold. At ten paces, she turns to face me without surprise. She knew I was here all along.

She is better at this than I am. This was her idea, meeting here; I never would have suggested it. I would wish Opal a happy birthday in my own way, but there is a mandatory, sacramental rigor to Amanda's approach that leaves me powerless to do anything except exactly as she says.

She smiles at me as I walk up, and I kiss her once. She smells the same, and her smile is kind. She has always been kind to me. When she left, she did not blame me. She told me that she loved me, that she was sorry, but that she had to leave. And although I believed her and knew she had no choice, I wanted her to stay. I wanted to say something to make her stay, but the only thing I could think of, she didn't understand. She had stood there, framed in the doorway, while on the street a black livery cab idled. "What did you say?" she had asked me.

I had said it again, weakly, embarrassed, pathetic. A plane flew overhead.

"That—?" she asked. "What? I—I'm sorry?"

Again I said it.

"I don't understand what that means, Andrew. Is that a poem? The car is here. Just—"

She drove away, and I repeated one last time in the echoing apartment, *"In all the world, my nest is best."*

Now we are talking as if nothing happened—

"Good, good," I say. "And your dad?"

"Good, good," she says. "Playing a lot of golf, you know. He hurt his hip—"

"Oh—"

"No," she says. "It's nothing. He's all right. But how have you been?"

"You know—good, good."

"You look good," she says, sounding clinical.

"Well, you look great, Amanda," I tell her honestly. She is beautiful—chilling now, though, with Opal's face inside hers.

And so we go, saying nothing. We are strangers on the subway.

When we are there she takes my hand, but it means nothing. *If you want to know, I don't blame you, either.* I know she had no choice. She couldn't even look at me. And still her eyes have not sought mine except in small, curious darts. She would never get past Opal with me in the way. Her persistent, illogical love for me is irrelevant, an impediment. She has a doctor's economy of emotion, and she told me that she loved me as though she was disclosing a mortal diagnosis. If we did not still love each other, we might have stayed in touch. I could have moved her boxes to the city. We could have caught a movie from time to time.

Holding on to Amanda, I look at the narrow, rectangular headstone set in the earth with her name upon it, my name. I don't think of her as *Opal Giobberti*—she is only *Opal*. Strange to see her name with mine tagged onto the end, cluttering her simple arrangement of letters with my vowel-littered tongue twister. She never could get it right herself, smiling self-consciously whenever she said it. My name near hers seems like a misplaced caption.

I try to bring her to mind, thinking that in this place there might be something. But still there is nothing.

I am staring intently at Opal's marble rectangle, and I am thinking not about her but about the dead girl. Her name was Kayla Harris. Her picture, a yearbook photocopy, sat on an easel next to her casket. She could have been any one of an infinity of girls; the exposure made her dark features unrecognizable. I know only how she appeared in death, from the crime scene Polaroids and the medical examiner's slides. (I've seen her perforated, Kodachrome heart.) I think about Utopia's reaction to her dead sister: "Her hair look so nice."

I am finally thinking about her.

"Andy," Amanda says afterward. "Working on anything interesting these days?"

"You know," I tell her. "Same old."

"I saw you in the paper," she says, and I wonder for a moment how she knows about Kayla—she doesn't read the *Post,* and *The New York Times* (her paper) left it alone—but then she says, "Why'd they call him Spiderman, anyway?" and I relax. She is not talking about the girl. She is not even talking about my job. This is her way to get around to something else.

"He just liked comic books is all," I tell her. "A whole stack while the jury was out—you wouldn't believe the guy."

More small talk, but still she has something on her mind. She asks, finally, "You're in the Windsor Terrace apartment?"

"Yes."

"Andy," she says.

"Yes?"

"Can we go there?" she asks. "After here."

"Yes."

"I was hoping I could get some things," she tells me as a matter of fact, but—now oddly tentative—she adds, "If it would be all right with you."

"Of hers, you mean?"

"If that's all right," she says. "There was a dress that she had, that I remember. I have a picture of her wearing that dress, the yellow one with the little collar like that?"

"You can have anything you want, Amanda," I tell her. "It's all there."

"You know, it's funny. I feel kind of—I don't know—asking you."

"Don't," I say.

"No, I do. Because I think of it as yours," she tells me. "My mother asked me where her things were, her clothes and all her other things, and I told her that I left everything with you. It made me realize that—in my mind, I guess—it's almost as though she's more yours, that she's more yours than mine. Do you know what I mean?"

"No, Amanda. Why do you say that?"

"I know that's not how I should feel," she says, frowning as she does, "but in my mind it seems that she is more yours. I don't know."

"No," I tell her.

"No, Andy, it's true. It's how I feel, anyway," she says. "It's good to talk about her. We can talk about her today."

"All right."

"I want to tell you, and I'm not telling you to hurt you, but when I think about what happened, you know? When I think about her and what happened, I can almost—hate you, more because of that—because you had more of her—than because of what you did."

"Amanda."

"I know it doesn't make sense. It's a stupid reason to hate you. I wish I had a better reason. It would be easier if I could really— hate you. But I can't. You can't hate someone for being stupid and careless—as much as you try, you can't. You just end up feeling sorry for him, and then where are you? You end up feeling sorry for yourself and the person who—"

She is talking and crying and talking. She has never talked this way about it, but she still can't say her name aloud. A moment comes and goes when I should reach out to her, but all I can do is read the letters on the marble.

"I know I shouldn't tell you," she says. "I'm not trying to hurt you, but I was so—I don't know, *envious* of you, I guess. She loved you so much, Andy. She did. She did. The two of you. *God!* Your secret words and the books you both knew—the two of you always completing each other's sentences and singing songs together. Songs about—mermaids—and *aphids*, for Christ's sake. That goddamn aphid song. I can't—"

"Amanda," I say.

"Oh, and that Cary Grant movie she likes, *Bringing Up*—whatever."

"You were so busy, Amanda—middle of residency—you can't blame—" I start to tell her, but it sounds like an accusation.

"You say something and she just cracks up. Just one word. Or a face. Just—one look—and I have to sit there—no idea—no idea. The way she looked at me when you two were together—like I was going to take her away. Put her in bed. But I didn't take her away. I didn't take her."

I let her cry, still untouched.

"I was never around," she admits. "I know that. That was my fault, I don't know why I blame you for that. She loved you so much. You were such a good father to her, Andy, and I hate you for that. Isn't that terrible and mean?"

"Amanda, don't."

"You have all of her, Andy. And now—you have—all those memories of her that I don't have. I can't even see her when I close my eyes. I thought if I had that yellow dress—"

"Amanda. God."

"I can't even see her face."

CHAPTER
31

"I really don't know why I'm here," the medical examiner says after a solid hour of gin martinis up with a twist—her order, not the drink I'd recommend at Batson's, where even the taps go bad, giving you a forty-eight-hour headache.

Her arms are crossed in front of her on a table in a far corner beyond the pool table, beyond Bloch and his crew, who all looked at me and at her as we walked through the door, past them, and to the rear. My pathologist is prettier here than I remember from my cubicle, and I was certain Bloch shook his head as I passed his too-obvious stare. He thinks he knows the deal, but it is not the usual with her.

"You never seem to know why you are where you are," I tell her.

"I never seem to know why I'm with you."

"Didn't I explain the grand jury the other day?" I ask.

"Now explain that." She unfolds an arm and points quickly at the wedding band on my finger. "That," she repeats.

"I thought this was just a drink, Doctor?" I ask her.

"There's no such thing as just a drink," she says. "Joe."

"Sometimes a drink is just a drink."

She frowns at me. "And a lay is just a lay, I suppose."

"No," I say. "I pay for my drinks."

"Oh. Ha," she says. "Aren't you ever serious?"

"You have no idea."

"I have some idea," she says. "I can guess the rest."

From the front of the bar, a loud cheer suddenly goes up. We both look. Men have their arms in the air, all of them looking at the television affixed to the wall, and we are looking at the men. Not golf—someone just beat the crap out of someone who now lies on the canvas, not getting up. There is Bloch the spectator, looking stupid and happy.

"I'm not married—not anymore," I tell her. "I'm legally separated." She looks skeptically at me. "You know," I say. "I don't think I've ever said that before—*legally separated.*"

"No?" she asks.

"Isn't that funny? It's funny to say, anyway."

"Funny," she says, sounding unconvinced. "What happened?"

"Kind of a depressing topic."

"You know any uplifting divorce stories?"

"She's a doctor—like you," I say for no reason. "I just realized you're both doctors. That's some coincidence, wouldn't you say?"

"Not a pathologist, I suppose?" she asks.

"No," I say. "Her patients are alive."

"That why she left you? You were on the wrong side?"

"Why do you think she left me and not—you know?"

"Because you're working so hard," she says. "Like you're trying to prove something with me."

"Like what am I trying to prove?"

"You tell me," she tells me.

"You brought it up."

"That you're—I don't know," she says. "Nice—that you're a nice guy after all."

"*Nice?*" I ask. "I'm not nice. Is that what I'm doing?"

"Yes," she says. "There's something on your mind, at least."

"Maybe you're just reading into it," I tell her. "Maybe you're not used to male attention, after those cocktail parties—you sitting alone at a card table in the kitchen and all."

She smiles.

"How am I doing, anyway?" I ask in a moment.

"Don't worry, Joe," she says, drinking. "You're doing all right."

"You mean you think I'm nice? How all right?"

"You're asking me am I going to bed with you?" she asks me. "Isn't that what guys want to know?"

"We may want to know it," I tell her as another cheer erupts from the front. "We may not want to be told, though—it's like watching a fight when you know someone's gonna take a dive."

She takes a drink that includes the lemon rind, which she pulls from her mouth seductively but perhaps unconsciously, since she drops it without ceremony into an ashtray, saying, "It's not a fight."

"What's not a fight?"

"This. You and me. Men and women," she says. "Women don't lose when they go to bed with you. They're not giving up anything, if you haven't noticed. And if you haven't noticed—that's probably why she left you."

"No, that's not why."

"Then why?" she asks.

"Look. I'm not going to get into this with you. You just want— No, let me tell you."

"Go ahead," she says. "I like this sort of conversation."

"Let me tell you the way women are."

"Tell me."

"You sure you want to hear?" I ask her.

"Tell me," she says. "You sound like you really know a lot about us."

"Believe me. A woman doesn't make her own opinion about a man. Her opinion about him is—a carbon copy of what other women think."

"Carbon copy?" she says. "That's just plain silly."

"No," I say. "You want to know why Amanda left so you can decide what you think of me. You want to know? You want to know why Amanda left? All right. Because she couldn't stand being around me—couldn't look at my face anymore. Okay?"

"How long were you married?" she asks.

"Eight—almost nine years," I say. "Listen. I know what you're thinking—an unwanted man. That's cool, because I tell you—an unwanted man doesn't want any woman who would have him."

She smiles. "If a woman would have him, he's no longer an unwanted man, is he?"

"Come on."

"No, really. Anyway, isn't that what love is?" she asks.

"What?"

"What you don't deserve," she tells me. "That's what love is. I think."

"But I want what I deserve. If it's free—it's like cheating," I say. "You don't value it."

"We never deserve love—"

"You sound like a card-shop poster," I interrupt. "I see kittens."

"Well, that's your opinion, Joe," she tells me. "Everyone's entitled to his own, you know—even women. Mine aren't carbon copies of anyone else's, thank you very much." She drinks a while by herself, then she tells me, "But if you're saying I want to know if your wife thinks you're a shit, then you're right. I do."

"She doesn't," I say emphatically.

"She thinks you're *nice*?"

"No. I'm not nice," I say. "I am a shit—I was a shit to her, but she doesn't know about that. She just thinks I'm stupid and careless. She doesn't hate me."

"Stupid and careless?" She frowns, not believing me. "That's the general opinion about you? That you *were* a shit, and now you're just stupid and careless?"

"No—the general opinion is that I'm an asshole," I say. "In big letters. No one likes me anymore."

"No wonder you're trying so hard," she tells me.

"Stop it."

"This is the part where we test your theory about women's opinions," she tells me. "I don't date assholes, Joe."

"Fair enough," I say, standing.

"But I'd like to come to that conclusion on my own, if you don't mind." She takes my forearm and pulls me back in my place.

"Maybe you're just desperate?" I suggest.

"I can see that the general opinion about you may have some merit after all." She sighs and says, "I'm really not, though. And if I were, wouldn't that say more about you?"

"Nothing I don't already know."

"Now *you* sound kind of desperate." She puts her head down in the cradle of her arms, a woman's head devoid of overt femininity—like a twelve-year-old boy's. She closes her eyes and in a minute tells me, "I don't want to talk about this anymore."

"I thought you liked this kind of conversation."

"Not this kind," she says. "Let's talk about something else. You said on the phone there was something you wanted to ask me."

"No, nothing. I was just thinking about that guy I told you about."

"What guy?" she asks.

"Milton Echeverria," I say. "The wheelchair guy?"

"You never told me his name."

"I wanted to ask you something about that. And see what you think."

"All right," she says.

"I was thinking you might be right about that," I say. "Anyway, I have another case now that's similar."

"Tell me about it."

"This guy's like driving his car, right? And he's got a passenger. His kid. His little—boy. Like six years old. Sitting on the seat next to him. And let's say he forgets to buckle up the kid and the kid's just sitting there without a seat belt on. And there's an accident— and the kid gets—you know—thrown out the window. And dies."

"This a real case?" she asks, lifting her head.

"Yes."

"That's horrible," she says. "What are you asking me? Are you asking me whether the father should be indicted for murder?"

"Not for murder, maybe—but something," I say. "Do you think he should just get to walk away from something like that?"

"I don't think he's ever going to walk away from something like that, do you?"

"So you think he should be indicted?" I ask. "Manslaughter, maybe? Negligent homicide?"

"God, I don't know," she says. "You know—that's so hard."

"Let me ask you this. What if I told you that the guy, the father, didn't forget to buckle the seat belt? What if I told you he was, like, hot and thinking about something else, and he couldn't be bothered—he just figured it was only a few blocks to drive."

"I don't know," she says. "I don't know."

"And what if I told you the air-conditioning in the car was broken and there was another car trying to cut into his lane—"

"Oh, God. I don't know."

"That's a tough one, isn't it?"

"It's horrible," she says.

"I'm just wondering, if—this father—this stupid-ass father—whether I should indict him—or just—let him go, you know? Just let him go. Figure he's—like you say—never gonna walk away from what he did. Just let him fucking live with it, you know?"

"I don't know. I don't know."

"I don't know either," I say.

"It's so sad."

"And then I was thinking about Milton Echeverria, and what you were saying."

"What about him?"

"You know. You were saying that it's not really my fault if he kills someone after I let him out. If he's, like, if he sells some of his shit to some junkie, and the junkie gets high and kills someone, is that my fault too? I mean, there's got to be some—cut-off, right? Isn't that what you were saying? That it's not my fault?"

"Oh, Joe, is that what happened?" she asks. "With Milton?"

"Yes."

"You can't blame yourself for that," she says.

"That's what you said."

"Have you been blaming yourself for that?" she asks me. "Is that what this is all about? You think you're like that driver?"

"It's the same thing, right—a stupid—mistake, really. Should we blame him—this father? He makes a mistake and now someone is dead. You can't really hate someone, blame someone, just because they're careless and stupid, can you? Can you blame him?"

"*Yes,*" she says quietly. "It's hard, but I think you have to. I don't know if it's a crime or whatever, but what he did—it's not the same thing as what, as what happened to you. You're not like him. Look at me." I do. "You're nothing like the driver," she tells me without blinking. I don't say anything, and after a moment she says, "If you're asking me, that's what I think."

After another silent moment, she stands.

"Let's go," she tells me, standing on her long legs, now visible and pale under a black skirt.

"Oh," I say, looking inside my wallet. "Don't suppose I could borrow a couple twenties?"

"Sure, Joe." She smiles. "But that will sort of ruin your rather witty *I pay for my drinks* comeback."

Outside, the sun has set above Court Street, and an airplane blinks and roars in a sky blue-black and entirely without stars. We walk to her car, not speaking. "Come with me," she then tells me abruptly, looking playful and free in a way I could never be, and when I tell her no, she hits me and coyly says, "You don't want me because I'd have an unwanted man!"

"No." I kiss her anyway. "I have to get something squared away first."

She nods, thinking she understands. We are walking to her car. When we get there, she says to me, "Why don't you, you know— come up and subpoena me sometime."

"Sure."

She smiles lightly from her car window as she pulls away, and that is not how I want it to end. I could be better with her than I am with myself or with someone else. When I am with her—*what is her name?*—I don't feel like I'm stealing. I don't feel like I might get caught. With her, I could be good for six months.

"Wait," I shout, now running into Court Street as her car mercifully slows in the face of a blinking yellow light. And then there she is at the open window, looking brightly at me.

"What's your name?" I ask her. "I mean your first name—I forgot it."

"Very smooth, Joe." She rolls her eyes and the light changes to green—and from her car, from a hundred feet, to me still standing in the street, she calls, "Ann!"

"*Ann,*" I repeat to myself as I walk to the F train. "Remember *Ann.*"

Should be easy—we're a pair. (Raggedy Ann and Andy.)

CHAPTER

32

"Good morning, ladies and gentlemen of the grand jury," I say, now on the record, the words from my mouth passing through the fingertips of the court stenographer and onto a white ribbon shooting slowly from the machine recording forever and for all what I am saying, what I am about to do. *What am I about to do?*

Too late to ask that question. (I have already decided.)

"Good morning," they repeat like good schoolchildren seated in this featureless beige shoe box—except for one in the back who says instead, "Morning, Mr. G!" Soon he will be asleep. "G-man." He laughs to himself. "G-man the *G-man*. Ha, ha, ha."

"Good morning, everybody," I say. "And if you don't remember, my name is Assistant District Attorney Andrew Giobberti. The grand jury number is seven-eight-three-three. Today I am going to present you with additional evidence in the case of the People of the State of New York against Lamar Lamb. Madam Foreperson, is there a quorum present?"

"Yes, there is," she says primly, taking her job far too seriously.

"Let the record reflect that there is a quorum present," I say. "Now, before we begin, let me ask the grand jury whether there is a request that I marshal the evidence in this case?"

A solitary juror looks at me and says yes from the front row. The twenty others look at him and shake their heads. They've been sitting for three weeks now—long enough to know the real deal about the grand jury. They—apart from this one up front and Madam Foreperson here—know not to take their job too seriously, and they don't. They eat and sleep and read magazines while an assortment of assistant district attorneys in cheap suits and skirts bring them case after case after case. Gun cases, for the most part, and drug cases—the facts varying only in the name and the place, the caliber and the narcotic. But there are assaults, too, which liven them up a little—nothing like a good tune-up with a pipe, or a shooting, or a knife in the neck. There are also robberies and rapes, and a defendant will sometimes testify—always a broken promise of excitement frequently ending in crocodile tears, leaving the jurors unmoved and stony-faced—except for the inevitable pain in the ass (inevitably white, inevitably an art therapist, inevitably from Park Slope) who ends up in every jury. She will cry her eyes out at the human spectacle laid bare before her, for she has never seen anything like this before. She will have cried her eyes out from day one, and the rest will ignore her thin protests and indict the son of a bitch to spite her.

There's the grand jury for you, if you want to know. And yet, of the twenty prosecutors who have presented evidence this week to this one of eight sitting juries, they remember me. Of the fifty cases they've heard this week, they remember this case. They all remember, except for this juror in the front who looks earnestly at me—not lazy or apathetic like the rest, just stupid.

"Let the record reflect that there is such a request," I say. "Now, before I marshal the evidence, remember that nothing I say constitutes evidence in this case or has any probative value. You must rely upon your recollection of the evidence because it is yours—"

"—and not mine that controls," the one in the back interrupts, completing my sentence, the sentence they all know now by rote.

"And not mine that controls," I repeat. "I still have to say it, you know? Having said that, it is my recollection that you heard evidence that on August fourth a fourteen-year-old girl by the name of Kayla—"

The juror up front nods. "Oh, yeah. The girl one. Okay."

"—name of Kayla Harris."

"Yeah, all right," he says. "The girl one. Sure. I got it now, chief. Go ahead there."

"Is the grand jury's recollection refreshed?" I ask them.

Heads nod. A woman looks up from her knitting. She is making me a sweater. "Not for now," she told me. "For when it turns cool outside." Nice, but it looks too big, too turquoise.

What happens next is part of the public record—the words I say, anyway, and the answers given. They are plain enough to see. They can be read in black and white on a typed transcript. I tell them, "You will now hear testimony from Nicole Carbon." And as the door to the grand jury room opens, the stenographer types, "Whereupon, the witness entered the grand jury room"—eight words comprising a sentence, the sentence itself framed between parentheses, and the entire parenthetical indented and offset on the transcript page—as if to acknowledge the implicit importance of it, of Nicole Carbon setting foot inside this room.

The record shows that Madam Foreperson asks Nicole Carbon to swear to tell the truth, and that she does so swear. I hear this as

I walk to the back of the grand jury room, my back to Nicole sitting in the witness box that nearly overwhelms her small self. I turn and see her inside it, looking like a lost child in a Pack N' Play.

The record also reflects the prosecutor's first question to his witness: "Can you tell the grand jury your name?" And her answer: "Nicole Carbon, as in carbon copy."

But the cold record also leaves much unrecorded—that a man in the back of the grand jury room is already loudly asleep, that a woman looks up from her knitting when Nicole Carbon enters the grand jury room, slightly stooped, and that her presence here—the mother of a girl dead from an act of violence—creates barely a ripple on the placid pond of the grand jury's collective face.

Nor does the transcript record whether the prosecutor's failure to extract a waiver of immunity from Nicole Carbon is a mere oversight on his part or something else entirely.

Lawyers may do what lawyers do; they may argue over when (that is, *at what precise moment*) Nicole Carbon receives complete immunity against the charge that she shot and killed her youngest daughter. And it is an interesting question, from a legal point of view. Does immunity attach the very instant she steps into the grand jury room? When the prosecutor asks her name and she gives her answer? Or some later point in the proceeding, such as when she is asked to put on the record her version of events leading to her daughter's death—already told and retold to the point where it has become (for her) the equivalent of truth.

I don't know; a fitting subject for a law-review article. I would be interested to read it.

But for now, I simply ask, "Miss Carbon, do you live with anyone?"

"My family," she answers. "My girls."

"I'm going to ask you if you're related to Kayla Harris?"

"Her mother," she says without emotion. "But she was killed."

"All right," I say. "Let me ask you when was the last time you saw her?"

"Livin, you mean?"

"Yes," I say.

"That night," she says. "The night he shot her up."

"Where was that?"

"My house," she says.

"I'd like to turn your attention now to about midnight, all right?" I ask. "That night. Maybe just a little after midnight, okay?"

"All right."

"At that time," I ask her, "were you still home?"

"Yes," she says. "I was there all night."

"Now, at that time and place," I ask, already knowing her answer (*"Sleepin"*), "what were you doing?"

"Sleepin," she says.

"Did anything wake you up?"

"Yes."

"What?" I ask.

"My daughter, the older daughter, Topia, had went in the back where Kayla sleep with the baby—she has a baby girl herself—and she had started screamin, which was what woke me up in the first place."

"What happened then?" I ask.

"She was dead," Nicole answers.

"Who was dead?"

"Kayla," she says, indicating her own sunken, breastless chest. "Shot here."

"You say she was shot?" I ask her.

"Yeah," she says. "Here."

"At any time that night," I ask, "did you see Kayla with any-one?"

"Not that I see," she starts, "but Miss Iris, that's my neighbor, she had seen the boy—"

"Ma'am," I cut her off, "I'm going to ask you not to testify about what anyone else told you, and I'm going to instruct the grand jurors to disregard the hearsay." (I almost smile. The case is finished. Over. Yet here I am, being a lawyer, going on about hearsay and instructing the jury—as if anything will come of her testimony apart from allowing Nicole to slip nimbly wrenlike from the cat's maw.) "Just tell us whether you—you yourself, ma'am—saw Kayla with anyone that night?"

"No."

"Did you see anyone shoot her?"

"No."

"Now, turning your attention to August sixth, at about eight-forty in the, um, morning, do you remember where you were?"

"No."

"Let me ask you," I say. "Were you at the Kings County Morgue?"

"Yes."

"At that time and place, did you see anything?"

"What do you mean?" she asks.

"Did you see anything at the morgue?"

"Kayla," she says. "They show me a picture. They say they used to let you look at the body herself, but now they only show you a picture of her."

"Thank you very much, Miss Carbon, I have no further questions. You may step down."

"Can I go home?" she asks from the witness box.

"Please just wait outside for minute."

When she has stepped back into the hallway and the door closes behind her, I address the grand jury. "Are there any questions for Miss Carbon?"

There are no questions for Miss Carbon. They are allowed to ask questions, but after three weeks on jury duty, their curiosity has evaporated. Besides! It is almost time for their break. (They are already gone.) A man is working on his crossword puzzle. A girl is wearing a headset. From the back, I hear the sound of sleeping. I hear knitting needles click.

"No questions," the foreperson tells me.

"No questions?" I ask again.

"No," she repeats.

"Let the record reflect that the grand jury has no questions," I say, and the court reporter types it all. They stir, ready for their break. My sweater (already two turquoise arms and a thin band of torso) is poised at the mouth of a plastic grocery bag. Someone farts loudly, and accusatory stares telegraph around the room. "No questions," I say, then abruptly I slap my blood-red file on the desktop. "In back. Hello. You sleeping, sir?" I walk to the back. "Hello?" I say. "Hello?"

"I'm awake, Mr. G," he says, waking. "I'm just resting my lids, you know? Have me a long night."

"Do you have any questions, sir?"

He looks sheepishly, sleepily, from side to side.

"Does anyone have any questions for this witness?" I ask. (Nothing.)

"I've been coming in here for what? Four days?" I ask them all. "And it's funny, because—I guess it never really came up, but no one has asked why. I mean, why was this girl shot? Why is she dead? Doesn't anybody—I mean, don't any of you want to know why this girl, this fourteen-year-old girl, died? Doesn't anyone want to know why? Why something like this could happen? Aren't any of you going to ask that question? I'm sorry." They are looking at me. "You're all looking at me like I'm, like I'm crazy or something. No, it's okay. I'm okay. You know, it's just that I have a few questions. Just a few more. Okay, everybody? I'm sorry. I know it's almost time for your break, but I have just a few more questions. All right. Sit down, everybody."

They sit.

And I say, "The People recall Nicole Carbon."

I look at the wide-eyed foreperson at her high table.

"It's okay," I tell her. "Go ahead."

"Whereupon, the witness reentered the grand jury room," the stenographer types, looking at me. They are all looking at me, Nicole included, who sticks only her head inside the room.

"You are reminded you are still under oath," the foreperson tells Nicole.

"Please sit down, Miss Carbon," I say.

She does, with reluctance, and looks at me with a sour expression. "I thought you say I was done?"

"Just a few more questions, all right?" I say.

I open my file and locate a folder marked "Photographic and Documentary Evidence." I withdraw a blurred Polaroid of a pistol set upon a faux wood tabletop. I hand it to Nicole.

"At this time," I say, "I am handing People's Exhibit Fourteen to the witness. Ladies and gentlemen of the grand jury, you may remember that People's Exhibit Fourteen is a Polaroid of a certain twenty-five-caliber Lorcin semi-automatic pistol introduced in evidence through Detective Ralph Archer of the Ballistics Squad, um—the Firearms Analysis Section."

She takes the photo, and I say, "Miss Carbon, please have a look at the exhibit and tell me whether you recognize it?"

She says nothing. A minute passes. I hear the knitting needles again, and the insect sound of a Walkman going.

"Miss Carbon," I repeat. "Do you recognize People's Fourteen?"

"A gun," she says. "Silver gun."

"I'm going to ask you again, ma'am, do you recognize People's Fourteen?"

"No," Nicole says, squinting. "No. Why you expect me to recognize a gun?"

"No?" I say—just *no,* not a facetious courtroom *no.*

"I told you no."

"Let me ask you this," I tell her. "Do you know a man by the name of Massiah Harris?"

"Yes, I know a man by the name of Massiah Harris," she says quickly, throwing the Polaroid down and crossing her bare, narrow arms.

"How do you know him?" I ask.

"My husband."

"Did Massiah Harris ever give you a gun?" I ask her.

"No he did not never give me no gun," she answers—not frightened, but angry.

"He ever give you a gun that you kept behind the refrigerator in your home?"

"He ain't never give me no gun at all," she says.

"He ever give you this gun?" I ask. "This gun in People's Fourteen?"

"No," she answers flatly.

"He ever give you this gun?"

"No," she says.

"Look at it again."

"No," she says. "How many times have I got to tell you no?"

"Did you ever take this gun—"

"Stop telling me I had a gun," she says.

"—on August fourth of this year to your daughter's bedroom—"

"No."

"—to Kayla's bedroom—"

"No."

"Lamar Lamb was there, wasn't he?" I ask. "Wasn't he?"

"I ain't seen him. Miss Iris seen him."

"You told Lamar to leave, didn't you?"

"Miss Iris—"

"Forget Miss Iris," I tell her now. "You saw him. You saw him."

"No."

"You didn't want him there. You didn't want him there because you thought Kayla was turning a trick on him, right? Turning a trick in her own bedroom, isn't that what you thought?"

"No."

"You told him to leave and when he didn't leave, you threatened him with this gun. You got this gun and you waved it in his face. Like this."

"No I didn't."

"You waved the gun—this gun—at him. And it went off."

"No."

"You killed her," I tell her.

"No."

"You killed her," I tell her again. "You weren't careful."

"He killed her."

"You were stupid and careless and stupid," I tell her.

"No."

"And now she's dead."

"He killed her," she says, standing in the witness box and pointing to an unseen he.

"She trusted you."

"It was LL," she says.

"You were her mother. She was a little girl."

"No," she says.

"She trusted you—she loved you—you were supposed to take care of her only you didn't."

"No," she says again and again. "No."

"You were supposed to take care of her but you killed her, you killed her, because you, you—"

"No." She is repeating the word, still standing. "No. No."

"You told her to be quiet," I tell her, and that is all it takes.

"That's it," I say. "That's all. That's all. Get out. Get her— Get the fuck out. Get the fuck out."

And the stenographer types it all in antiseptic black letters. "Whereupon," she types as Nicole falls out the door into the hallway where Solano waits for her, "the witness left the grand jury room."

"The fuck happened in there, counselor?" Solano asks me when I, too, leave the room.

Nicole is still barking harsh sobs on a wooden bench ten feet away. It is what I wanted to hear, but I don't want to hear it anymore. She doesn't matter anymore, if she ever did. Her head is nearly between her legs.

The grand jurors file past us and around us, looking ashamed as they come into the hallway. One—the one who was asleep before—silently pats Nicole's sharp shoulder.

"Yo," he says to me as he comes by. "Some cold shit, G."

"Nothing," I tell Solano when we are alone with Nicole in the hallway. "Just some fun. Now put her under."

"What charge?" he asks.

"You were right—she shot her. Get her out of here."

And he does, taking her gently away, away to the perfunctory process at the Seven-Five, where she—fingerprinted and under arrest, free but not yet, unaware she cannot be touched by law—should promptly fall into a dreamless sleep, the fresh ink still blackening her yellow fingertips.

"You stupid, stupid, stupid—" Bloch struggles for the precise word, but the best he can do is "*fucker*! You know what you did?"

That is what he says when I tell him what I did.

"Yes," I say to him. "I know, Phil. I just told you."

He tells me anyway: "You put Nicole Carbon in the grand jury without her waiving immunity!"

"I know."

He is paging through the typed transcript of Nicole's testimony, reading it over and over again as I sit not unhappily looking out his office window. I see Stacey there, alone.

"What the fuck happened in there?" Bloch says, echoing Solano's words. He says it after trying unsuccessfully to make a big noise with the twelve-page transcript by slapping it onto his garage-sale desk. "Did you lose your *fucking mind*? Do you know what this means?"

This is good for Bloch, I think. He will go home to Cranford tonight and put his peachy nurse across the table. Dogs will bark.

"Yes, Phil. I know what it means."

He tells me what it means. "It means she's got a walk!"

"I know."

He halfheartedly swats at a dangling fly-streamer, missing it. Embarrassed, he swings again, curses pathetically, and this time the streamer attaches itself to the back of his swinging hand, snaps loose from an acoustic tile overhead, and alights along the arm of his pressed white shirt.

"*Ew*," he says, recoiling, looking over his shoulder for the end of the thing while at once turning about like a dog after its own tail. "*Ew*—fuck—fucking asshole thing!"

"Here," I say, peeling off the streamer and brushing sticky fly raisins from his shirt.

"There's another one there," he says, pointing. (I brush it off.)

His anger spent, Bloch falls onto the couch.

"Gio," he says, reverting now to his old self. "Gio. What did you do? You know the spot this puts me in upstairs. The press is all over this—I've had four calls from the *Post* in the last forty-five minutes."

"I'm sorry, Phil." I am sorry for Phil.

"Just tell me this," he says. "Tell me you had no fucking idea she's your shooter and that's why you didn't make her waive. Just tell me that and I'll die happy."

"All right," I tell him. "I had no idea she's my shooter, so I didn't make her waive."

"Bullshit," he says, rubbing his head. He knows, of course. "That's what I'll have to tell them. I mean, I can't tell them you just forgot. *You* can't tell me you just forgot—not after what happened with that other one."

"What other one?"

"You know," he says, waving his hand. "The one whose name I could never get right."

"Milton Echeverria?"

"Yes. You can't tell me you just forgot, Gio," he says. "Not again."

"No," I admit.

"It was an accident, though," he says hopefully. "Right?"

"Yes, Phil. I was stupid and careless."

"At least there's that. They won't fucking crucify you—me." He calms down for a moment; then, thinking of something, he lights up again, standing. "Goddamn it! What happened in there? What am I gonna say?"

"Well," I say. "Tell them *necessitas vincit legem.*"

"What?" he asks as I pull open his door, which snags itself on a wave in the scratchy red carpet. "What did you say? Giobberti, come back in here! Who said that? What is that? Fucking Latin?"

"It's Latin, Phil," I tell him as I leave. "Look in the law dictionary."

Bloch thinks I've snapped again. He thinks this is the half-longed-for crack-up. He saw it coming and told people so. He'll find someone to tell "I told you so" if he hasn't done so already. In a few days, he'll sit me down and we'll have a talk. He'll be very sincere and concerned about my well-being, asking me how I'm doing and whether I might need a rest. He'll call me brother. Maybe he'll suggest a reassignment to a sleepy bureau, like Appeals—a place where I don't have to be around people or talk to people or risk letting a child-killer go free. He'll say a great many things, and for the most part he'll be sincere and he'll be right. I'll be unable to say anything in reply. I'll just sit there with my hands crossed in front of me, sitting on his dog-shit-colored couch, looking at the air-conditioning compressors through the window.

"Giobberti, you stupid fucker."

"Stace. Holy Mother—not you too."

Stacey looks wryly at me. I am on her wooden walkway, where she is alone with her cigarette. The gray skies are closed for the moment, although the morning's downpour has fertilized the garden of ash and bird shit at our feet. She says nothing more for a moment. She smokes prettily, her cigarette smoke disappearing against the gray clouds—woolly and fat—roiling behind her.

"Heard about Lamar Lamb?" I ask her then. Only the clouds and her cigarette hand move.

"No," she says. "What's that bad boy been up to?"

"Seems he got his punk ass snatched up last night."

"Didn't take long—he was only out a few days," she says, with interest. "Another homicide?"

"Yes, in fact."

"Get out of town," she says, evidently surprised. "Who you set up the poor motherfucker for this time?"

"No one you knew, Sharp."

"Someone you knew, then?" she asks.

"Old friend of mine," I say. "By the name of Echeverria, but his friends called him Pirelli."

"Didn't think you had any friends, Giobberti."

"We weren't too close—we just had a few things in common."

"With you?" she asks. "Must've been an unlucky, sorry bastard then."

"An unlucky, sorry bastard," I say. "He got shot up and had to use a wheelchair."

"A wheelchair?"

"Then he lost his girl."

"Sounds like a country-western song."

"And now he's dead," I tell her.

"You got my attention," she says skeptically. "What's the punch line? Why's Lamar wanna do your old friend?"

"Always asking why, aren't you, Sharp?"

"Boys want to know how. Girls want to know why. There's always a reason why things happen," she says. "Even accidents, Gio."

"So, name a classic motive," I tell her.

"Money."

"Guess again," I say.

"Love."

"Closer," I say. "But you surprise me."

"Why?" she asks.

"I thought you were unimpressed by that emotion."

"In general," she says, flicking ash. "What about hatred? No. Revenge."

"Yes. Revenge, Sharp."

"Revenge for what?" she asks.

"Kayla."

"Kayla?" she asks, all frowning doubt.

"Yes," I tell her.

"How's this mope Eck-whatever down with that?"

"He's the babyfather," I say. "LL didn't like that. Plus he dealt—got Nicole hooked. Lamb blamed him, I suppose. For what happened to the girl."

"Lamar doesn't blame Nicole?"

"Guess he figured she was just stupid."

"And neither do you? Blame her?" she asks me, and I don't touch it. Then she says, "You have any evidence of this, or are you just pulling it out of your ass?"

I shrug to indicate the latter.

"Jesus, Giobberti," she says. "Last time you had all the proof but no motive. Are you telling me you finally have a motive but no proof?"

"Less than that, Sharp," I say. "I got Dirty Dread. Remember him."

"The wheelchair!" she realizes immediately, laughing. "From LL?"

"Right."

She is still laughing. "The little guy," she says. "Surprised he didn't confess himself to homicide, you scared him so bad." We are both laughing now, thinking about Dirty. "You're right about one thing, though."

"What's that?" I ask.

"If he's all you got on LL, you got dick."

"Suppose."

"Why'd you scoop up LL then, Giobberti?" she asks. "You just wanted to make a point?"

"I suppose I did, in a way. Sometimes necessity is stronger than law, but usually you have to play it by the book."

"That's pretty funny. Coming from you," she says. "Everyone thinks you've lost it."

"What do you think?"

She inhales on the cigarette. "I think it's so you."

"You think?"

"That's right," she says. "Always some theatrical bullshit at the end. Everything going to hell, and then there's you—my fucking hero."

"You're such an authority on the subject of me," I tell her.

"No," she says. "I don't know what you think."

"You don't. So why don't you lay off it?"

"Because this was my case, Giobberti," she says. "This was my case too."

"You're not talking about the case, though."

"The case is about us," she tells me. "Don't be stupid."

"And now it's over."

"You're not talking about the case, either," she says in a moment.

I shake my head no.

"No, idiot," she says. "This is where you're supposed to do something theatrical."

"What do you want me to do?"

"You know what to do," she says, all sarcasm. "Be my hero. Fucking save me."

"Stop it."

"Save me. Tell me you love me again." She laughs then turns on me, still thinly laughing. "You shit. You're not my fucking hero."

"Stace, it's not about—" I say, moving to her.

"No, Giobberti," she says while she pulls back. "You don't have to be nice to me. I knew what you were going to say. I've known it since that first night."

"Since then?" I ask. "I always thought you supposed we were meant for each other."

"No," she says. "I only thought we deserved each other—there's a big difference."

"No, Stacey," I tell her. "I don't deserve you."

She looks at me. Then she kisses me for the last time, whispering, "You asshole."

"I'm sorry."

"No," she says, almost laughing again. "That's not what I'm looking for. Everyone's always sorry—you know I'll let it go."

"Stace."

"You are sorry, aren't you?"

"Stace."

"Say it again," she tells me, brushing away my hand, finally showing hard emotion.

"I'm sorry."

"No," she tells me. "Really say it."

"I'm sorry."

"Say it again."

"I'm sorry. Stacey. I'm—"

"No—stop saying it now," she says. "Now it just sounds ridiculous."

CHAPTER
34

Soon it is time.

In the afternoon, the rain has come and gone, but the sky is still muddy with the promise of more. I stand silently for a long while beside a brown column in front of 210. The man who lives behind the column is noiselessly asleep (perhaps even dead). Just visible in the distance, three miles away, the deco spire of the Empire State Building alone pushes through a field of low, scudding cloud— menacingly, like a periscope in the frigid North Atlantic. Fog shrouds the towers of the city, and Brooklyn becomes what it was a hundred years ago, independent, a city in its own right, where there were honest farms and paddocks to be seen and Manhattan was distrusted as a place of rollicking debauchery.

On the rain-darkened pavement bloom bright broken umbrellas with inverted canopies and snapped spines. I walk over them, across Joralemon Street, past Borough Hall, through my little plaza, to the steps of the Supreme Court, where on the damp stone a man does one-arm pushups. I come into the courthouse lobby, through a crowd collectively deciding whether to dash out into the accumulating weather.

"Well, Mr. Giobberti," Justice Harbison says upstairs, ruining my name. We are off the record but in full hearing of all present in his courtroom. Only a moment earlier, he was flossing his teeth; the white thread still is wrapped around an index finger, reddening the tip of it. "A few days ago you had one dead girl and two defendants. I said to myself, He's got one too many. But then upon reflection I thought, Well, Christ, he can always get rid of the one he doesn't need."

"Yes, Judge."

"But now, Mr. Giobberti, I understand that you don't have any. Not a single one. Is my understanding correct?"

"Yes, Judge."

"One of them walked out of my courtroom few days ago," he says. "He looked pretty happy—didn't he look happy?"

"Yes, Judge."

"He did look happy. You have the second one here right now. She doesn't look too happy, does she? But that's going to change in a minute. What do you think?"

"I wouldn't know, Judge."

"Well, what about you?" he asks me.

"Judge?"

"What about you? Are you happy, Mr. Giobberti?"

"I don't know, Judge," I say.

"Well, just between you and me and the fifty other people in my courtroom, let me tell you that you shouldn't be happy," he says. "You should be fucking miserable, Mr. Giobberti."

"Yes, Judge."

"That's not the way it's supposed to work, Mr. Giobberti," Harbison tells me. "You're letting defendants out of my courtroom faster than the police department can round them up. And I believe it was a year ago, Mr. Giobberti, when a certain gentleman in a wheelchair left looking rather happy as well."

"Yes, Judge."

"Are you rehearsing for the defense bar, Mr. Giobberti?"

"No, Judge." (*Fuck you judge who is you?*)

Harbison shakes his head in unaffected disgust with me. "Call the case," he says to his clerk, and the court reporter begins to type.

"Number nineteen on the calendar, People of the State of New York against Nicole Carbon. Nicole Carbon. Defendant is produced and present in the court. Your appearances, please."

"Jonathan Gruber for Nicole Carbon. And a most pleasant afternoon to you, Judge."

"Andrew F. Giobberti for the People."

Nicole Carbon sits handcuffed beside Gruber.

She sneezes unattractively.

And then I let her go.

Downstairs, another wave of rain, and the crowd in the courthouse lobby now throngs happily as strangers sometimes do together, as if it's a holiday decreed just for them. People who would not ordinarily speak or even acknowledge one another talk noisily and gather, as outside, the summer rainstorm sweeps across the plaza. They all seem to say, "Oh well!"

Oh well, I, too, am thinking when I hear a familiar voice calling.

"Mr. A.D.A. Giobberti." (Nicole.)

She comes through the crowd, muscling her small way until she is beside me, and with her—looking embarrassed or simply shy—is Utopia, holding the baby.

"Mr. A.D.A. Giobberti, I have somethin I wanna say to you. I wanna shake your hand. I wanna ax you a question." Her awkward face is beaming, her yellow palm displayed. I take it.

"I wanna know somethin," she tells me. "You got children?"

"A girl."

She laughs wickedly. "Oh, ho. Girls are worse than boys. How old is your girl?"

"Seven."

"Oh, ho. You just wait," she says, reaching out for me, then turning instead on Utopia and putting a sharp finger into her side. "Girls give you all *sorts* of problems you never expect. You see what I mean."

"All right."

"I know you got a child," she says. "I know that's why you let me out. You don' want them children of mine to be without a mother. You did me right."

"I didn't do anything for you."

"You did me right, mister," she says, turning grave. "And I ain't forget it. That lawyer told me you done somethin that let me out and I hear that and I say, That man's a good man. He must be somebody father. I din't understand at first, but then I remember somethin you say. Remember what you say when you come over to my house?"

"No."

"You say, Children are a blessin," she says. "You remember now?"

"Yes."

"That's how I know you was somebody good father. Children are a blessin from God. That's right."

With that, she is gone.

I walk into the rain, and suddenly I want to know if they will make it. Utopia was right after all. I am part of her family—not much of a family, but then look at mine—

I am thinking about Opal now, and as if a curtain is drawn away,

I can see her face as clearly as I ever have. I can feel her in my arms. I can smell her hair. I can hear her voice, high and pure. And as I stand there, bracing in anticipation, waiting for the sudden welling of blame and hatred that has kept her from me, waiting for it to wash over me with the rain and make me sick with it—it does not come.

There is only the feel of the rain and the sound of the people and the warm beauty of seeing her once again, softly breathing in my arms.

ACKNOWLEDGMENTS

Three beautiful women made this book what it is. Jennifer Rudolph Walsh—to say she is my agent would barely suffice. Courtney Hodell, my editor, who is so very good she makes you believe you can write okay. And of course Christine Reuland, without whom I am nothing.

Many thanks also to Ann Godoff and Random House—
To my parents—
To Lauren Yaffe—
To Adrienne, Allison, Anthony, and Geraldine (Abbates all)—
And to Sarah Almodovar, Sheryl Anania, Coleen Cahill, Lauren
   Miller, and Ken Powell.

ABOUT THE AUTHOR

ROB REULAND is an assistant district attorney in the Homicide Bureau of the Brooklyn District Attorney's office. A graduate of Cambridge University and the Vanderbilt University School of Law, he lives in Brooklyn with his wife, Christine, and their two children. He can be reached at robreuland@mindspring.com.

ABOUT THE TYPE

This book was set in Caledonia, a typeface designed in 1939 by William Addison Dwiggins for the Merganthaler Linotype Company. Its name is the ancient Roman term for Scotland, because the face was intended to have a Scotch-Roman flavor. Caledonia is considered a well-proportioned, businesslike face with little contrast between its thick and thin lines.